W0006327

Sissi: The Last Empress

Danny Saunders

Copyright © 2015 by Danny Saunders
All rights reserved. No part of this book may be reproduced in any form or by
any means without the prior written consent of the author.
This book is a work of fiction. Names, characters, places, and incidents either are
products of the author's imagination or are used fictitiously. Any resemblance to
actual persons, living or dead, events, or locales is entirely coincidental.

ISBN: 1511733063
ISBN 13: 9781511733069

Images: 123rf.com

To all Sissi nostalgics

"I long for death, I do not fear it, for I cannot believe that there could be a Power so cruel as to add to the sufferings of this life and keep on tormenting the soul once it has left the body."

— Sissi (a few days before her death)

Foreword

$\mathscr{E}$ lisabeth of Wittelsbach, more commonly known as Sissi, undoubtedly remains one of the most popular sovereigns in History. As Empress of Austria and Queen of Hungary in the 19th century, she attracted the admiration of her people with her rebellious temperament. She, who did not wish to ascend to the throne of the Habsburgs, was for many historians the cornerstone of the Austro-Hungarian Empire. A true patron of the arts, Sissi made it her mission to protect the artists of her time. A passionate woman, she was madly in love with her husband, Emperor Franz Joseph I. Despite her sincere feelings for the monarch, Sissi could not bear the pressure of her imperial rank. And her frail health only added to this torture. Constantly ill, she would suffer from multiple physical indispositions. Forced to face an unhappy existence, she would seek refuge in the several trips she took in her lifetime, which allowed her to break free from her adoptive land. Only death would grant her deliverance from her pain, in 1898, when an Italian fanatic would assassinate her in Switzerland.

Portrayed on the big screen on many occasions, including the brilliant performance of the actress Romy Schneider,

Empress Sissi survived in the collective memory of her country, but also throughout the world. Her legendary beauty, her exemplary refinement and her independent nature earned her the love and idolatry of many people from different generations. The "untamed girl", as her mother-in-law used to call her, left History with an important legacy. To this day, the presence of Elisabeth of Wittelsbach can be felt both in Vienna and Munich. But who was she really?

Reading through the chapters of this book, you will discover an emotional and combative Sissi. A determined woman who was willing to keep her freedom at any cost. This historical fiction novel is by no means a biography of the Empress of Austria. Although many facts are true, the story you are about to read is in great part the sole fruit of my imagination.

In order to facilitate the reading, the official titles 'Duke in Bavaria' and 'Duchess in Bavaria' have been replaced by 'Duke of Bavaria' and 'Duchess of Bavaria'.

PART I

An Inauspicious Start

CHAPTER 1

A Carefree Youth

Possenhofen Castle
1837-1852

"**S**ISSI! COME back here immediately!" thundered the duchess of Bavaria.

Once again, she had run away in the forest surrounding the family estate. As soon as it was time to receive the teachings of her governess, she escaped. It wasn't that she hated the Baroness of Wulfen, but rather that she loathed European geography. Remaining seated on a wooden chair for hours was unbearable. Sissi much preferred walking in the woods, in the open air.

Elisabeth of Wittelsbach didn't like her first name very much; it's why she decided from an early age to give herself the nickname Sissi. Shorter, less formal and very original, it somewhat looked like her. Her circle accepted this decision and very rarely used her real name. Only customary formalities required that she state her true identity. Despite her undeniable beauty, the young woman had pinkish skin, black eyes and reddish chestnut hair. She loved activities reserved for men, and horseback riding was by far her favourite one. She never went a day without mounting her mare. Polly, with her brown coat, was her best friend in times of sadness. In good weather and bad, every time the slightest sorrow came over her, Sissi climbed on the back of her fateful companion and galloped along the land of her country for a long while. She was in harmony with the nature that surrounded her. If she hadn't been a member of the nobility, she would have made a great farmer.

Amid century-old trees, Sissi walked slowly in the dewy grass. On this autumn morning, a cool wind blew on the mountainous region.

"Why should I learn such nonsense? I do not need to know the location of Paris or Rome... I will never go to such places," she whispered to herself.

Wearing a simple white dress and leather shoes, she started dreaming about a handsome and valiant prince charming. In her vivid imagination, he came to her on a magnificent black horse. The dark-haired man had blue eyes and immaculate white teeth. Nothing in the world could prevent her from believing that this famous stranger would eventually show up.

Her long walk had tired her, so she decided to rest. Sissi sat comfortably on a small rock, not far from a huge tree. She was gazing at the vast clearing that reflected against her twinkling eyes.

"There's nothing quite like this anywhere else...!" she thought without a doubt.

She was nearly fourteen years of age, and she did not worry much about her future. She was of a rather carefree nature, but she was by no means foolish. Very early on, her father, Duke Maximilian, familiarly nicknamed Max, had showed her how to avoid life's pitfalls. He, who had been forced to marry Sissi's mother, knew more than anyone that freedom was the most powerful weapon any individual could possess. Having been obliged to marry the youngest daughter of the King of Bavaria, he had lost a great deal of his independence. The nobleman had sworn to protect his children from a similar fate, particularly Sissi, his favourite. The man had made it his mission to watch over the fate of his offspring.

Sissi's mother, Duchess Ludovika, was the complete opposite of her husband. Assuredly elegant and refined, she was inclined towards the etiquette of high society. Wasn't she a member of the royal family of Bavaria? She had been sacrificed by her parents to maintain the union with the youngest branch of the Wittelsbach family. By marrying her cousin, the princess guaranteed the continuity of the dynasty. But did she have a choice? All her sisters were living similar situations. Sophie, for example, was the mother of the Emperor of Austria, Franz Joseph I. Truth be told, Ludovika was the only one in her family who married a nobleman without any royal or imperial blood. The pride of Sissi's mother was hurt, and she would suffer in silence all her life.

"Sissi, here you are!" let out Helene, one of her sisters.

"Mother is still looking for me... I suppose? When will she understand that I am not one of her servants? I do not have to obey each and every one of her orders," she retorted.

"You are unfair to her. Mother cares a great deal about our future. A lady of our rank must have a certain education," declared Ludovika's eldest daughter.

Sissi turned to her sister and looked her in the eye as a sign of provocation.

"Of course! You are the perfect child of the ducal couple..." she uttered spitefully.

Helene's heart sank, and a tear of sadness fell on her cold cheek. The smallest thing upset her as she was emotional and sensitive. The hurtful words of her younger sister humiliated her and her pride. She admitted that she wanted to please her parents, but she wasn't a slave to their every desire. *Why disobey them if they're only looking out for our best interest?* she told herself each time.

When she saw her sister's sorrow, Sissi was stricken by remorse. Her words had exceeded her thought. She loved Helene tenderly, and she did not want to sadden her.

"Forgive me! I've acted badly, and I apologize," she said taking Helene's hand into hers.

"Don't worry about it! I'm hypersensitive... a real fountain of tears."

They hugged, and then burst out laughing. The two sisters were the best friends in the world. For as long as they could remember, the daughters of the ducal couple had always confided their secrets to each other. There were no taboos between them. They both told each other everything about their lives. Three years earlier, when she entered womanhood, Helene told Sissi that her body was starting to change. Her breasts were getting bigger and hair was growing on different parts of her body. Intrigued by this piece of information, Sissi asked if these transformations were painful. Her sister, who was protective of her, reassured her and explained that it wasn't the case.

The Wittelsbach family counted ten children: five boys and five daughters. Unfortunately, two of the ducal couple's sons died in early infancy: one was stillborn and the other died a few months after his birth. The clan, as Duchess Ludovika liked to call it affectionately, was made up of the eldest child, Ludwig Wilhelm, followed by Helene, Sissi, Karl Theodor, Marie Sophie, Mathilde, Sophie Charlotte and Maximilian Emanuel. The blood that was flowing in their veins was not the only reason why they were so close; the endless love that they shared for each other explained their tight-knit bond. Never had a family in Bavaria lived in such harmony. Helene, more so than the other members of her family, was very close to Sissi. According to those who saw them together, they were two inseparable souls.

"Let's return to the castle! Mother must be biting her nails right now," suggested Sissi, smiling to her sister.

"You're right… Let's go!"

As was their custom, they challenged each other: the first one to get to the castle would win. The two young women ran to their residence as fast as they could. Nevertheless, an obstacle was awaiting Helene on her path: she tripped over a tree root. But she stood up right away and continued her furious race. The eldest daughter did not want to leave victory in the hands of her younger sister. Despite her determination, she was unable to catch up with Sissi.

"I win!" exclaimed Sissi as she walked through the gate of Possenhofen Castle.

"It's not fair! I fell on the ground," retorted Helene.

"You must accept defeat, my dear sister."

Out of breath, she did not have the courage to confront Sissi. *Why waste my words when my sister will never prove me right?* thought the loser. Indeed, Sissi couldn't settle for a second place. She always had to be in the lead, particularly in her father's heart. It was of the utmost importance to her to stand out from everyone else in all matters.

Once inside the building, Sissi headed to the drawing room where her mother was impatiently waiting for her. The duchess was sitting straight in her favourite Louis XIV-style armchair.

"My dear child! Why did you run away from class once again?" asked Ludovika.

"Mother, I am sorry... I won't do it again!" she lied, lowering her head.

It wasn't that Sissi enjoyed fooling the people around her, but she knew that it was better not to contradict her mother. Prone to bursts of anger, the duchess took offence at the smallest things. To avoid making a scene, she convincingly played the part of the repentant daughter.

"Good! Go back to the Baroness of Wulfen and try to behave yourself," demanded Ludovika.

She bowed briefly before her mother and walked up to the upper floor unhurriedly. *Sissi, get a grip on yourself, it's a subject like any other,* she convinced herself. She entered a small, poorly lighted room, and sat on a wooden chair, in front of a desk. She waited for the return of her governess to go on with her education. To help pass the time, she returned to her daydreaming. The same magnificent prince charming came back to her. He walked to her, offered his hand and helped her climb behind him on his horse. Completely absorbed by her romantic fantasies, Sissi didn't notice that the baroness was standing right in front of her.

"Miss!" said the teacher, nearly shouting.

Torn from her reverie, Sissi seemed quite troubled by her governess' bitter tone. She shook her head to come back to reality and looked at the noblewoman.

"Sorry, Madam! I lost my way...," she said, lowering her eyes, trying to explain herself.

"Enough! Once again, Miss thinks she is above everyone else. When will you understand that you must try to earn your place in society? Do you sincerely believe that a kind man would consider for even an instant marrying an uneducated woman?" asked the governess with an authoritative voice.

Sissi, flushed with anger for being rebuked in such a way, raised her eyes and replied in a tit-for-tat manner.

"Madam, do you believe that being free to think for oneself is more interesting than thinking through others?"

Shaken by this observation, the baroness swallowed her words. She understood all too well what Sissi's statement meant? Before her marriage with the Baron of Wulfen, she had considered getting an education. Nonetheless, governed by the obligations of her rank, she had to forget about her personal aspirations. Since then, the governess had confined herself to a role that made her bitter.

"Sissi, please listen to what I have to say. For a woman growing up in a man's world, education in the key to freedom. Without it, you will always live in the shadow of your future husband," she explained calmly.

Surprised by the confession of her governess, Sissi thought about each word that she had just heard. She conceded that this assertion made a lot of sense. For the female gender, knowledge was the most formidable asset to face men. She, who found so much pride in her freedom, had to make sure she kept it for the sake of her future. *Perhaps I should find a way to enjoy geography?* she thought.

"Madam, teach me how to become a free woman."

"Gladly, my little Sissi. You will have to work relentlessly, but you will appreciate the reward even more," said the baroness, smiling.

Without giving it a passing thought, Sissi opened her book and listened keenly to the teachings of her governess. Sitting on her chair, she took pleasure in learning the capitals of European countries. London, Vienna, Copenhagen... so many wonderful places available to her. The tutor, by opening up to Sissi, radically changed her pupil's perception of education. Learning was no longer a chore but rather a tool for the future, her future.

Early in the evening of December 24, 1837, Duchess Ludovika of Bavaria was lying on her bed, in great pain. Surrounded by an army of servants, she was suffering in silence in her cold room. While large snowflakes were falling on Munich, the Wittelsbach family was expecting with great joy the birth of the ducal couple's new child.

"Madam, we don't know where to find the duke," announced one of the servants to her mistress.

"Find him!" she shouted.

Everyone began searching the premises to locate their master and let him know that his wife was about to give birth. Some combed every single room on the top floors while others foraged the first floor through and through. Nothing! There was no trace of the nobleman anywhere. In a stroke of genius, one of the menservants went to the stables. He tiptoed inside and was suddenly attracted by a source of light. He moved forward and found the duke lying on the ground. Maximilian was completely drunk and deeply asleep. *Poor master!* thought the manservant. Realizing that he wouldn't be able to carry the hefty man by himself, the domestic fetched some help. Together with two other menservants, the trio managed to carry the head of the household in one of the castle's drawing rooms.

"Heidi, please let Madam know that her husband will not be able to stand at her side," ordered the manservant.

The young woman, who had a crippled arm, walked to the upper floor to give the message to the duchess. Exasperated by her husband's attitude, Ludovika burst into tears.

"Why is my man so immature!" she cried.

The contractions were unrelenting and the mistress of the premises contorted in pain. Unable to contain her suffering any longer, she let out screams that reverberated through the palace. Upset to see her in such agony, the servants wiped off her forehead with fresh water. While about ten people surrounded Ludovika, three men were trying to wake her husband up on the main floor. He was still under the effects of alcohol and the scene would certainly look quite peculiar for anyone who would dare show up unannounced.

Around 10:45 pm, after more than three hours of unbearable pain, the duchess gave birth to a pretty little girl. After he made sure that the newborn was healthy, the doctor reassured the mother.

"Madam, the child is well!"

As she heard the physician's comforting words, she was relieved of a heavy burden. Losing her offspring was the greatest of concerns for a royal descendant. She had to give the throne of Bavaria a lineage just like her mother had taught her. This perilous mission was finally accomplished.

After wrapping up the child in a warm blanket, one of the servants placed the baby girl on the bed, near the duchess. Despite her weariness, she took her into her arms. She noticed that the newborn already had a tiny teeth. *How strange!* thought the mother. She pressed the infant against her chest and fell asleep light-heartedly. So that Ludovika could rest, the servants and the doctor left the room without a sound.

Early the next morning, Duke Max woke up abruptly when his children, Ludwig Wilhelm and Helene, barged in the room. Singing, they jumped on the couch where their father was lying.

"It's Christmas!"

Still confused after last night's drinking binge, the man did not understand what was going on straight away. He shut his eyes a short while to regain his senses. When he opened them again, Max rubbed his head. What had happened? Where was his wife? The duke suddenly realized the gravity of his lapse of judgement. The previous night, he had celebrated the arrival of his newest child. Completely intoxicated, he had gone beyond what was reasonable. His body was saturated by the impure liquid that filled his stomach.

"Ludovika!" he murmured.

He recollected the image of his pregnant wife, about to give birth. He grinded his teeth as if to illustrate how much trouble he was in. She would never forgive him for this misconduct. He rubbed his nose and paced around the drawing room. Noticing the uneasiness of his master, the eldest manservant walked to the duke.

"Milord! Congratulations on the birth of your daughter. She is adorable," he said to reassure Max.

"A daughter!" exclaimed the father.

He adored children, especially girls. The family had just gotten bigger with this baby. *I must go up and see her,* he convinced himself. Nearly running across the residence, he rushed to the apartments of the duchess. The man slowly opened the door and walked inside the dark room. He headed to his wife's bed. She was sound asleep. In her arms, he found a sleeping angel. *A true godsend on this Christmas day,* thought Max. The eyes filled with tears, he placed his hand on the girl's head. With a soft touch, he caressed her hair. He had never seen anything so beautiful.

"We shall call you Elisabeth," the man whispered, smiling.

If the child were female, the ducal couple had decided to name her in honour of her aunt, the Queen of Prussia. The latter, one of Ludovika's sisters, was going to be her godmother. Everything had already been planned out for the birth of the Wittelsbach descendant.

When the duke was about to exit the room, his wife opened her eyes.

"Max! You are a thankless man...," she thundered.

The man turned around and raised his arms.

"Sweetheart, I was intoxicated with joy!"

Amused by her husband's silly answer, the duchess burst out laughing. Her anger suddenly faded. She waved at him, so that he would come closer. He walked towards the woman who shared his life with a big smile on his face. Behind the door, Ludwig Wilhelm and Helene were spying on them though the keyhole.

"Max, here is your second daughter. A great destiny awaits her... I can feel it!" declared Ludovika.

"I don't doubt it! She is our godsend," asserted solemnly Max household, sliding his little finger into the child's delicate palm.

In the autumn of 1851, just like every year, with the arrival of multicoloured leaves also came the departure of the ducal couple. During the cold season, they preferred living at Ludwigstrasse Palace. Located in the heart of Munich, this residence was, in all likelihood, closer to the Bavarian activities. Ludovika was happy to return to the city since she loathed the countryside. When she stayed in the capital, the duchess could more easily frequent salons and other places coveted by her rank.

Unlike his wife, Duke Max despised the end of sunny days. He couldn't bear the superficiality of Munich. The head of the household wasn't the type to strut about the city in public. When he lived in his urban residence, he often gazed at the window in his library. He always hoped to catch a glimpse of the first sun rays. The presence of the sun meant the return to the fields of Possenhofen Castle.

Just like her father, Sissi didn't enjoy living in busy places very much. She loved horseback riding and could not indulge in this activity in the Bavarian capital. Her sister, Helene, who cared about her younger sister's happiness, attempted in vain to entertain her during their stay at Ludwigstrasse Palace.

"Sissi, come with me! Baroness Zazie organizes a ball in honour of her nephew," begged the eldest daughter of the ducal couple.

"No! You know that such evenings aren't my cup of tea," answered Sissi, lighting a candle on the centre table of the sitting room.

"I promise that you will enjoy yourself..." added the other to convince her.

Looking into Helene's eyes, briefly, Sissi understood her supplication.

"I agree!"

She didn't even have time to finish her sentence that her sister was jumping for joy.

"Helene... I will go with you, but I shall leave early," clarified Sissi.

Helene bounced over to her sister and hugged her as hard as she could. Exhilarated, the eldest sister was laughing loudly at the thought that her confidante would be by her side. Helene, who was eighteen years old, was hoping to fall in love with a highly-placed man in society. She wasn't the only one with such a dream. For a while now, her mother had been devising a plan to marry her to a good prospect. If she, Ludovika, daughter to the King of Bavaria, didn't have the privilege of marrying a blue-blooded man, her children, at the very least, would not make the same mistake.

"Sissi, what will I wear for the ball?" asked Helene, panic-stricken.

Astounded by her sister's words, Sissi walked to the closet. She opened the doors of the narrow cabinet nimbly and plunged inside. The shelves were filled a huge collection of clothes. There were dresses of all colours: blue ones with white lace, pink ones with puffed sleeves or yellow ones with a matching train. Sissi just couldn't understand her eldest sister. How could she be worried about finding suitable attire with so many clothes at her disposal?

"Helene, you are blowing this out of proportion!" she said, taking a dress from the closet.

"What are you telling me? These are merely peasant clothes," replied the other.

"I have rarely seen countrywomen wear similar outfits," she answered.

Offended by Sissi's attitude, the eldest sister sprang out of the room. *How could she not understand the importance of this ball?* thought Helene. It was true that Sissi was barely fourteen year old. Marriage wasn't a priority for her, and for good reason.

Disappointed by her sister's lack of solidarity, Helene sought advice from her mother. The latter, who was delighted that her child turned to her for guidance, comforted her at once.

"Honey dearest, we will go shopping to buy the perfect dress for you. You can rest assured that you will be glowing for the event," declared the duchess, pinching her daughter's pink cheeks.

As promised, the next day, Ludovika went to the business district with Helene. It was snowing lightly, and they spent part of the day looking for a dress that would fit the occasion. Finally, they found the perfect attire. A white dress adorned with hundreds of glittering little pearls. In her outfit, Helene resembled a true descendant of the illustrious Wittelsbach dynasty.

"You look ravishing!" exclaimed the boutique's saleswoman.

Satisfied with the purchase, Helene hurried back to Ludwigstrasse Palace. She wanted to share her joy with her confidante, Sissi.

"Look!" she cried as she walked into the sitting room.

Over the moon, she took out the dress from its box and laid it out on the sofa. Standing in front of the clothing, which she considered to be a true wonder, Helene was waiting for her sister's reaction. Sissi examined the object closely; she remained speechless and pensive a long while before she decided to speak.

"My dear sister, if you finish the evening without any suitors, it will be because these men are all blind," she finally said with a wink.

Thrilled by Sissi's words, Helene snuggled around her sister's neck, kissing both her cheeks. She was certain that an opportunity would present itself at the much anticipated ball.

She had prepared herself with so much dedication that it could not be any other way.

A few days later, when the cold had spread across the streets of Munich, the two sisters were about to leave the family residence. A carriage and some horses were waiting in front of Ludwigstrasse Palace. They were richly dressed for the occasion. As planned, Helene was wearing her new dress. The white fabric paired with her black hair gave her an angelic look. As a present for the evening, the duchess had loaned her a diamond necklace. As for Sissi, she gladly wore one of her usual dresses. A blue outfit embellished with simple white lace. Despite her plain attire, she remained the prettiest daughter of the ducal couple.

"Helene, you are adorable!" exclaimed Ludovika, spreading out her arms.

"Thank you, mother!"

"There is no doubt that you will find you future husband. Such a pleasant face to look at can only attract glances," she added as she turned around her daughter.

A servant let the duchess know that the coachman was waiting outside.

"Hurry up! The ball will start without you if you keep dawdling."

The two sisters immediately left the Wittelsbach residence. Helene was the first to climb into the carriage. When she was about to get on board, her father suddenly appeared. He came near Sissi and looked into her eyes tenderly.

"Sissi, you will always be the most beautiful in my heart," he whispered to her.

Delighted by the remark of the head of the household, she replied with a charming smile. Once again, the duke had found the right words to compliment his favourite.

Baroness Zazie's castle, on the outskirts of the capital, was one of the most imposing residences in the area. Dating back to the fourteenth century, an inimitable sumptuousness oozed from the building, unparalleled in all Bavaria. Even the sovereign, although he was very wealthy, envied its beauty. In the summertime, intricate gardens adorned the building and perfumed the estate with a delicate and sweet fragrance. During snowy days, the noblewoman enjoyed ordering the carving of ice sculptures. Visitors were captivated by the divine creations that came to life through the expert hands of local artists.

After a fifteen-minute ride, the carriage with the two Wittelsbachs on board came to a halt, before the castle's copper doors. Several people were strolling around the property's estate.

"Sissi, do you think that I will have the chance of meeting the ideal man?" worried the eldest daughter of the ducal couple.

"Fear not! If you do not find your soul mate tonight, then no other woman will either," answered the other to reassure her.

Helene gently kissed the cheek of her younger sibling and got off the vehicle gracefully and with flamboyant femininity. She walked inside the castle with exquisite elegance. Sissi followed, a few steps behind her eldest sister, with as stately a gait as hers. When she arrived in the hall, she immediately noticed a man, in the distance, among the crowd. She didn't know his face, and yet an unusual feeling came over her. Sissi had a nervous feeling in the stomach. Never before had she felt such excitement. Curious, she tried to push her way through the guests, to reach this individual.

"Sissi, where are you going?" asked the eldest sibling in a fright.

Deadened by the surrounding racket, Helene's words did not reach Sissi's ears. The latter was only a few steps away from the mysterious man. Suddenly, an insuperable timidity took hold of Sissi. She wasn't herself. The most courageous child of the ducal couple now had shaky legs.

"Pull yourself together!" she told herself in a muted voice.

There was nothing she could do. The emotion was so intense that her heart was pounding in her chest. She decided to hide behind a shrub to spy on him from afar, discretely. Through the thick leaves of the bush, Sissi admired the one who troubled her. The stranger had a perfect silhouette in the eyes of the young woman. He was tall and well-built. Moreover, he had a well-defined jaw and pleasant features. His black hair reached his shoulders. When he smiled, she could see his dazzling white teeth. There was no doubt that this man was Sissi's dream come true.

"I must speak to him!" she told herself.

Sissi kept observing him several long minutes. He spoke with guests, exchanged a few handshakes and drank in a crystal glass. Unfortunately for her, a woman with golden blonde hair took his forearm and decidedly pulled him into a sitting room.

W*hat is she doing?* wondered Sissi. From her hiding place, she could not see the unknown woman. She moved towards the room where the man who made her heart miss a beat was going. From the squared window in the wooden door, she could see him kissing the young lady. A tear fell on Sissi's cheek. Since he wasn't available, the charming individual could not be the ideal man. Humiliated, she ran across the ballroom. She hastily headed to the front doors, crying. In the distance, her sister noted that her younger sibling, looking downhearted, was running away. A true soul mender, Helene hurried behind her and joined Sissi on the porch of the castle.

"What's going on?" asked the eldest sister in a worried voice.

"It's nothing, really!" she replied.

"Sissi... Why are you crying?" insisted the other.

Sissi did not want to answer, for she feared that Helene would mock her. She, herself, was feeling quite silly for shedding tears for a complete stranger. Despite her apprehensions, she confided in her sister and told her the reason behind her sorrow.

"Helene, do not laugh at me. I noticed a man among the guests. I do not know his rank or even his name, but he made me feel a way that I had never experienced before," declared Sissi reluctantly.

Surprised by such a revelation, Helene remained speechless a short while. Then, she tried to find the right words to console her younger sibling.

"I understand... It's love at first sight, my dear sister," she said, smiling.

"What are you telling me?" said Sissi, astounded.

"You've just experienced your first love. You are becoming a woman, my dear Sissi."

Sissi slowly turned her head towards Helene, who was looking at her. How could she become a woman? Yesterday, still, she was playing with her porcelain dolls. *There must be some mistake?* she thought.

"Show him to me! I could ask about him and you could get to know him," suggested the protector.

"Never! I saw him lay a kiss on the lips of a woman," replied the younger sister, almost angrily.

"Don't be too hasty a judge. You know nothing about the situation. Maybe this kiss didn't mean anything to him," explained Helene.

"You think so?" stammered the other.

The two sisters returned inside the castle and walked into the ballroom. Sissi searched for the stranger who had just made her head spin. Despite her efforts, she couldn't find his glance. It seemed that he had literally vanished.

"I don't see him!" let out Sissi to her elder sister.

"Are you sure?"

She looked across the room. No, he was no longer there. Disappointed, Sissi came closer to her sister and whispered in her ear that she wished to return to Ludwigstrasse Palace. Helene, out of compassion, suggested that she accompany her to the family residence. The younger sister refused and bitterly left the premises. Alone, under swirling snowflakes, she regretted ever coming to this ball. If Sissi hadn't let herself be convinced to attend Baroness Zazie's event, she would have never experienced such turmoil.

"Fräulein, you have dropped your handkerchief," said a manly voice.

Without thinking, she turned around to face the man behind her. She immediately recognized the gentleman who was standing right in front of her. There he was, the one who had made the heart of Sissi shiver. His face was even more beautiful than she had imagined in the distance.

"Fräulein, did I frighten you?" he kindly asked her.

"I'm so foolish... Thank you for this thoughtful attention," she managed to utter without stammering, as she took her handkerchief.

"Forgive me, but I'm afraid I cannot agree with you," replied the individual.

Bewildered by his beauty, she didn't understand what he meant.

"You are by no means foolish! Believe me, I've encountered more than my fair share of silly women in Munich. Your handkerchief has merely fallen on the ground," he declared.

"You are very kind. What can I do to thank you?" she asked.

"You don't have to do anything, believe me. Simply tell me your name and I will be quite content with the turn of events," he suggested with a mischievous look.

"My name is Elisabeth of Wittelsbach, but my friends call me Sissi."

"May I invite you inside, Sissi?" he said politely.

Unsure whether she wanted to accept his offer, she remained on her guard.

"A man of your rank must certainly have a pretty woman at his side."

"Absolutely! Now that you are here..." he concluded.

Hearing this, Sissi held out her hand to the individual, hence showing her approval. The gentleman, who was delighted to be accompanied by Sissi, brought her to the ballroom.

"Would you care to dance?" he asked.

Without hesitation, she welcomed the proposition with undisguised pleasure. They walked to the middle of the majestic room and danced eagerly. Not far from them, Helene was in the company of three elderly men.

"I think that your sister is enjoying herself," declared Baroness Zazie's husband.

"I think so too!" she replied, pensive.

She recognized the mysterious man that Sissi had become enamoured with. Richard von Hazon belonged to a small Prussian dynasty and had inherited the title of count upon his brother's death. Known for his lightness of character, he was by no means the ideal husband for a Wittelsbach. Rumour had it that he was an infamous womanizer. Many of his conquests, often young and innocent noblewomen, found themselves with child. Some even called him the Casanova of Berlin. *How will I separate my sister from this individual without hurting her?* thought Helene. She decided to let her younger sibling know the hidden side of Count von Hazon. She took advantage of his momentary absence to get closer to Sissi.

"Do you know this man, my dear?" questioned Helene, making sure that no one overheard their conversation.

"Not really! Should I?" asked Sissi.

"I believe so! He's not right for you. His name is Count Richard von Hazon. Some people call him Casanova… Do you understand the kind of man you are dancing with?" added the eldest daughter with caution.

"Helene! Since when do you care about other people's gossip? I didn't think that you were that kind of person," exclaimed Sissi angrily.

Helene did not continue the discussion, for she knew about her younger sister's stubbornness all too well. She returned to the three guests she had been talking with for quite some time. *Why try and help her if she didn't want to hear it?* she told herself.

After this warning, Sissi was quite puzzled. *Was her sister right?* she asked herself. In order to be certain, she decided to face the man and ask him about the rumours that existed about him. She set out to look for him. He was supposed to leave her for a few minutes only, just so he could get himself a glass of wine. She went through the room, but she couldn't find him anywhere.

"Baroness, have you seen a certain Count von Hazon," asked Sissi when she saw Zazie by the bar.

"No, my dear friend…, I'm sorry!" replied the noblewoman, holding one glass too many.

Sissi decided to walk to the castle's porch. *Perhaps he had gone out to take some fresh air?* she convinced herself. When she was about to set foot outside, she recognized the individual, kissing the same young lady he was with earlier. Shaken by the scene, she walked to him nimbly.

"Richard von Hazon! What are you doing here?" she let out furiously.

He immediately turned to Sissi nonchalantly, and stared at her with disdain.

"What do you want with me?"

"And you dare ask! I've been waiting for you forever," she answered promptly.

A witness to Sissi's outburst, the young aristocrat did not understand the reason for this improper attitude. She was even beginning to think that it was a bad joke.

"Richard, who is this person?" she asked.

"A certain Wittelsbach," declared the individual, pretending not to know her.

"What does she want with you?" she continued.

"I assure you that I do not know."

Bitterly disappointed by the assertion of the Prussian count, Sissi felt a dreadful pain tear her chest. Her sister wasn't lying, he was a real Casanova. Her first love had just betrayed her. Would she ever recover? With her pride in shreds, she ran back to Helene in the ballroom.

"I'm going back to the palace!" she exclaimed without explaining herself.

Helene didn't even have time to open her mouth before Sissi hopped into the carriage and headed back to the family residence.

On the way back, she wept and wept. She promised herself never to open her heart to a man again. As attractive as he may be. She had just experienced her first heartache.

CHAPTER 2

An Arranged Marriage

Ischl Castle
1853-1854

I N EARLY summer of 1853, Duchess Ludovika received a letter from her sister letting her know that her son, Emperor Franz Joseph I, would be coming to Bavaria. Indeed, for a few years now, members of the imperial family stayed at Ischl Castle. Since it was located nearby Munich, the residence of the Habsburgs was used as a haven during the summertime. It was less formal than Schönbrunn Palace, and allowed the emperor and his entourage to rest.

"Max!" yelled Ludovika upon reading the message.

She raced around Possenhofen Castle to tell her husband the news. The noblewoman screamed the duke's name throughout the building. Nothing! He seemed to have vanished into thin air.

"But where is he?" she thundered impatiently.

A servant let her know where the head of the Wittelsbach family was hiding. As usual, the man had gone fishing very early that morning. Behind the estate of his residence, Max had already been tackling the fish for over an hour, without success. A true example of perseverance, he patiently waited for his hour of glory. In the distance, the duchess was running in the meadow to find her husband. Holding on to the bottom of her dress, she energetically dashed through the vegetable field.

"Max!" she cried, out of breath.

The duke thought he heard his wife's voice and gazed up to find the mother of his children. He eventually saw her: she was getting near him hastily. *What does she want with me this time?* he told himself.

"Honey! I have the most important news to give you," she said, catching her breath.

Surprised by Ludovika's words, he laid his fishing rod on a small rock and met his wife halfway to better hear her message.

"My sister, Archduchess Sophie, sent me a letter announcing that we would receive the visit of our nephew, Franz, in the weeks to come," she said, bouncing with joy.

"I'm happy to hear that the emperor will be among us shortly," answered the duke.

"You don't understand! The monarch will be in Bavaria," added the noblewoman.

"I know..." replied her husband.

"Max, Franz Joseph is still unmarried," continued Ludovika.

"I see! You are considering marrying him to our beautiful Helene..." he declared.

"Absolutely! She is perfect for him and the emperor is the ideal husband for our daughter," she asserted.

The duke understood that the young nineteen-year-old woman had to start her own family. And yet, he would have preferred to keep his children by his side until he took his last breath. He was the type of man who wanted to protect his offspring, even when time had come for them to fly with their own wings.

"I will write back to my sister at once. She would certainly approve of marrying her son to our Helene," she told herself.

Ludovika quickly returned inside the family residence, and spent part of the morning writing the perfect letter to convince the Archduchess of Austria.

> *My dearest sister,*
>
> *It is with great pleasure that the duke and I have heard about the upcoming visit of His Majesty on Bavarian soil. We are eager to see our nephew again and welcome him among us. As you know, the emperor must get married to ensure the continuation of the Habsburg dynasty. I believe that I have found a more than interesting solution to solve this issue. Do you remember my eldest daughter, Helene? She is said to be one of the prettiest women in the kingdom, and would make a perfect*

*companion for the monarch. Her beauty,
her refinement and her education render
her the ideal candidate to produce heirs for
the Empire. If it's in agreement with you,
I propose that we introduce my daughter
to your son. Franz Joseph has surely met
her before, since they are cousins, but in
the recent years her beauty blossomed like
a rose in early summer.*

Your affectionate sister,

Ludovika

With this letter, the duchess was hoping to allow her eldest daughter into the Habsburg lineage. It was by far the most powerful dynasty in Europe. If she, Ludovika, hadn't married a royal dignity, her daughters wouldn't suffer the same fate.

During the evening meal, the ducal couple announced the arrival of the Emperor of Austria. All were excited to know that their precious cousin would be among them in a near future. All but Sissi, who considered Franz Joseph to be arrogant and inconsiderate. On the rare occasions when she had actually met the monarch, he had given her very little attention. Her young age being the main cause of his disregard.

"You do not seem happy about the news…" asked the father to his youngest daughter.

"Well, I cannot see any reason for all this agitation. What I know of His Majesty doesn't please me much," she answered indifferently.

"Sissi, I ask you to show more respect towards the Emperor of Austria," reproved the mother.

"He isn't our monarch! You, of all people, should know that…" she replied, getting up from the table.

Sissi, who was offended that she had to confront her parents about her personal opinions, ran to the forest. As always, nature was her favourite refuge. Truth be told, Sissi was fond of her cousin, but his lack of interest towards her had hurt her more than once. Rejected by Franz, she did not wish to see him again.

More than a week passed before Ludovika received an answer to her proposition. In her letter, the mother of the emperor approved of her sister's idea. Not only did she give her support to the initiative of the duchess, but she had also decided to accompany her son in Bavaria. It was time for the monarch to find a wife and Helene was a rare jewel. To ensure the success of this endeavour, the archduchess would be present during Franz Joseph's stay at Ischl Castle. Sophie's offer was more than welcomed by Ludovika. She would see her sister again and would be encouraged in her attempt to marry her daughter to her nephew.

As soon as she knew the purpose of the message, she requested Helene's presence in the sitting room. The eldest daughter of the ducal couple complied with her mother's demand.

"My dear child, come sit near me. As you may know, I take the future of my family very seriously," said the duchess by way of introduction.

"Of course, mother! We are very grateful."

"Your aunt Sophie and I think that His Majesty, your cousin, would be a dream husband for you. He is twenty-three years old while you are nineteen," specified Ludovika.

Helene, enthralled by her mother's words, listened carefully to each syllable that came out of the duchess' mouth. She had never told anyone, but her heart was beating in her throat each time Franz was at her side. He met all the criteria she had set for herself about the male gender, and so much more.

"I strongly suggest that you get ready for this memorable meeting," concluded the duchess.

Completely exalted by the news, the eldest daughter eagerly sought out her younger sister to share her state of mind with her. If everything went according to her mother's and her aunt's plan, she would become the wife of the Emperor of Austria. To this day, Helene had pictured her wedding in so many of her nightly dreams that it had become seemingly real in her mind.

"Sissi, you won't believe your ears," she let out as she entered her confidante's room.

"Tell me, perhaps you will surprise me," replied the other, smiling.

"Aunt Sophie and mother wish that I marry His Majesty."

"Really?" replied the youngest.

She suspected that the duchess was hoping to wed her off-spring to the best suitors in Europe. Since her childhood, her mother constantly repeated that her daughters would not end up like her. A marriage to the Emperor of Austria would be the summit for anyone. Should she rejoice at the thought of seeing her sister leave for Vienna? In a way, Sissi had to congratulate her eldest sister since she was leaving her for an exceptional fate. In spite of it all, she felt a huge sorrow overwhelm her. After Helene's departure, she would lose her closest friend and confidante. *I must not think about myself but rather about my sister's happiness,* she convinced herself.

"Helene, I am happy to know that such a great future awaits you," she said caressing her hands.

The eldest, concerned about her sister's feelings, looked into her eyes and discerned some bitterness. She tried to understand where this emotion, which contradicted her words, was coming from.

"Sissi, you are the most precious thing to me," declared Helene, as she gently stroke the chin of her sister with the back of her hand.

"You too!" let out Sissi, crying.

"Don't be sad. We will still see each other regularly. I will have you visit me at the Imperial Court," offered Helene to comfort her young sister.

Satisfied with this proposition, Sissi threw herself into Helene's arms. Surprised by her sister's change of attitude, she gladly welcomed the joy of her younger sibling.

In early June, Franz Joseph I and his mother arrived at their summer residence. During their stay, the monarch had only planned one official activity. He had scheduled a – short – formal visit to the King of Bavaria. In order to strengthen the commercial exchanges between the two nations, the emperor had to ensure the continuity of the friendly agreement between them.

"Franz, do not forget that you must meet with your aunt Ludovika," declared the archduchess when her son was about to go into the woods to spend some time alone.

When he was in Austria, the monarch could never have some time off, even for a very short period of time. His obligations towards his empire were more and more demanding and pre-vented him from fully enjoying life. At times, the head of state had to preside over his country's Supreme Council meetings. In other circumstances, he looked after the economic affairs of his territory. Days went by very quickly for an emperor.

Franz hiked – supported by a stick – in the steep paths of the estate. Even if he wasn't the sturdy type, he was still in good physical shape. He most probably had his mother's features. Sophie was still in good physical and mental health despite her advanced age. In the company of his dog, the man walked into the dark woods surrounding the palace.

"Tatu, do you think that I must marry a woman? Why couldn't I govern the Empire alone?" he asked his faithful com-panion, obviously not expecting an answer.

He kept on strolling across the trees, not paying much attention to where he was going. The further he went into the forest, the less he seemed to recognize his surroundings. After about an hour, Franz stopped to assess the situation. He seemed completely disorientated and troubled by the heavy rain that was falling on the estate.

"I must find shelter, or I risk getting cold," he told himself aloud.

Even his dog, who was used to the rain, did not want to stay under the pouring water. Franz Joseph finally saw a log cabin, near a brook. Without further delay, he headed to the improvised shelter to protect himself from the massive rainfall that was piercing him through.

The inside of the building was not designed to welcome a noble dignity with imperial blood. The furniture was limited to a wobbly chair and a huge wooden table. Walls were rather thin and could barely withstand the bad weather. A sole four-pane glass window, which let in very little sunshine, light up the room.

"My good dog, I think that we will spend a few hours here."

Hours passed by and the emperor still hadn't returned from his stroll. Worried by his extended absence, the archduchess feared that her son had had an accident. Unable to stand still, she sent an officer to Possenhofen Castle. Sophie wished that her brother-in-law, Duke Max, intervened by conducting a search party for the monarch. The nobleman knew the region very well and could offer inestimable assistance in these circumstances.

As soon as the messenger sent by Franz Joseph's mother let Max know about the alarming situation, he ordered some of his men to join him, for he needed their help to search the forest.

When he was about to mount his horse, Sissi ran near him.

"Father, I'm coming with you!" she proposed forcibly.

"No! It's too risky. The sky looks threatening and a thunderstorm can come down at any time," replied the duke, showing her it was time to return to the residence.

"I insist!" she interrupted.

The nobleman did not listen to his daughter and asked his team to leave at once. Standing in front of the family dwelling, Sissi had to do something. Whoever thought this Wittelsbach would obey her father's orders was mistaken. She had it in her to take part in the search party for her cousin. She ran to the stables and mounted her favourite mare.

"Polly, we must save Franz. I'm counting on you to fulfill this task brilliantly," she whispered in her horse's ear.

Sissi and her mount came out of the barn at full speed, under a nearly torrential rain. Informed of her daughter's spontaneous initiative, Ludovika ran outside. She moved nimbly on the muddy ground and yelled out to Sissi not to leave the castle. Her words did not by any means change Sissi's mind. *As stubborn as her father,* thought the mother bitterly.

The rainfall turned into a violent thunderstorm and flashes of lightening streaked the sky on the southern part of the kingdom. The duke and his men combed through the forest that circled Ischl Castle. They examined each corner of the area. Max screamed out his nephew's name in the hope that he would show a sign of life.

The search party lasted over an hour, with no results. Winds were incredibly strong and considerably hindered the progress of their undertaking. It had become impossible to continue the search in these conditions.

"We must return to the castle. As soon as the storm eases off, we will come back," yelled the duke to his team.

They all left the forest and not without difficulty. Some even thought that their time had almost come. Max, the sturdiest, offered his help to the men who were weaker than him. They were finally received by the archduchess inside the imperial residence. Panic-stricken, Sophie ran to the head of the Wittelsbach family.

"My dear brother-in-law, did you find Franz?" she asked with trembling lips.

"Not yet! Sophie, I swear on my honour that I will rescue him as soon as the conditions clear up," promised the nobleman, looking at the emperor's mother.

She was distraught at the thought that her son could be lost in the forest, with such a mighty storm raging. He was the monarch of a powerful empire but, for her, Franz Joseph was above of her child. Despite Sophie's authoritative demeanour, the duke could see the distress in her eyes.

Hidden in his makeshift shelter, the monarch prayed the Lord to protect him. Franz wondered if the building would resist the violent gusts. Even his faithful companion howled after each tremor. He regretted leaving the castle without letting his mother know exactly where he was going. *I'm such an idiot!* he thought.

Suddenly, a swift flash of lightening tore the sky and hit a tree near the emperor's shelter. A fire started in the branches and quickly spread to the trunk. Up in flames, the thick leafy tree fell on the shed where Franz had taken refuge. Destroyed by the force of the impact, the wooden hideout immediately burst into flames.

Not far from there, Sissi witnessed the frightful scene. She had her brave mare gallop to the ablaze shelter. Perhaps there were some people inside? She absolutely had to rescue them. She got off her mount and cautiously walked near the blaze.

"Is there anyone?" she yelled out.

The sound of the thunder and the fire consuming the shed deadened any voice that could have been asking for help. Sissi examined the premises as best as she could. She wanted to make sure that no human being stood prisoner to this situation. *There is no one here*, she told herself. She headed back to her horse to keep searching for her cousin, despite the storm.

When she grabbed the bottom of her dress to climb on Polly, she heard a noise. Sissi paid close attention to it, hoping she would hear it again. And she did. There was no doubt that a dog was barking. *This animal must have a master,* thought the courageous damsel. She retraced her steps and tried to get inside.

"I am here to rescue you! Please show yourself!" screamed out Sissi with force.

She looked left and right, but it was nearly impossible, nay insuperable, to see through the thick smoke. Concentrating her attention on part of the collapsed room, she distinguished a shape under the debris. Then, another – much smaller – shape was moving nervously. Her eyes got used to the blurred vision.

She finally spotted where the noise was coming from. A small black dog was whirling around in circles. He was imprisoned by the reddish flames that surrounded him.

"I'm coming my cutie!" cried Sissi to the poor furry victim.

How can I reach the animal? she asked herself. All of a sudden, she had an idea. If she managed to knock over the wall behind the shed, she could reach the dog more easily. With the help of her mare, she could destroy the wooden construction.

"Polly, we must help out this small creature," she told her horse, petting her muzzle.

Sissi walked to the rear of the building and got on her mount. She was hoping to break down the wall with the animal's legs. After many attempts, the obstacle finally crumbled. She got off her mount and entered through the narrow opening, tearing her clothing in the process.

"Come here!" she demanded, clapping her hands.

The canine remained near the motionless shape that was hidden under the debris. Intrigued by the protrusion, Sissi walked to the dog. She was quite surprised to see that a man was lying, face down, on the floor. She turned him over, not without difficulty, and immediately recognized her cousin.

"Franz!" yelled out Sissi, stricken with worry.

She wished with all her heart that the monarch was still of this world. Using all her strength, she pulled on the emperor's arms. She miraculously managed to get him out of the blaze. A few metres away from the horrible scene, Sissi lay down on the wet grass, near Franz Joseph. Exhausted from the physical effort she had just performed, she fell asleep on the spot.

The sun was at its peak when Sissi opened her eyes the next day. Lying on a cosy bed, she did not recognize the room where she had been carried. With one leap, she hauled herself out of the bed, wearing a simple nightgown. She walked to one of the windows to see if she recognized where she was.

"I am at Ischl Castle!" she told herself in a low voice.

"Franz!" cried Sissi when her memory came back.

Without thinking, she left the room in a rush and ran to the apartments of her cousin. A guard, who was snoozing on his chair, had been given the orders to watch the door. He didn't even have time to intervene that she opened the doors of the antechamber and walked in speedily.

"Franz!" yelled out Sissi.

Once she was at her cousin's bedside, she noticed that he still had fresh scars all over his body. He seemed in bad shape, he who was usually so strong.

"Where are your manners, my dear..." blurted out the archduchess, looking at her niece.

"Forgive me, my dear aunt. I was worried sick about Franz Joseph," she replied, lowering her head.

Sophie had always frightened her because of her authoritarian temperament. The emperor's mother was the only one who could disconcert her. Was it her rank or her authority that embarrassed Sissi? Although she knew not the answer, she knew, on the other hand, that she better obey the instructions of the archduchess.

"My child! His Majesty needs to rest... And so do you!" declared Sophie.

"You are right!" replied Sissi, although she did not believe a word.

She returned to her room, just like her aunt had asked her to. Now that she had seen Franz, she was reassured. She had saved his life and she was to thank for this gesture.

A while later, the duke knocked on his daughter's door. Sitting on a chair, Sissi was brushing her hair.

"Come in!"

Max entered Sissi's room and shut the door behind him. He walked to his favourite and placed his hand on her shoulder.

"Sissi, I'm mad at you. You risked your life by leaving the castle. Your mother must be worried to death," declared the man, in an annoyed voice.

She stood up gently and took her father's hands in hers.

"Father, I know that I acted recklessly, but Franz was in danger. I couldn't sit back and do nothing when my dear cousin was wandering in the woods," she explained, trying to touch the nobleman's heart.

Unable to resist the words of his Sissi, Max hugged her close to him. She had his temperament, and he knew it all too well. Could he hold it against her?

"You should apologize to your mother," he kindly advised her.

"Of course!"

The duke asked his daughter about the turn of events, after she ran away in the forest, searching for her cousin. She described in detail the course of the much talked about evening. Feeling very proud of Sissi's courage, the father congratulated her on her bravery. He saw in his offspring's act his own character traits. She was indeed Maximilian's dignified daughter.

Nearing the end of the afternoon, Ludovika headed to Ischl Castle after being informed of her daughter's extraordinary adventures by a messenger. As expected, Sissi was lectured by her mother who scolded her for being reckless.

"Sissi, I forbid you from ever acting that way again. You will certainly kill me if you keep on like this," said the duchess bursting into tears.

"I promise!" answered the young girl to clear the air.

Early in the evening, after dining in the company of the Archduchess of Austria, Sissi asked for a brief meeting with her cousin.

"I will allow it, but it is solely because you're the one who rescued him," added Sophie.

Happy to see Franz again, Sissi hurried upstairs. She knocked on the doors of the monarch's apartments and opened them without waiting for his permission. She tiptoed inside the first room. Then, she walked stealthily to Franz Joseph's bed. He was still sleeping.

"Franz!" she said in a soft voice.

The emperor slowly opened his eyes, and stared at the ivory ceiling for a few seconds. The man moved his eyeballs fearfully as he did not know where he was.

"My dear cousin, I'm so grateful to the Almighty to see you alive," uttered Sissi.

He immediately recognized the voice of his aunt's daughter. The emperor turned his head towards her.

"Sissi, you were there!" he said almost unintelligibly.

She was surprised that her cousin could remember that she was present at the scene the night before. He seemed unconscious when she rescued him.

"Indeed, Your Majesty. You were in a bad position. Polly and I knocked over the wall that kept you prisoner so we could rescue you from the flames," she explained.

A tear fell down the man's cheek as he heard these details. He understood that he had had a brush with death. Franz Joseph wished to thank Sissi for saving his life.

"My dear cousin. How could I repay you? This was such a courageous act!" he told her.

"I'm not asking for anything!"

"I insist! I must reward you for your action," added the emperor.

For Sissi, knowing that her cousin was alive was more than enough.

"Well! If you demand it... I would like to keep you company while you recover," she suggested with a smile.

Delighted by this proposition, Franz Joseph could not refuse Sissi's offer. Much to the pleasure of his cousin, he gladly accepted.

"Good! In this case, starting tomorrow, I will read to you," said Sissi as she left.

As planned, early in the morning, she arrived at Ischl Castle by horse. A blazing sun was soaking all of Bavaria on this day. For the occasion, the archduchess went to Munich to meet with the imperial ambassador of Austria. She had to give him the monarch's latest instructions with regard to politics. Unable to go to the capital himself, Franz had asked his mother to replace him.

Sissi walked inside the sumptuous residence of the Habsburgs. On her rare visits there, she had always been surprised to see so much wealth. Possenhofen Castle certainly was a magnificent building, but it did not equal the emperor's in any way. She headed directly to her cousin's apartments. So she would avoid disturbing him, she opened the door to his room gently.

"Franz, are you up to receiving me?" she asked, sliding her head in the doorway.

"Of course! Come in, my dear Sissi," replied a manly voice.

She entered the dark room and walked to the monarch's bed.

"Would you like me to open the curtains?" she suggested.

"That's a great idea!"

Like a fairy, she moved to the imposing window and drew the linen fabric apart. Lying on his bed sheets, the man noted the refinement in her gesture.

"I brought you a collection of tales. You can clear your mind by listening to the stories I will tell you," declared Sissi.

She sat on a small stool, not far from Franz, and began reading him a tale. For about an hour, she entertained the monarch with her book. Some amusing passages managed to create a joyful atmosphere that sometimes led to uncontrollable bursts of laughter. Never before had Sissi been in such close company of her cousin. To this day, the few occasions when they had actually talked together had been very short, and always in public.

"Sissi, why did you look for me?" asked Franz, intrigued by the young woman's answer.

"You are my aunt's son," she said honestly.

"Indeed, but there was a storm and you put yourself in danger," he added.

Sissi put the book on the corner of the bed and stood up slowly. She headed to one of the windows, which was slightly open. Through the frame, she could admire the multicoloured gardens of the imperial estate.

"Do you think that I should have left you in this ablaze shelter?" she declared.

"No, of course not! But, at first, you didn't know where I was. So, why did you do it anyway?" he asked again.

"I would have done the same thing for anyone in my family," she replied simply.

Franz Joseph wasn't convinced of his cousin's argument, but he didn't have the physical faculties to continue the interrogation. He had to regain his strength as fast as possible so he could announce his engagement to Helene. He barely knew this relative from the Wittelsbach dynasty. She was said to be of refreshing beauty and outstanding intelligence. The monarch, upon the recommendation of the archduchess, had decided to find a wife as soon as possible. The eldest daughter of the ducal couple certainly represented the perfect choice to hold such a coveted position.

"Sissi, tell me about your sister," asked Franz.

She returned to her cousin's bedside to talk about the beautiful Helene.

"Where shall I begin?" she said in a low voice.

"She is my best friend. Since we were children, we have always been there for one another. We've never been mad at each other for more than half a day. My sister is kindness itself," she said by way of introduction, looking at the emperor.

Intrigued by Sissi's wording, he asked her to be more specific.

"Well, you see, I have a more difficult character than Helene. Despite my childish behaviour, she has always remained gentle and sensitive towards me. Last month, I was horseback riding with her. A dog that came out of nowhere barked so loud that her poor beast knocked her down. Even if she had just hurt her ankle, she showed incredible kindness. Helene is just made that way!" let out Sissi.

Satisfied with the description he had just heard, the emperor was convinced that his cousin was the ideal wife.

The day went by very quickly and Sophie swiftly thanked her niece for her attentive care. She told her that it was time for her to leave and that Franz had to rest.

"My dear child, we will be expecting you in the morning. Do bring your sister for the occasion," demanded the aunt.

Sissi immediately climbed on Polly's back and headed to Possenhofen Castle. Along the way, she thought about the day she spent in the company of her cousin. She even came to believe that perhaps Franz Joseph wasn't as uninteresting as she had thought.

"I am very happy to get to know the monarch," she murmured.

When Sissi finally arrived at the family residence, everyone hurried around her to hear the latest news about Franz. She told them every detail, without leaving out anything, about her presence at the bed side of Franz. At night, exhausted, she fell asleep earlier than usual.

As required by the archduchess, the next morning, Sissi and Helene arrived at Ischl Castle. Sophie welcomed them in person as she wished to speak in private with her future daughter-in-law. She needed to question Helene about her intentions as potential wife. It was decided that they would amble around the imperial gardens.

Meanwhile, Sissi sat on the same stool she had the day before. Impatient to see his cousin again, Franz had been waiting for her since he was awake.

"Dear friend, your presence is a relief to me. I only have good memories of the day we spent together," declared the man, smiling.

Sissi, embarrassed by the compliments of the monarch, immediately blushed, which did not go unnoticed by Franz Joseph.

"Sissi, forgive me… I didn't want to put you in an uncomfortable position," said Franz, looking ill at ease.

"Don't worry about it! You've taken me by surprise, that's all!" she replied.

Sissi had also enjoyed keeping her cousin company. So it was not a burden for her to visit his apartments.

To relax the atmosphere, Franz suggested that they go down to the drawing room. He needed a change of setting since he hadn't left his room in days. Sissi took leave of the monarch so that he could put on decent but – most of all – comfortable clothes. With the help of two servants, Franz barely managed to get dressed. As soon as he was finished, he asked for his cousin.

"My dear, would you be kind enough to help me walk," he asked politely.

She didn't have to be asked twice, so the emperor placed his arm on the shoulder of Sissi. He moved slowly with the support of his cousin. They managed to reach the ground floor rather clumsily. They entered the room and walked to the long, black piano.

"Sissi, my aunt told me that you played this instrument beautifully. Would you agree to play some soft music for me?" Franz Joseph almost begged.

She did love to sit at the piano on rainy days. While saying that she played beautifully might have been a slight exaggeration, she just couldn't refuse since Franz had asked her so kindly.

Franz sat in a velvet armchair while his cousin settled at the piano. She lifted the small wooden flap that covered the keyboard. She threw a timid glance at her cousin and placed her frail hands on the instrument. For over fifteen minutes, Sissi's refined fingers danced on the keys. A nearly divine melody filled the huge room. With his eyes closed, Franz listened to each and every note. He was exhilarated to hear such beautiful music. Although he was used to listening to musical compositions, to him, there was nothing more gracious than the sound of these voluptuous notes.

In the middle of the afternoon, after talking about everything and nothing with the archduchess, Helene set out to keep her cousin company. After she was told where she could find Franz Joseph, she headed there. As she opened the doors slowly, she saw her sister, sitting at the piano. Not far from her, the emperor seemed very relaxed in her presence. The scene almost appeared trivial, but not in Helene's eyes. She knew her younger sister better than anyone; just by looking at the movements of her body, it was obvious that Sissi enjoyed playing for him. It was more than a simple relationship between relatives.

Uncomfortable, she shut the doors and walked in the corridor. Surrounded by paintings from the greatest European artists, she didn't know what to think. Was her imagination playing tricks on her? Had she jumped to conclusions? *I mustn't think about such nonsense*, she thought. Not to disturb the monarch and Sissi, Helene patiently waited in the emperor's antechamber.

At lunchtime, Franz returned to his apartments to eat some hot soup. When he entered the anteroom, he noticed the presence of Sissi's sister.

"Helene! Have you been sitting here long?" asked the man, surprised to see his future wife.

"Your Majesty! I was waiting for you… If you agree to it, I would like to spend some time with you," she suggested reluctantly.

Could he refuse such a thoughtful attention from the woman who was about to become empress? Without really wanting to, he accepted her offer. It wasn't that Franz Joseph disliked his cousin, but rather that he preferred the company of Sissi. She just seemed more entertaining and less formal than the eldest. Franz had Sissi notified that her presence was no longer needed for the remainder of the day. Sensitive to Helene's happiness, she returned to Possenhofen Castle without protest.

The next day, she repeated the exercise, always with more conviction. The emperor, who was feeling better and better, spent long hours with his cousin. Soon, the monarch had completely recovered from his injuries. For that, he had the doctors to thank, but he also knew that the true miracle came from Sissi's constant presence. The man was convinced of it, and he thanked her on many occasions.

In early August of 1853, when everyone was impatient to hear the emperor's official proposal, Sissi was beginning to have real feelings for the emperor. She, who had once considered her cousin to be insensitive and proud, had to face the facts: she was madly in love with Franz Joseph of Habsburg. Sissi and the monarch were alike on many levels. They both adored horseback riding, hunting in the forest and the opera. But a sizeable obstacle remained, he was twenty-three years old and she was almost fifteen. And the issue proved to be even more problematic since Franz was to marry her sister, the beautiful Helene. For now, she would keep this secret to herself.

On the second week of the month, the archduchess and the emperor invited Max and Ludovika, along with their children, to a costumed party. Most of the noblemen and women from the south of Bavaria were asked to attend this big event. As per her custom, Sophie was hoping to solidify the historical ties between Vienna and Munich. She also wanted to show the extent of the Habsburgs' power, and it was certainly the best occasion to do so.

The members of the ducal family arrived early in the evening. Except for Sissi, who preferred to show up later. She did not want to attend the emperor's official announcement. She knew very well that her cousin would take advantage of the celebration to ask her elder sister's hand in marriage. No one suspected that she had feelings for the monarch. Only Helene had suspicions about her younger sibling's state of mind. Unsure of the situation, she did not say anything about it to Sissi.

It was planned that Franz Joseph would share a waltz with the daughters of the ducal couple through the course of the evening. He began the first dance with the youngest, Sophie. She was awfully loquacious and wouldn't stop talking pointlessly. Despite her young age – six years of age –, she had an opinion on everything. The second one, Mathilde, was only four years older than the first one. More refined, she was disconcertingly timid with anyone. Although Franz was used to exchanging civilities, he could not find the words to start a conversation. Maria, the next one, had a strong personality in spite of her twelve years of age. She was clearly very ambitious. The emperor saw in her a determination to climb up the ranks of power. When it was Sissi's turn to dance with the emperor, she remained invisible. Everyone started looking for her across Ischl Castle. At this exact moment, Helene grasped the scale of her doubts concerning her sister's feelings towards her cousin.

"My aunt, do you know where my dear cousin was the last time you saw her?" asked Franz, worried.

"Dearest nephew, I think that she was taking a stroll in the gardens," answered the duchess of Bavaria.

Without giving it a passing thought, the monarch hurried outside to find Sissi. She seemed to have magically disappeared since no one had seen her. *But where is she?* Franz fretted. Suddenly, the answer became very clear to him. He rushed back inside the castle and asked one of his servants to give him a lighted torch. Franz ran out to the forest. Behind him, the archduchess was shouting to her son, telling him to come back to the guests. It was no use since he only had one thing in mind. Franz Joseph rushed to the cabin that was destroyed by the fire. If there was one place where Franz was certain to find his cousin, it was there.

"Sissi!" he called out.

He circled the ruins of the building and, as he had expected, saw Sissi sitting in the grass. She was crying her eyes out in the dark woods. Not to interfere in her private moment, he put out his torch. With a light step, he walked closer to her and looked at her, so fragile yet so strong. Without her courage, the emperor probably would have perished in the fire. Moreover, she had helped him recover by spending entire days with him.

"Don't cry my dear!" said Franz softly not to scare her.

Surprised by his presence, since she thought she was alone, Sissi jumped. She tried to see the face behind this manly voice, but it was dark.

"Cousin, is that you?" she asked, restless.

"Of course!" he replied, caressing her cheek with his soft hand.

"Franz, I am sorry I didn't come this evening. You see, my heart is aching, truth be told."

"And what could be the cause of your sorrow?" he asked.

Sissi, uncomfortable to face the one she loved, did not utter a word. Worried by her silence, Franz Joseph wrapped his arms around his cousin. Pressed against him, she felt her heart skip a beat. He, too, was nervous to be in her company.

"Dear cousin, I love you!" declared Sissi, closing her eyes.

Upon hearing this, the man understood that his fate was about to be decided. What she didn't know was that the emperor also had tremendous feelings for her. He had fallen madly in love with Sissi during the days they had spent together. She had become the main source of his daily joy. In the morning, when Sissi arrived at Ischl Castle, Franz was already awake for quite some time. At night, upon her departure, he looked forward to the next day with delight.

"Your feelings echo mine," he replied with trembling lips.

After he uttered these words, she burst into tears. Never would she have imagined that he would open his heart to her. The man responsible for her paced heartbeats humbly shared his emotions with her.

"Franz, I couldn't live without you. I know that you are to marry my sister… Despite all my efforts not to give in to temptation, I cannot help it. I long to live by your side till death do us part," she confessed to him truthfully.

"I feel the same way. Without you, my life is meaningless," declared the emperor, kissing her forehead discretely.

They both fell silent for endless minutes in the arms of one another. For them, the Earth had just stopped spinning. The wind brushed away the sounds of the night. These two completely enamoured beings had come to understand that their destiny would now be intertwined.

"How will we face your mother, and my parents?" she asked, breaking the silence.

"With the truth! I am the Emperor of Austria, and I shall decide who I want to share my life with," exclaimed Franz Joseph to convince himself.

"Franz, I don't want Helene to suffer because of me. I would die of sorrow if I knew my sister were devastated by my happiness," she explained in a grave voice.

"Fear not, my dear Sissi. Our situation will have to be accepted by all," he said to reassure his beloved.

The Emperor of Austria and the daughter of the Duke of Bavaria would have to remain discreet for a few more days. Before making their love official, they had to ensure their passion was enduring. Was it a deep feeling or a mere fondness? Franz suggested that she return to the imperial residence. Their lengthy absence would eventually be noticed by the guests, and most of all by the archduchess.

On the porch of Ischl Castle, Sissi saw her eldest sister with Sophie in the distance. The situation would likely upset her. Would she be able to put on an act? She had never lied to anyone, much less Helene.

"Be brave, my dear!" whispered the monarch into Sissi's ear.

In fact, Franz Joseph was as nervous as her, and perhaps even more so. He had to face his mother, the terrifying and strong-headed woman of the imperial family. This certainly wasn't the easiest thing to do, even for a dignity of his rank.

"Franz, where were you?" thundered Sophie, raising her arms in despair.

"Your Imperial Highness mustn't worry, I went to look for Sissi," he told precisely.

"I see that you have discovered her hiding place," replied the archduchess, looking at Sissi with disdain.

She, intimidated by her aunt's attitude, couldn't say a word to defend herself. Her only reaction was to lower her head before the archduchess.

"My dear child, could you leave His Majesty and me alone?" demanded the emperor's mother with a discourteous voice.

Against her wishes, Sissi immediately obeyed. What other choice did she have at this evening where more than a hundred people were invited? She bowed before the monarch and her aunt, then walked in the palace.

"My son, let's go for a walk in the gardens, shall we," suggested Sophie, pointing in that direction.

"Of course, mother!"

Franz Joseph knew very well that she would speak about his marriage to Helene. The purpose of their stay in Bavaria was, after all, precisely to wed the emperor to his cousin, wasn't it? As he had anticipated, they discussed lengthily this very important project for the archduchess.

Meanwhile, Sissi spent part of the night dancing with a handful of noblemen, each one wealthier than the last. A minute didn't go by without the young woman thinking about Franz.

On the following days, the two sweethearts met regularly at the shed. In the greatest secrecy, they spent long stretches of time together, without worrying about the future. But reality caught up with them soon enough when the emperor's stay came to an end. Indeed, his imperial duties forced the monarch to return to Schönbrunn Palace. A war in Eastern Europe required Franz Joseph's presence in the centre of Austrian power.

On August 19, the night before the departure of Franz Joseph and his mother, the ducal couple was invited to the Habsburg residence. None of their children, not even Sissi, was present for the occasion. Sophie, who was always behind her son's initiatives, did not know the reason for this mysterious meeting.

Standing in the drawing room, the emperor was surrounded by the archduchess, the duke and Ludovika. Each one was sitting in an armchair, waiting for Franz to speak. The two sisters were convinced that an impending wedding would be announced, to their hopeful delight. Both were mistaken and would be greatly astonished at the outcome.

"Dear mother, uncle and aunt… I have asked you here today to announce something that, I sincerely hope, will make you as happy as I am," he said to begin.

Sophie was ecstatic at the very thought of hearing the words "marriage" and "Helene" come out of the emperor's mouth. Since the birth of her eldest child, she had been waiting impatiently for this day.

"Duke, as you probably know, a man, particularly a monarch, must share his life with a woman. The time has come for me to marry the woman who will become the Empress of Austria. This is why I'm asking for the hand of your daughter Sissi in marriage," declared Franz Joseph, staring at the father of his beloved.

A heavy silence hit the enormous room. Rendered speechless by the surprise, the authoritarian Sophie could not believe her hears. Her son had mentioned the name of this Sissi. A Wittelsbach unworthy of wearing the crown of the Habsburgs, and much less of being heir to the Empire. She jumped up, in an uncontrollable fit of anger.

"Have you lost your mind, son? You were supposed to marry Helene, not this girl," she exclaimed, furious.

"Mother, I thank you… and my aunt, but my heart belongs to Sissi," replied the emperor.

"I cannot support your project… She isn't capable of complying with the tasks needed from a supportive wife and sovereign," hurled the archduchess cursing fate.

Hurt by his sister-in-law's slanderous words, Max spoke, on the defensive.

"Sophie, I believe that you got carried away and that you didn't mean what you said."

"Absolutely not! You daughter is not the one who should marry my son," she thundered.

"I won't accept that you insult Sissi. You are not in any position to judge her," he shouted.

Cornered between her sister and her husband, the duchess closed her eyes a split second. It was true that she would have preferred to see Helene marry Franz, but if he had feelings for Sissi, why not approve of their marriage.

"Enough!" she cried.

Astounded by the intervention of Ludovika, everyone ceased their ear-splitting racket.

"Sophie, I also think that my eldest daughter would be the ideal person, but... If Franz Joseph wants to marry Elisabeth, why should we prevent it?" she declared, trying to meet the eyes of the archduchess.

"Ludovika, I understand your reaction. Sissi is your daughter and you think highly of her, but be reasonable... She cannot become the emperor's wife," replied the other one, in a conciliatory tone.

Noting his mother's stubbornness, the monarch had no other choice but to impose his idea. For the first time, Franz did not agree with the woman who had offered him the throne of the Habsburgs. He was torn between his mother and his feelings, but he couldn't act any other way.

"Mother, I love you like a son should, but I will marry Sissi... Whether you want it or not!" he said in conclusion.

Humiliated before her sister and her brother-in-law, the archduchess retired to her apartments, in a terrible fury. It was better not to get in her way. Alone in her room, Sophie sat on her wooden chair, in front of her Renaissance-style secretaire, to write in her personal journal.

> *On this nineteenth day of August, His Majesty has decided to hurt me as a mother. With the arrival of Elisabeth of Wittelsbach, misfortune shall fall on the Empire of Austria. May the Almighty enlighten the emperor in his project of marriage with this young woman.*

Franz Joseph had decided, in agreement with his future wife, that she would stay with her family until their wedding day. It wasn't that the two sweethearts weren't sure of their feelings, but rather that it was more practical that way. On the one hand, a war was threatening Eastern Europe, which forced Franz to be away quite frequently and, on the other hand, the monarch wished to let the dust settle for the good of his relations with the archduchess. Satisfied with this decision, Sissi would make the most of the months that remained by spending some leisure time with the Wittelsbachs.

One winter's night, the duke took a stroll around the estate of Possenhofen with his daughter. Since they were alone, they took advantage of this relaxed setting to discuss her future. In this peaceful location, the father wanted to know the true feelings of his favourite.

"Sissi, do you love Franz sincerely?" he asked, staring at the moon.

"Why this question?" she replied, rubbing her hands to keep them warm.

"Well, you see, I only want your happiness. Knowing that my child is happy is my first priority for my old age," answered the man, lighting his pipe.

"Father, I may not have the experience of Franz Joseph, but I know that all my thoughts are for him. Ever since that stormy night, my heart only beats for him," added Sissi.

Max, exhausted by his hike in the snow, sat on a flat rock. He didn't doubt for a minute the sincerity of the relation between his daughter and his nephew. His worries were related to the role and the responsibilities that would fall upon her as Empress of Austria. Love was one thing, but duty was another.

"Sissi, do you know that by marrying the monarch, your life will change radically?" he continued, putting emphasis on the last word.

"Your concern for my future touches me deeply… I understand what awaits me in Vienna very clearly," she declared, smiling to the nobleman.

Half-reassured, Max had to face the facts: his daughter was serious. As the good father figure that he was, he had to support her as best as he could.

On April 23, 1854, on the stroke of noon, a golden carriage drawn by six attired horses, crossed the streets of the

Austrian capital. Tens of subjects from the Empire had gathered along the itinerary that was planned for the event. The most powerful took part in the cortege of the imperial family. Everyone was curious to see the future sovereign. For months now, rumours of the emperor's marriage with Elisabeth of Wittelsbach were going around from house to house.

Nervous, Sissi timidly waved at the cheering crowd. She had never seen so many people packed together, screaming her name, especially in a foreign country. She, sitting on a leather bench, was experiencing larger-than-life moments. Franz, who was by her side, tried to entertain her by whispering tender words in her hear. He understood the scale of the task that awaited his fiancée.

"My dear, do you think I'm capable of successfully undertaking what is expected of me?" she asked.

"Absolutely! I have no doubt about your talent," answered the monarch.

The imperial cortege continued its way to the gate of the Habsburgs' residence. In the main yard, Austrian dignitaries along with the members of the monarch's family were waiting for him and his bride-to-be. Nearly fifty people bowed when Franz Joseph got off the vehicle. A few seconds later, Sissi followed, but an unfortunate event happened. As a result of her inexperience, she did not lower her head enough when she came out of the carriage. Her diadem, an imposing diamond-set jewel, hit the door and fell onto the stony ground. The blunder did not remain unnoticed by the archduchess.

"Foolish child!" she told herself in a low voice.

She instinctively bent over to pick up the precious jewel. Franz helped her place the valuable object back on her head. He took her hand and guided her amid the important figures of the Empire. The two sweethearts headed directly to their apartments.

Since she was child, Sissi had never entered the famous Schönbrunn Palace. Her mother had described it to her with so much precision that she thought she recognized the emperor's room. Canvases of the greatest painters were hung on the walls, a gigantic bed filled the room and a few pieces of furniture were placed here and there.

"Honey, to respect the custom and the laws of the Church, I will not share your bed tonight. Tomorrow, once we have exchanged our vows before God, we will spend our first night together," declared Franz, kissing Sissi on the mouth.

She had to obey the rules of the Holy Scriptures and had no intention of becoming estranged from the Almighty. She spent the remainder of the day preparing the ceremonies for the next day. For this special occasion, the wedding celebration was to be held in one of the sacred temples that Sophie had selected. Despite the weariness of the last few days, Sissi worked relentlessly to carry out her task well. She stayed up very late and only went to sleep when she was completely satisfied with the instructions to be followed.

During the night, she couldn't get any sleep. She was so nervous that she couldn't relax at all. At dawn, she was sitting in her bed, waiting for the turn of events. The servants brought her breakfast, but her stomach couldn't hold down any food.

Around eight o'clock, the archduchess walked to the apartments of her future daughter-in-law.

"Sissi, get up! A memorable day awaits you," she said right away.

Sissi obeyed her aunt, without uttering a word. *Why argue with Franz's mother?* she told herself, knowing that any other attitude would be pointless.

"The servants will help you get dressed for the ceremony. Afterwards, join me in my private parlour," ordered Sophie, clicking heels.

"Very well, my aunt!"

As mentioned by the archduchess, the women serving the imperial family followed the instructions of Franz Joseph's mother. Some were styling the bride's hair while others were helping her put on her bulky dress. After quite some time, Sissi was finally ready to face her big day. She went down to the tenth floor and – not without difficulty for her clothes hindered her movements – headed to the room where the archduchess was expecting her.

"Here you are, my dear!" exclaimed the authoritative woman, getting up from her armchair.

Without much discretion, the mother of the emperor looked at Sissi from head to toe. A white dress, with golden lace embellishments, and a train of the same colour enhanced the shape of Sissi's body. She was enchantingly beautiful, most certainly one of the prettiest young women in Europe. Even Sophie had to admit such a striking truth.

"Everything is perfect! Stand up straight, my child… we aren't in the countryside of your Bavaria, here," she hurled spitefully.

Humiliated, Sissi lowered her head, to her aunt's greatest pleasure. Sophie did not want her niece to be her daughter-in-law, so she had decided to make her life unbearable. Such was her revenge on her son's unilateral decision.

According to the protocol of the Imperial Court, the monarch had to be the first one to get to the Augustinian church. There, he would wait for his wife-to-be for the marriage ceremony. Afterwards, a sumptuous cortege with Sissi on board would head to the religious building. As planned by the archduchess, everything took place in an orderly fashion, without a hitch.

The vehicle carrying the future Empress of Austria came to a halt before the copper doors of the edifice. An impressive crowd had gathered on-site. Men, women and children joyfully expressed their happiness. Even before she was crowned, Sissi had won the hearts of her many subjects. They saw that her character was in opposition with the despicable temperament of the monarch's mother. According to them, it could only prove to be profitable for the people that a foreign noblewoman marry their monarch.

"God, please guide me in my new life," begged Sissi, getting off the carriage.

Escorted by soldiers in uniform, she graciously walked into the church. Four pages were holding the bride's white train. When the master of ceremonies was told about the presence of Sissi, he nodded to the musicians so they would start playing their instrument. A celestial melody resonated inside the walls. Alone before her fate, she light-footedly advanced towards the altar. Along the central aisle, she stared at the man of her dreams. Franz was wearing a white and red suit with some Empire insignias. In the eyes of Sissi, the emperor was probably the handsomest man of Austria.

Franz Joseph of Habsburg was born on August 18, 1830 at Schönbrunn Palace, in Vienna. The eldest son of Archduke Franz Karl of Austria and Princess Sophie of Bavaria was third in line of succession. Early on, he understood that the frail health of the first two heirs, namely his uncle and his father, would propel him to the imperial throne. The young, open-minded man would receive a classical education, and famed tutors would teach him the important subjects. A hunting aficionado, he spent his rare leisure time travelling the woods with his rifle. He was crowned on December 2, 1848 under the name Franz Joseph I, after some revolutionary riots in the capital.

Sissi paraded under the curious eyes of the people gathered at the cathedral. Nearly three hundred people were attending the celebrations of the imperial wedding. Members of the House of Habsburg, princes from other European countries, representatives of the Holy See, foreign ambassadors, the Empire's nobility, Hungarian diplomats and the bride's family, the Wittelsbachs. Wearing their most beautiful attires, everyone was impatient to hear the first words of the clergyman. When she arrived by her husband's side, he smiled at her to reassure her. Sissi appreciated the thoughtful attentions of the man she loved passionately. Standing before the cardinal of Vienna, the bride and groom listened to the speech of the prelate.

"Ladies, my lords, were are gathered here today to join together this man and this woman before God and the Crown," he said to begin.

Joseph Rauscher knew the emperor personally since he had taught him philosophy as a child. Today, the Catholic was presiding the religious marriage of the monarch with his young bride.

"Do you, Franz Joseph Charles of Habsburg, take Elisabeth of Wittelsbach to be your wife, to love and cherish her until death do you part?"

"I do!" asserted the man with slightly trembling lips.

"Do you, Elisabeth Amalie Eugenie of Wittelsbach, take Franz Joseph of Habsburg to be your husband, to love and cherish him until death do you part?"

"I do!" replied Sissi.

Sitting on a wooden bench, Helene shed a few tears. She was happy to see her sister marry the man she adored, but also felt somewhat bitter that she had lost her place. She spent all her lifetime preparing herself to seal such a sizeable wedding. *God had other plans for her*, she thought.

As for Max, losing Sissi to the archduchess didn't reassure him at all. He knew her well and was sure, without a doubt, that she was ecstatic at the very thought of controlling her niece. Incapable of watching his daughter fall into such a trap, the man preferred to look at the magnificent setting.

Colourful stained-glass windows enlightened the solemn atmosphere of the religious ceremony. Each one represented scenes of the Holy Scriptures: from the birth of Christ to his crucifixion. Red roses embellished the naves along with golden candelabra. A marble dove was suspended from the ceiling. The Augustinian church was probably Vienna's stateliest Christian building.

When the cardinal finished his speech, a priest brought a gold diadem set with precious stones to the emperor. Franz climbed on the first step and turned to his wife. This moment was certainly the most important of Sissi's new life. She kneeled down on a small padded stool and kept her head straight.

"As emperor and sovereign of Austria, I, Franz Joseph, crown you empress. May the Almighty help you with the duties that fall to you as of now," declared the monarch, placing the symbolic object on Sissi's head.

She was officially becoming the most important woman of the Empire and the main advisor to the emperor. The times of her carefree walks in the forest of the estate of Possenhofen were long past.

The bride and groom headed to the exit, waving to the guests. Everyone, but the duke, applauded when the imperial couple walked in the central aisle. The greetings outside were as warm, perhaps even more so. The subjects of the monarch shouted for joy in response to the marriage of Franz Joseph and Sissi.

"Long live the emperor! Long live the empress!"

CHAPTER 3

A Threatening Mother-in-law

Schönbrunn Palace
1854-1855

AFTER THE emperor and the empress' wedding ceremony, the archduchess demanded to meet with her new daughter-in-law. She wanted to give her advice about her duty as a wife. It was paramount for the Imperial Crown that a lineage be ensured as soon as possible. Although the monarch was still quite young, a problem could present itself at any time. Sissi had to understand her obligations towards Austria.

A valet knocked on the door of Sophie's antechamber while she was reading.

"Come in!" she declared without raising her head.

"Your Imperial Highness, Her Majesty the Empress is here," said the individual, walking into the room.

Sissi headed towards the piece of furniture where her mother-in-law was sitting. In a familiar gesture, she wanted to lay a kiss on the woman's cheek. Before Sissi even had time to do so, the archduchess threw her a snubbing glace.

"My child! Do you still think that you are on your father's land?" exclaimed the authoritative aunt.

Speechless before such words, the empress took a step back. She saw no harm in showing a mark of respect for Sophie. At Possenhofen Castle or Ludwigstrasse Palace, her parents would have never lectured her for such behaviour. Evidently, Sissi hadn't gasped the role that was expected of her from the Imperial Court.

"Please take a seat in this armchair," demanded the woman, looking towards the object in question.

Sissi carried out the request of her husband's mother. Alone in the antechamber, they began talking.

"My dear, you must understand that a wife must appeal to the man who shares her daily life. To do so, I suggest that you make sure Franz is continually attracted to you. A male will swiftly lose interest in his wife, and turn to other creatures, if she stops pleasing him," added the archduchess.

The sixteen-year-old Sissi was terrified to hear this. According to Sophie, if Franz Joseph eventually found a mistress, only she would be to blame. However, throughout her childhood, her father had taught her that both the man and the woman involved in a romantic relationship had to maintain it. Today, her mother-in-law was showing her that life at the Imperial Court was utterly different from the one she had had with her parents. In the building from the previous century, the sole purpose of the emperor's wife was to attend to the well-being of the monarch.

"I will do everything in my power to keep the flame alive in my marriage," replied Sissi, disoriented by her aunt's words.

"I knew that you would eventually acknowledge your lack of experience in this area... and in many others also," responded the woman who was named the strongman of the Habsburg family.

An endless silence filled the room, located in the left wing of Schönbrunn Palace. Sissi no longer wanted to open her mouth, for fear that Sophie would humiliate her again. As for the monarch's mother, she was ecstatic to see her daughter-in-law fret about her marriage, right before her eyes.

"That will be all, you may resume your activities," concluded the archduchess.

The sovereign came out of her enemy's apartments, and nearly ran to hers. She collapsed on the floor of her room, without being noticed by anyone.

"Why does this woman hate me so much?" cried Sissi against a pillow to deaden her words.

She stood up gently, adjusted her dress with her hands and light-footedly left the room. She had decided to visit Schönbrunn Palace, the imperial residence where Sissi would have to live for the rest of her existence. Accompanied by a small dog, which Franz Joseph had given her for their wedding, she walked throughout the innumerable sitting and drawing rooms, bedrooms, hallways and other locations within the palace.

The residence of the imperial family was one of the most out-standing in all Europe. Schönbrunn Palace, which was built starting in 1696, grew in square metres following the sover-eigns who resided there. Each one of them wished to leave their personal touch, so the monarchs converted the premises according to their preferences. The building's original design was that of Emperor Leopold I from the Holy Roman Empire of the German Nation. He gave it the name Schönbrunn because it meant water fountain in German. Indeed, not far from the foundations, there was a natural spring. So as to prove the hegemony of his reign, he had wanted to compete with the architectural wonders that existed elsewhere. Since they had ascended to the country's throne, the Habsburgs had always preferred living there. Everyone considered this construction to be of unparalleled magnificence and practical convenience.

Sissi spent half a day discovering the thousand and one rooms of the huge castle. Nothing seemed to have been left to chance. The sparkling colours and the gorgeous furniture were exqui-sitely paired up. *I think that I will like it here*, she thought. Satisfied with her excursion, the sovereign returned to her apartments.

"Sissi, honey! Where were you? Your absence worried me," said Franz Joseph when he saw his wife enter the room.

"Franz, I was exploring the castle. It's such a magnificent place..." replied Sissi, embracing him tightly.

"Your words comfort me... I was waiting for your opinion about our residence," admitted the man, holding the young woman against his virile body.

The emperor let Sissi know that he had to go to the neighbouring city right away. His marshals had to report the state of the current situation in Eastern Europe to him. The problem lied mainly in the Hungarian uprising against the Austrian authority.

"Will you return tonight?" she asked.

"Don't worry, I will be back here sooner than you think," declared the emperor to reassure hear.

During her husband's absence, Sissi set out to begin a book of poetry. She enjoyed writing very much and this passion allowed her to relax. The inspiration of the moment was obviously related to love. This powerful emotion that the sovereign felt for Franz. She spent the evening, shut in her apartments, writing free-verse poetry. Exhausted by her eventful day, the empress fell asleep on the huge bed with her clothes on.

Around midnight, a warm hand gently caressed her face. Taken by surprise, she awoke in a jolt. Franz Joseph, seated beside her, had been looking at her body without her knowledge for quite some time. He was in love with his wife and proved her so in every way possible. The emperor swamped her with gifts and other presents.

"My darling, I would like to make you a woman tonight," whispered the emperor, looking at the angelic face of Sissi.

Mixed emotions took hold of her at the thought of having sexual intercourse with him. Would she measure up to his expectations? It was too late to back down; she had to face her fears. In a surge of abandon, Sissi lay down comfortably on the satin sheets. She shut her eyes and felt her husband's hand fondling her body. Never before had a man touched her this way. Franz passed his fingers over her body as if she were a goddess. Her skin was so soft and so fresh that it couldn't rival that of any other woman. Was it because of the love between them?

"My darling, I want to press my lips all over your body. My feelings for you are so deep," whispered Franz Joseph kindly.

Only a handful of candles lighted up the room. She was excited by this first night as a woman.

"Honey, we should take you out of these bulky clothes," said the monarch, untying Sissi's dress.

A feeling of modesty came over the young sixteen-year-old woman, who was completely naked. It was the first time that she encountered herself in full nudity. He was her husband and he had the right to show her all the love he had for her. In a surge of passion, the monarch laid a thousand kisses on the empress' breasts. This initiative made the sovereign uncomfortable. The arousal she had initially experienced gradually transformed into a sense of obligation towards her wifely duties.

"Franz, I'm not feeling well," she murmured.

"Don't be afraid!" replied the emperor, without stopping.

The most repulsive moment for Sissi was when the man drove his member inside her. It was such an unpleasant sensation that she let out a shriek. Franz had no intention of stopping in the heat of the moment. For her, the sex act seemed to last almost an eternity. It wasn't that her husband was rough in his manners, but rather that she did not like what he was doing at all. Half an hour later, after giving himself to his better half, Franz Joseph fell asleep by her side. That night, the monarch made a real wife out of Sissi, a status that she had obtained without truly wanting it.

The next morning, before the first sunrays peeked through the window, Sissi slipped a green dress on and headed to the gardens of Schönbrunn Palace. What had happened the previous night had terrified her greatly. She still felt pains in her lower abdomen, even several hours after the sex act. She begged the Almighty to intervene so that the emperor wouldn't take a liking to this carnal pleasure. Amidst the scented flowers, a shiver came over her loins. Sissi didn't much enjoy this new sensation that possessed her body. Suddenly prone to dizziness, the empress had a hard time standing up. She looked for an area where she could rest for a little while, but there didn't seem to be any bench nearby. The sovereign unexpectedly fell down, not knowing why. A boy, having witnessed the scene, rushed to her assistance. He helped her lean against a tree trunk, located a few steps away from her.

"Thank you, my friend," uttered Sissi, unaware of the individual's identify.

"At your service, Your Majesty," answered the young masculine voice.

When she had come to her senses, she looked at her brave knight. He had brown hair and his features were that of the Eastern European nation. He limped with one leg, but it didn't seem to bother him much.

"What is your name?" asked Sissi.

"Vlad Bavòry."

"What are you doing on the Habsburg estate?" she continued, curious.

"My father is the ambassador of the Magyars. I'm accompanying him during his stay in Vienna," added the foreigner.

"Forgive my ignorance, but what country are you from?" asked the empress.

"You, Austrians, call it Hungary," replied Vlad.

The governess of the ducal couple's children had told her about this nation when she was a child. Bordering the Empire, they were frequently forced into submission to the power of imperial capital. Known for their rather unsophisticated temperament, the Magyars were more or less peasants without education. Despite that, they were rising up against Franz Joseph's army.

"Madam, forgive my lack of civility, but you are different from the other members of the imperial family," asserted the boy.

"I'm not from around here... Bavaria is my homeland," declared the woman.

She was speaking to the foreigner without worrying about her rank or the rules prescribed by the protocol. Indeed, an empress couldn't, under any circumstances, discuss with enemies. Hungary had rebelled against the authority of Vienna, and the son of the Magyar emissary was the enemy that needed to be vanquished. But not for Sissi. He was merely an angel on her path. He had helped her when she wasn't feeling well. Why should she hate him?

"Sissi!" cried a familiar voice in the distance.

"Hurry on, Vlad… You must return to your father right away," whispered the empress, looking at her husband who was getting nearer.

The boy obeyed and sneaked out of the garden through the flowers. When Franz arrived near his wife, the foreigner had disappeared.

"What are you doing here, my dear?" asked Franz Joseph.

"I wanted a breath of fresh air… I miss the breeze of Bavaria in the morning," added Sissi to support her claim.

"My darling, I only seek your happiness. If you wish to see Possenhofen Castle again, we shall go in the beginning of summer."

"I am so happy to hear that," declared his wife, clapping her hands.

Like every year, the arrival of the warm season was synonymous with rest for the imperial family. Everyone went to the Habsburg estate for a few weeks. For Sissi, this was the perfect occasion to see her relatives and her land against.

"Sweetheart, my mother wishes to meet with you after breakfast," announced the emperor.

"Is it really necessary that I meet her in private?" let out sovereign with a disagreeable voice.

"Why do you refuse the advice of the archduchess? She has your well-being and the Crown's at heart," added Franz, smiling to his wife.

"Very well! If such is your desire, then I will do it for you," replied Sissi half-heartedly.

As promised, she met her mother-in-law in her apartments. The two women, who were alone once again, talked about the day before. Face-to-face, they could speak to each other in secrecy. With a cutting tone, Sophie interrogated Sissi lengthily.

"My child! How was your first night of intimacy with His Majesty?"

The empress, who refused to tell the truth, did not know what she should say to avoid bringing the archduchess' wrath upon herself. She decided to go for a cautious lie.

"Very well, Madam! A small pain made me somewhat uncomfortable, but that's all," asserted the sovereign.

"Don't worry about this minor unpleasantness. We all feel such a pain at the beginning... but time will take care of the situation," declared Franz Joseph's mother.

Sissi was relieved by the understanding reaction of the archduchess. She had feared the worst and it hadn't happened. She had just avoided yet another humiliation.

Archduchess Sophie of Austria, born Sophie Friederike Dorothee Wilhelmine of Wittelsbach, was the daughter of King Maximilian I Joseph and Queen Caroline of Bavaria. She descended from a royal family and had received the best education of her time. The princess was very close to her sisters and her mother. Ever since she was a child, she had been prepared to be joined in matrimony to a dignity of her rank. Surrounded by powerful women – her aunts had married monarchs and noblemen of Russia, Sweden, and German territories –, she was hoping to ascend to this coveted status. This moment would finally present itself on November 4, 1824 when Sophie would wed Archduke Franz Karl of Austria. Through this union, she would officially join the imperial family and the House of Habsburg. She would give birth to five children: Franz Joseph (1830), Maximilian (1832), Karl Ludwig (1833), Maria Anna (1835), and Ludwig Viktor (1842). Two of her sons would become emperors, one of Austria and the other of Mexico. The loss of her only daughter, who was barely five years old, would break her heart forever. Out of love for her eldest son, she convinced her husband to abdicate the throne in his favour.

On the weeks that followed, Franz headed to Hofburg Palace daily. Located in the heart of Vienna, the building was a nerve centre for the affairs of the Empire. The man left Schönbrunn Palace very early in the morning and came back late at night, often around midnight. He was a real workhorse, and he took his position at the top of the Austrian power pyramid very seriously. As time passed by, the monarch would go away for longer and longer stretches of time. Abandoned by her husband, Sissi spent her tedious days writing poems in her notebook or walking in the gardens of the imperial residence. She was in love with Franz Joseph, but she was starting to hate her life as an empress. Moreover, the young woman's mother-in-law continuously spied on her. Her every move was commented on by the archduchess, negatively more often than not. Everything was going wrong for Sissi.

She would receive some good news in early June when the emperor would inform her of their upcoming departure for Bavaria. The imperial couple was going to Ischl Castle for the summer vacation. Franz's mother had declined the invitation because of her husband's health, so the two sweethearts would be alone on the Habsburg estate.

On June 15, 1854, after about two months of marriage, Sissi returned to her motherland. The journey between Vienna and Munich took place without a hitch. The monarch had decided that he and his wife would pay a courtesy visit to the king. For the occasion, Duchess Ludovika was invited by Maximilian II to receive the imperial couple. The mother of the Austrian empress was the aunt of the new Bavarian sovereign.

When the horses stopped before the wrought iron gate of the king's castle, Sissi hastily got off the carriage. Holding on to her hat with one hand and waving at the passers-by with the other, she even came to forget her manners due to the extent of her enthusiasm. Standing behind her, Franz admired the energy with which Sissi ran across the royal estate.

"My darling, you are going to trip if you keep on hopping this way," let out the man, roaring with laughter.

"Don't worry, my dear husband... I am like a butterfly darting from flower to flower," replied Sissi with a melodic voice.

She was the happiest woman in all Europe. Nobody had ever missed their land as much as her. The empress even shed a few tears, which did not go unnoticed by the emperor.

"Come, we must meet His Majesty and your mother," he declared somewhat moved.

Holding hands, they walked inside the castle of the King of Bavaria. It wasn't the first time that Sissi laid foot inside. During her childhood, she had gone there on several occasions with the duchess. Wasn't she a member of the royal family after all? When the imperial couple entered the palace, the sovereign and her aunt came to greet their distinguished guests warmly. The empress literally jumped into her mother's arms. Astonished by her daughter's reaction, Ludovika did not know how to react. Sissi thanked heavens for bringing her back home. Given the emperor's position, such familiarity made him feel uncomfortable.

"My darling, please get a grip on yourself... May I remind you that we are in the presence of the king," he said with a soft voice.

She didn't hear him, for she was too happy to be reunited with the members of her family. She was constantly lectured by the Archduchess of Austria and needed some motherly comfort. She was barely sixteen years old and her character didn't measure up to Sophie's.

"My child, get hold of yourself! I understand your excitement, but you are now the Empress of Austria… Please behave accordingly," whispered Ludovika in her daughter's ear.

Sissi slowly moved away from her mother, wiped her face with her silk handkerchief and returned beside the emperor. She had been mistaken about her mother's feelings. She thought that Ludovika would have showed her just as much gratitude. Sadly, it wasn't so. Bitterly disappointed, she would keep a rather painful memory of the event.

"Your Majesty, it's always a pleasure to see you," said Franz straight away.

He then leaned over his aunt to lay a kiss on her cheek. She thanked him politely and smiled affectionately. Kinder to her nephew than to her daughter, Ludovika wanted to show her attachment to Franz Joseph. This gesture, not without consequence, hurt the empress harshly. *How can she ignore me when she opens up to His Majesty?* she thought.

After the appropriate greetings, the imperial couple spent an hour with the sovereign. They talked about the political affairs of the Empire and the kingdom. The two men seemed to enjoy speaking about their favourite topics. As for Sissi, she hated these long and dull conversations.

"My husband, may I be excused? I would like to take a stroll in the backyard?" asked Sissi.

"Go ahead, my dear!" replied Franz without paying any attention to his better half.

She would have preferred being in the company of her mother, but she had returned to Ludwigstrasse Palace to attend to her affairs. Alone, once again, she paced around the plot of the royal estate. It was insipid and completely uninteresting.

"At least Schönbrunn possesses wonderful gardens," she told herself in a lower voice.

"Perhaps! But the air of Bavaria is beyond comparison," replied a woman.

Sissi wondered where the words she had just heard came from. A familiar face suddenly appeared from behind a bush.

"Helene!" cried the empress with boundless joy.

The two sisters ran to each other, dropping their personal effects in the process. So many events had taken place in their lives since the famous summer of 1853. They had parted in a more or less serene atmosphere. The eldest, the first choice of the arch-duchess, had seen the imperial crown slip through her fingers. The youngest had won over the heart of the Emperor of Austria.

"Your Majesty!" replied Helene, raising the bottom of her dress to curtsey.

"Stop it! There is no empress between us. We will always be the best friends in the whole world," exclaimed Sissi, taking her sister's hand.

They sat together on a small wooden bench, slightly warped from the bad weather, and looked at each other closely for a short while.

"You are even prettier today," asserted the sovereign.

"That's very kind of you, my dear sister. You are well aware that you will forever hold the first position."

"Helene, you must know that I never wanted to hurt you," let out Sissi, holding her hands tightly.

"I know that! The last thing I would want is to lie to you, so I will tell you the truth. When you were chosen by His Majesty, my heart stopped beating. I despised you…" admitted the eldest.

Sissi, who had imagined her sister's sorrow on that memorable summer, had never weighed the extent of her anger. She was revealing the essence of her thoughts. Troubled by this truth, the empress listened carefully to Helene's words.

"Today, I think that I understand the turn of events. Franz fell in love with you, your kindness and your beauty," her sister continued.

"You must understand that I did nothing to gain an advantage in his eyes. I think that the long days we spent together during his recovery brought us closer tougher," interrupted Sissi.

"I know! One day, while you were playing the piano for him, I caught a glimpse of you through the doorway of the drawing room. You seemed so comfortable with one another."

Surprised to hear her sister's well-kept secret, Sissi remained speechless for several minutes. She sat on the bench, listening to Helene.

"I finally understood everything on the night of the emperor's masquerade ball, at Ischl Castle. You absence spoke loud and clear of your sadness, since you knew that His Majesty would officially announce our engagement… The pain of hearing the news straight from his mouth would be unbearable for you. I would have probably done the same thing if I had been in your shoes. The question was whether Franz felt the same way about you."

Still under the shock of her sister's recount of events, Sissi could imagine the bitterness that Helene had experienced. Her secret must have eaten away at her for nights at a time.

"I knew that the die was cast when he went to look for you. Franz Joseph showed the Wittelsbachs that he had chosen you," she concluded, with a lump in her throat.

"My dear friend, I thank you from the bottom of my heart for opening up to me in such a way. I fear that I won't be able to obliterate your scars, but you can rest assured, as God is my witness, that my intentions have never been to inflict any kind of pain on you," swore Sissi with trembling hands.

The two sisters wept and wept; they were finally reunited after spending so many months apart. They pledged, for the rest of their lives, never again to leave any quarrel between them unresolved.

"Enough with bad memories! Tell me, how is your life at Schönbrunn Palace?" asked Helene, replacing the collar of her coat.

"I'm learning about the duties of an imperial wife. I admit that I find it difficult to please our aunt, but Franz is very supportive," explained Sissi.

"Is it exciting to have so many privileges?" wondered the other.

"Not really! Each word that I utter and each action that I take is judged by the Imperial Court. I feel like I'm doing everything wrong... The archduchess never congratulates me if I succeed at something," confessed the empress.

"My dear sister, if the monarch gives you his support, that's the most important thing," said Helene to comfort her younger sister.

"Maybe you're right!"

During Sissi's stay in Bavaria, the two confidantes would meet regularly. They spent hours talking to each other. The Wittelsbachs would also enjoy their favourite pastime, buying clothes in the shops of Munich.

The duke and his favourite left for a hunting excursion in the woods surrounding Possenhofen. Alone with their dogs, father and daughter would reminisce about their strolls in the forest. They had embraced nature so many times when they needed a safe haven from daily worries. Once they reached the lake, Max stored his rifle in his leather holster. Since his daughter's departure, he had been looking forward to this meeting to find out about her new life.

"My child! I'm anxious to know that you are so far away from me," he said, taking a stone in his hand.

"Why is that?" asked the empress.

"I know you... When you are unhappy, I know it," added the man, throwing the pebble he was holding in the water.

She could not lie to her father because, for as long as she could remember, they had always shared an unshakable bond.

Telling him lies could only damage their unique relationship. So she decided to go for it.

"Indeed, father, I'm having a hard time adapting to my role as sovereign and wife. According to aunt Sophie, I only do foolish things," confessed Sissi.

"I knew that the archduchess would cause you some troubles… I will speak to her…" thundered the nobleman.

Sissi came closer to the duke and looked him in the eyes. She did not want him to intervene in her personal affairs.

"No! I must overcome this hardship myself. I accepted to marry Franz and I will solve this issue on my own."

Despite his protective side, Max had to listen to his daughter and leave it up to her. The sovereign demanded to take care of her own life and he had to respect her wishes. They both agreed to stop speaking of the disagreements related to the Imperial Court.

On August 20, after spending a restful summer, the emperor and his wife returned to Schönbrunn Palace. In the vehicle that was bringing her to the Austrian capital, Sissi hoped that things would go back to normal for her. During their stay in Bavaria, the two lovebirds had been able to find each other again and share some moments of intimacy. They had also managed to solidify their union, to the sovereign's greatest delight. *Perhaps Sophie will stop intimidating me if I prove my loyalty to the Empire and the Habsburgs?* she convinced herself. Determined, the woman wanted to rise to the challenge of earning the consideration of her mother-in-law. Sissi would do everything in her power to prove that she was the ideal wife for her eldest son.

Sexually speaking, Sissi still hated offering herself naked to her husband, no matter how in love with him she was. In spite of that, she had to carry out her task as empress by trying to give an heir to the Austrian Crown. To do so, she made sure that she shared Franz Joseph's bed regularly. The emperor was attracted to his wife and loved the nights of intimacy he spent with her. The feelings he had for Sissi made the sex act much more exciting.

She finally became pregnant in the summer of 1854. The news was sent to every corner of the Empire and Europe. Relieved by the announcement, the archduchess took the unilateral decision to watch her daughter-in-law closely. She wanted to ensure that she didn't encounter problems during the pregnancy. Every day, she kept the empress company. Each of her actions was examined by the emperor's mother. Sissi had become nothing less than Sophie's prisoner.

One night, she burst out sobbing and demanded the intervention of her husband. She explained the situation to him, but he did not seem to understand what burdened her.

"Sissi, you should be thanking the archduchess for her thoughtful attentions," he declared after an argument about the subject.

"Your mother is willingly interfering in our couple and you aren't taking any action," thundered the empress, slamming the door of their bedroom.

The atmosphere had become tense in the imperial family and everyone blamed Sissi.

"Her Majesty does not seem to grasp the position she is holding," some said.

"The sovereign is ungrateful for the support of Her Imperial Highness," argued others.

Only one of the emperor's brothers, Archduke Karl Ludwig, stood up for his sister-in-law. It was not uncommon to see him beside himself when he witnessed some gossiping about Sissi. He, himself, suffered from the presence of the archduchess in his private life. On more than one occasion, she organized receptions attended by young women who belonged to the noblest of European families. The objective was always to find him a suitable wife.

In the middle of autumn, Sissi asked the monarch to allow her sister to come visit her. The pretext was that she missed the Wittelsbachs. But, in fact, she was hoping to count on an ally within the Imperial Court. For his wife's happiness, he granted her request.

Helene arrived at Schönbrunn Palace in early December of 1854. White snow was beginning to shroud the Austrian land. It was agreed that the confidante of the empress would only be staying for two weeks. After that, she would have to leave the imperial residence.

When Sissi's eldest sister entered the sitting room adjoining the apartments of the sovereign, she found her younger sibling lying on the ground. Concerned about her health, she ran to the room of the archduchess to find some help. As was her custom, Sophie put the blame on Sissi.

"This foolish child is putting the heir's life in jeopardy," she declared in the presence of Helene.

Shaken by her sister's condition, she was speechless before the words of the emperor's mother. Nevertheless, she was more preoccupied by the empress than by the cutting words of her aunt.

Franz Joseph ordered that his wife be surrounded by the most competent doctors of Austria. Sissi was bedridden for an indefinite period of time, so she could regain her strength. No visits were allowed except for those of her eldest sister.

"Helene, thank you for being by my side," said the ill, extending her arm out to her.

"My heart suffers to see you like this," she admitted, holding the empress' hand.

"Don't worry about me, I am strong you know."

The frail health of the sovereign lasted more than a week. Throat aches, headaches, and stomach aches tortured the young woman night and day. The eldest looked after Sissi throughout her stay. Every night, Franz spent long hours lying by his wife. When she was asleep, the monarch left the room to get some sleep himself. All the Empire was moved by the physical suffering that afflicted Sissi.

"Helene!" uttered the empress feebly.

The confidante had the archduchess informed of her sister's recovery right away. Sophie ran to the apartments of her daughter-in-law to assess the veracity of this piece of information.

"Your Majesty!" cried the emperor's mother when she entered the room.

Sissi, sitting on the edge of her bed, raised her head towards her aunt who was nearly hysterical.

"Madam, I am well!" she said half-heartedly.

"Ask for the doctors... Her Majesty needs to be examined along with the child that she is carrying," demanded the archduchess.

Helene, happy to see her younger sibling in better health, thanked heavens for their intervention. She had feared the worst for her favourite sister. *Now that she is out of danger, the empress will recover easily*, she thought.

The sovereign, somewhat lost in the surrounding uproar, tried to pull herself together. How long had she been lying in this bed? Had she offended Franz Joseph with her frail health? So many questions rushed in her head.

"Where is Franz?" asked Sissi to her aunt with strength and energy.

"Calm down! His Majesty is in a meeting with the Supreme Council. A messenger has left to give him a letter from me," explained Sophie.

Meanwhile, two doctors – the most renowned in Vienna – arrived at Schönbrunn Palace. They were escorted to the room of the empress. Once inside, the men of science demanded that everyone leave the room. The ill woman had to rest, and their racket caused her unnecessary stress. Equipped with their medical instruments, the practitioners carefully examined Sissi's body. The sickness seemed to have cleared up and the health of the empress was improving. All was well, according to the doctors' assessment.

As soon as Franz Joseph received word from his mother, he left Hofburg Palace. The monarch had been waiting for this moment for several days, and he certainly wasn't going to wait any longer.

After fifteen minutes, the monarch appeared in the doorway of his beloved. Her eyes were closed and it looked like she was peacefully at rest. Franz moved slowly towards his sleeping wife. Standing beside her, he looked at her carefully. This woman, his woman, was the most precious thing in the world. Franz may have been reigning over a powerful empire, but he would have given it all away not to lose Sissi.

Her eyes suddenly fluttered open and the most adorable image was right in front of her. Her husband, the love of her life, was smiling at her with an infinite tenderness. Their gaze was welded to one another and a unique energy was flowing between them. This powerful feeling had been uniting them since that summer of 1853. Nothing around them was important in this inexpressible moment. They were alone in the universe. There was no Sophie, no imperial family, but only two beings who truly loved each another.

"My darling, here you are once again among the living," exclaimed the man with teary eyes.

"Franz, all my thoughts were for you. You were in my dream… You were holding my hand, reassuring me, telling me that everything would be just fine," she described, her eyes filled with wonder.

"I am by your side. Not a day has gone by without me saying a prayer for you," he said caressing her cheeks.

"Your Majesty, I love you… My heart will never stop beating for you," declared Sissi, emotional.

The emperor leaned towards the sovereign's mouth and kissed her softly. She put her arms around his neck and embraced him tenderly. The imperial couple was closer and stronger than ever.

Hidden behind the wooden door, Helene had overheard the conversation between the two sweethearts. She was very pleased that her younger sibling and her cousin were so in love with each other. She promised to prevent anyone, especially the archduchess, from destroying such a unique bond. The eldest sister was far from done with her role of protector towards Sissi. She would carry on her mission with even more conviction now that her sister was at the top of Austrian power.

Seven days later, Helene left Schönbrunn Palace to return to her homeland. When they were about to part, the two sisters swore to remain in close contact with one another. They couldn't live without each other. The Wittelsbachs were like two parts of one whole.

"Be strong!" she let out when she bid Sissi farewell.

The empress benefited from a month of truce. At the request of Franz Joseph, Sophie stayed away from her daughter-in-law for a while. Not out of compassion, but rather as a result of strategic calculation. The Christmas celebrations had to take place at the imperial residence in Bavaria. For the occasion, Sissi's family would be invited at Ischl Castle. It was more advisable, according to the archduchess, to maintain a healthy relationship with the sovereign.

Sissi, about five-month pregnant, had a rather comfortable pregnancy. She did not have any pains in her belly or anywhere else. In spite of that, Franz asked to reduce the physical efforts of his wife to a minimum. At twenty four years of age, Franz Joseph had to provide the Imperial Crown with male offspring. Without any heirs, the dynasty would not survive the passage of time.

The whole Wittelsbach family was reunited for the winter period. Gathered at Ischl Castle, Sissi's brothers and sisters were all very happy to see their sibling again. Apart from Helene, no one else had been in her presence since the visit of the imperial couple the previous summer. Their reunion took place in sheer joy. Even the severe Sophie seemed to be affected by the nostalgia surrounding the birth of Christ.

While a thick snow covered the Habsburg estate, the empress – despite her round belly – wished to go for a walk outside. Wearing warm clothing, she left the building with a wooden cane. Should she feel faint, she could hold on to the object. As the considerate husband that he was, Franz Joseph accompanied Sissi. Even if she was a crowned head, her passion for excursions in the woods had not waned. The country-woman that she was still lay dormant inside her.

"Be careful, my darling!" declared the monarch, walking behind her.

"I know Bavaria like the back of my hand," she replied as she kept on hiking.

The imperial couple moved forward strenuously in the snowy paths surrounding the palace. Her pride had gotten the best of her, and she did not allow the superhuman efforts that were required of her to be seen. Her pregnancy hindered her movements and her breathing. Clearly, she had overestimated her strength, given her current state. After hiking for half an hour, she felt a painful cramp in her lower-abdomen. She grinded her teeth because the physical hardship was unbearable. Unable to go on, the empress fell to her knees on the white ground. Witnessing his beloved's moment of weakness, Franz quickened his pace to come to her assistance.

"Sissi! What's going on?" he yelled, out of breath from the effort.

"Franz, I'm in pain!" she cried, in tears.

Franz Joseph walked to his wife. He saw that she was holding her rounded belly with one of her cold hands. He tried to lift the empress up in his arms, but it only increased her suffering. What could he do? Abandoning his beloved, alone in the middle of nowhere, was out of the question.

"Honey… I must lift you from the ground to take you into my arms," he said, touching her hair.

Sissi understood that it was the only way she could get out of this unfortunate situation. She nodded to her husband that he could carry her to safety. She gritted her teeth to ease the pain. When he was able to haul her from the ground, Franz took his wife into his arms. With the strength of his love for her, he carried her to Ischl Castle.

Completely exhausted, the emperor collapsed on the portal of the imperial residence with Sissi against him. Weakened by the enduring pain, she had lost consciousness. Under the accumulation of snowflakes, the two sweethearts lay before the copper doors of the palace.

"Mother, I forgot Sissi's present. I'm going back to Possenhofen quickly," said Helene when she realized her mistake.

She hadn't even stepped outside that she saw the horrible scene: her sister and her cousin were lying in the snow. Their face was reddish and their lips almost blue. A fit of panic seized her at the terrifying sight. She threw herself on her younger sibling to check if she was still breathing. Luck seemed to have been looking over Sissi since her heart was still beating.

"Come here!" shouted Helene, nearly damaging her vocal chords.

Her words reverberated through the building's doorway and caught the attention of Max. The nobleman, who was about to go out to smoke his pipe, rushed to the scene. At the sight of his favourite, lying inert on the ground, he feared the worst.

"Sissi! Franz!" cried the man, taking his offspring into his arms.

A manservant, who witnessed the tragedy, immediately informed the archduchess and her sister of the situation. Both of them, holding the bottom of their dress, headed to the entrance hall as best as they could. Ludovika was petrified by the brutal shock. With one hand covering her mouth, she was unable to move or speak. In better control of herself, Sophie ordered one of her servants to send a letter to Munich. In the message, she demanded no less than the presence of the personal doctor of the Bavarian king.

Meanwhile, the emperor's guards carried the two bodies inside the palace. It was decided that they would put the two crowned heads in separate rooms. This was done to avoid causing potential pain to the spouses should one eventually awake without the presence of the other. Everyone was on the alert because of the uncertainty that stemmed from the monarch's and his wife's frail health.

"Yet another of your daughter's vagaries," vociferated Sophie towards her brother-in-law.

"Madam, know that I forbid you from despising Sissi. If your kindness were as vast as your malice, you would be the most amicable woman on Earth," he replied in a burst of rage.

Caught between the two sworn enemies, the duchess didn't pay attention to their words. Her only concern was that of a mother for her child and nephew. The incessant disputes between her husband and her sister did not get to her.

An army of servants surrounded the sovereigns, lavishing them with the best of care. While one wiped off Franz Joseph's forehead, the other one wrapped up Sissi's frozen limbs with warm towels.

The doctor arrived more than an hour later. The roads were snowed in, so the man of science had a hard time getting to the palace. Equipped with his medical kit, he climbed the stairs that lead to the apartments of the imperial couple quickly. He entered the room of the empress with as much promptness, and forgot to greet the people who were there. His first action was to give the pregnant woman a morphine injection, to ease the physical pain.

"She caught the flu because of the cold," were the doctor's first words.

"Do you think that Her Majesty will make it?" asked Ludovika with trembling lips.

"Definitely! Apart from her chilblains, her condition is far from serious," he replied, manipulating his medical instruments.

The archduchess, her sister and the duke were relieved to hear the doctor's medical verdict. Sissi and the child that she was carrying were out of the woods; their lives were no longer at risk. The empress would have to spend this time of festivities in a comfortable bed to regain her strength.

Reassured by his patient's condition, the man of science went to see the emperor. He examined meticulously Franz Joseph's body: his eyes, his ears, his heart, his breathing, and his articulations. The monarch was merely tired from carrying his wife in the snow on such a long distance. Rest was the practitioner's only recommendation.

"We will make sure that His Majesty does not do any unnecessary effort," declared Sophie, looking at her brother-in-law from the corner of her eye.

By saying this, she was putting her message across. There would be no hunting while the imperial family stayed in Bavaria. Franz had to follow the doctor's advice.

The convalescence of the empress spread over nearly two weeks. Throughout her bedridden days, Sissi's husband read to her. Sitting in an armchair, Franz spent long hours keeping his sweetheart company. For nothing in the world, he would have changed places with someone else. The sovereign was delighted to receive this much attention from her husband.

In January of 1855, the imperial couple and the archduchess returned to Schönbrunn Palace. They all had to go back to their respective lives in Austria. Sissi, bitter at the thought of leaving her motherland, would have given anything to stay in Bavaria. To her, the city of Vienna represented much sorrow. Night after night, before shutting her eyes, she prayed to God that he would help her overcome her suffering. Each day was the same. The monarch left regularly to go to Hofburg Palace; Sophie controlled the behaviour of the empress, and Sissi locked herself into her apartments to cry in silence. This clearly wasn't how she had pictured her life.

The sovereign, who was eight-month pregnant, felt her first contractions in early March. Informed by her daughter-in-law, Sophie decided to take control of the imperial delivery. A group of specialists, made up of about eight practitioners, looked after the emperor's wife. Their sole task was to make sure that the childbirth went smoothly. Tens of servants, some of which who had experience in this field, assisted the men of science. At the top of the pyramid, there was the authoritarian Archduchess of Austria. As for Franz Joseph, he was told about each stage of the labour on a permanent basis.

"Madam, would you be so kind as to have my sister Helene over?" asked Sissi to her aunt.

"Absolutely not! We're enough people here as it is… Moreover, she would be of no use to you," she answered.

Why involve another Wittelsbach in a State affair? thought the mother of the monarch. An ally of the empress certainly wasn't welcome in this crucial period for the future of the Austrian Crown.

On March 5, 1855, around noon, after some interminable physical anguish, Sissi was completely exhausted. The child was blocked in her uterus and did not seem eager to leave its comfortable nest. The doctors' interventions did not manage to extract the baby from its mother's womb. Franz, worried about not being present on the scene, put his daily work aside to support his wife. Sitting in the antechamber of the empress' apartments, he nervously waited for the seemingly endless delivery to come to an end. At his side, his brother Karl Ludwig tried, in vain, to entertain him with some jokes. Too troubled by the shrieks of his beloved, he was unable to take his mind off things. The monarch was broken-hearted and would have willingly switched places with Sissi if her pains hadn't eased.

The empress was no longer able to withstand this torture. The suffering was so unbearable that she lost consciousness in the middle of a contraction. Clearly, the childbirth wasn't going according to plan. The life of the mother and the child were now at stake. The doctors, who were debating the situation, concluded that a drastic choice had to be made in order to save one or the other. The eldest practitioner, Ernest, was given the difficult mission of announcing the delicate news to the imperial family. He came out of the room, closed the door behind him, and looked at the Habsburg.

"Your Majesty! Things aren't going as well as we had hoped," declared the man of science, taking his glasses off.

Troubled by the doctor's words, the monarch stood up abruptly. He did not quite grasp the gravity of what he had just heard.

"What do you mean by that?" questioned Franz.

"We are unable to save both... You must choose between the empress and the child," added Ernest, stammering.

Being hit in the stomach would have been less painful than having to choose between the life of his wife or his child. Before such a heavy responsibility, Franz paced back and forth a long while. Karl Ludwig, who witnessed his brother's distress, did not know what to do to help him. Not far from there, the archduchess had heard the conversation between her son and the doctor. Realizing that her eldest son was in no position to make such an important decision, she invited herself into the discussion.

"Franz Joseph, you must choose the continuity of the Habsburgs," she said by way of introduction, putting her hand on his forearm.

"What do you mean by that?" he exclaimed.

"My dear, we must save the infant. He will ensure the survival of the Imperial Crown," added Sophie, replacing one of her rings so that its diamond would stand proudly on her hand, face up.

Astounded by his mother's words, the emperor flew into a rage. Never before had he lost his temper against the archduchess, but this time, she had gone too far.

"Madam, do you realize what you are suggesting? You are asking me to let the woman I love die. I would give up my own life for Sissi... and you want me to leave her to her fate?" thundered the monarch.

Disconcerted to be humiliated in such a way before witnesses, she raised her voice. She was the strong head of the Habsburgs, and she wouldn't let Franz intimidate her.

"Stop this childishness! For once, behave as an heir who is worthy of his ancestors," she cried so that everyone understood her tenacity.

"Mother, is your heart made of stone? Never, do you hear me, never will I let my wife die!" shouted the angry man.

Ernest, embarrassed to have seen such an outburst, returned inside the room of the empress. He told Franz Joseph's order to his colleagues. God seemed to have witnessed the argument. In his great goodness, he spared the mother and the child. Both were saved from the ill fate that awaited them. Tired, Sissi closed her eyes an instant. She had just escaped certain death. Despite everything, she had fulfilled her duty towards the Austrian Crown. A new member had joined the dynasty.

"Madam, your daughter is in perfect health. You've just overcome quite an ordeal," announced one of the domestics, presenting her with the young baby.

She had not succeeded in giving the imperial family a male heir even though she had asked, even begged, the Almighty to fulfill her dearest wish. A daughter! *How will the emperor and the archduchess react?* immediately thought Sissi. A few tears fell down her sweaty cheeks.

The youngest servant came out of the room, with the baby wrapped up in a warm and fluffy blanket. With a smile on her face, she presented the young offspring to its father. Happy about the birth of his child, he pressed the small being against his chest. The sex of the infant was of no importance to him. His wife had just given him the prettiest daughter of the Empire.

"The next time, it will be an heir," he said, looking at the baby's angelical face.

Content with the fact that her daughter-in-law had just given birth to a female child, Sophie could still hope that the empress would eventually vanish. A woman who proved to be incapable of giving birth to a son risked repudiation at any time. As long as Sissi honoured her main responsibility, she could afford to lose her title as the Austrian emperor's wife. The archduchess, after fighting with her eldest son, hated Sissi more than ever. Never before had Franz stood up to his mother. The love he felt for this scatterbrain blinded him, thought the authoritarian Sophie.

CHAPTER 4

Empress under Obligation

Schönbrunn Palace
1855-1856

THE MORNING after the birth of the imperial couple's first child, the archduchess, in her ruthless fight against her daughter-in-law, had the baby's bed and personal effects placed in her own apartments. Sophie had decided that it was up to her to bring up her son's offspring. As an experienced woman, she was in the best position to fulfill this important task.

"Nene, where is my daughter's furniture?" asked the empress, worried.

"Her Imperial Highness had the personal effects of the young archduchess moved to her quarters," replied the servant innocently.

Upset by what she had just heard, Sissi rushed to her aunt's private parlour. Wearing a simple nightgown, she demanded an explanation from her mother-in-law. On the spur of the moment, she opened the door. Emotional, she headed to the armchair where her Sophie was sitting.

"Madam, how dared you?" she cried in a vehement outburst.

"Calm down, my dear! You will wake the baby if you do not stop right away," replied the archduchess arrogantly.

Even more infuriated, Sissi looked daggers at her sworn enemy. She wanted an answer, and she would get it whatever the cost.

"I'm asking you to explain yourself," protested the empress.

"Sissi, do you sincerely think that you are able to take care of a child? You're hardly able to control yourself as it is," added Sophie, smoothing out the front of her dress.

"You have no right to meddle in my private life. I am this baby's mother and it is up to me to decide."

"It doesn't matter, she will remain under my supervision…" concluded the archduchess, turning her back to the empress.

Without speaking another word, Sissi returned to her apartments. She paced around her room. *It's my child, I should raise her,* she murmured. She immediately asked one of her servants to help her get dressed properly. She also demanded that a carriage be prepared and asked a valet to keep it waiting in front of the gate of Schönbrunn Palace. As soon as she was dressed, she walked to the main floor decidedly.

"Madam, where are you going?" asked the eldest servant.

"I'm going to find His Majesty!" answered the empress.

Sitting in the vehicle, she told the coachman to head to Hofburg Palace. Sissi had no intention of caving in to her aunt's unilateral directive. Her influence had run its course, according to her.

At the same time, the archduchess was informed of her daughter-in-law's hasty departure. She knew very well that Sissi was going to the heart of the capital, where her son worked.

Once she had reached her destination, after a fifteen-minute journey, the empress ran to the emperor's ante-chamber. Without being announced, she rushed in the richly adorned room. Portraits of previous monarchs and stylish furniture adorned the premises. Gathered around a circular table made of carved wood, a handful of men were discussing military affairs.

"Franz!" let out Sissi, crying.

"Gentlemen, please leave us," demanded the emperor.

"Did you know that your mother had decided that she would be taking care of our daughter's education?" thundered the sovereign, clenching her fists.

"Yes, the archduchess told me this morning," replied her husband calmly.

Disappointed by her husband's statement, she remained speechless a brief moment. Once again, Franz Joseph was taking his mother's side. In the eyes of Sissi, this attitude was unacceptable.

"My darling, an empress shouldn't demean herself by undertaking such a common task. Her Imperial Highness has a lot more experience than you in this area," he explained clumsily.

Sissi did not want to hear another word from the mouth of the man she loved. It was clear that she would not be able to change things in her favour. Without adding anything else, she promptly left the antechamber, holding on to the bottom of her clothing. Franz, astonished by the strong reaction of his wife, tried vainly to catch up with her.

Shaken, the empress sat in the carriage like an automaton. She decided, without weighing the consequences, to head directly to Munich. The distance between the two capitals was extremely long, especially after a snowfall. But the empress had only one thing in mind: seeking the comfort of her family.

The vehicle ventured on the poorly maintained roads of Austria. When the coach was about to cross a slippery ravine, it immediately overturned. Stunned by the blow when her head hit the cabin's walls, Sissi lost consciousness. The coachman died on impact when the carriage crashed into a pointy rock. As for the horses, they ran away into the wilderness. She was alone in a corner of the Empire that she did not know.

When she came to, three dark-skinned women were surrounding her. Lying on a straw bed, Sissi glanced around her. The cart she found herself into was in a piteous state. An icy wind was blowing through the cracks. Some thick, grey blankets kept her warm, so she did not feel cold at all. Her eyes were drawn to the odd objects that were hanging from the vehicle's walls. Rabbit feet, multicoloured scarves and mysterious jewels decorated the place. The trio of strangers was speaking to her in a foreign language. She had never heard it before. Her saviours, who were wearing dirty, worn out

dresses, constantly moved their arms. The empress was starting to fear the worst. The convoy eventually stopped after a
long journey. The women left the caravan one by one. Alone
once again, the sovereign sat up on her makeshift bed, not
without difficulty. She was wondering why the strangers had
left the caravan.

"Madam! How are you feeling?" asked a manly voice.

Surprised, she glanced around to find where these words
came from. They were spoken with a distinctive intonation.
Sissi didn't see any man around her. Suddenly, the beige curtains behind her bed magically spread open.

"Allow me to introduce myself, I am Yourik. I am the head
of the Bohemians of the mountains," he explained, mispro-
nouncing his words.

"Sir, can you tell me where we are presently?" asked Sissi
with all her courage.

"We are on the border between Bavaria and Austria," he
specified.

So she wasn't very far from her motherland. How had she
gotten herself in such an unexpected situation?

"My brave man, where is my carriage?"

"You were alone on the road when we found you."

The man told the story of his people throughout the centuries. Hunted by the crowned heads, they were constantly
forced to roam over the roads of Europe. And so they had
become travelling nomads. Bohemians originally came from
the Eastern countries of the Austrian Empire. Today, they
went from land to land to feed themselves, trying to survive.

"Tell me, if you are the leader of this area, then who leads all the land?" questioned the empress.

"This is a long story. Formerly, my ancestors reigned over wealthy and prosperous kingdoms. One day, the first Habsburg invaded what belonged to us. Since then, we no longer have a true monarch. In reality, the Emperor of Austria is our king, but we do not pay allegiance to him. He obtained this title through the blood of our forebears," he explained in detail.

Sissi feared that the Bohemians would discover her true identity. She, Franz Joseph's wife, could easily be made a scapegoat of, should they wish to avenge their fate. Caution was her best ally in such circumstances. For the time being, no one among them recognized her.

"Madam, may I know your name?" asked the individual.

The sovereign had to find an answer to this question quickly, without giving away her identity. The simplest explanation was often the best solution.

"I am Elisabeth Markel... I live in Bavaria, in a small northern village," lied Sissi.

"Interesting! What were you doing in a carriage with the coat of arms of the imperial family?" replied the Bohemian.

Sissi's heart was pounding in her chest. What could she say without putting her foot in it? She felt a burning heat inside her.

"I am a servant at Schönbrunn Palace. The Empress of Austria is my mistress," she added.

"Really! Well, that explains it..." he declared, smiling.

After this conversation, the leader went back outside with his people. He invited Sissi to join them around a big fire. About twenty caravans were placed in an arc of circle. Amidst them, hundreds of people were bustling about. Some were preparing the meal while others were melting snow to drink. A small community was created in complete nature. It did not only include adults since there were children playing among the older members. The sun was about to set as delicate snowflakes filled the sky. Life seemed so simple among the Bohemians. There was no archduchess present to dictate everyone's conduct. Sitting by the fire, the empress was warming her hands. She was wearing a fur coat on top of her clothes.

Meanwhile, at the imperial residence in Vienna, Franz Joseph learned that his wife hadn't returned to Schönbrunn Palace. The monarch grew worried. Where was Sissi? Why hadn't she returned immediately after her stop at Hofburg Palace? The emperor suddenly fell prey to remorse.

Taking advantage of her daughter-in-law's blunder, Sophie went to her son's apartments. She could not miss the occasion to prove, once again, Sissi's immaturity. Since her marriage, she had never ceased to behave foolishly. With all the arrogance in the world, she walked into the monarch's sitting room.

"Franz! Don't you see how this impudent woman isn't fit to hold such a function."

"Will you stop destroying my marriage with Sissi one day? Why do you work so hard at hating my wife, who also happens to be your niece, might I remind you," he exclaimed, raising his arms in despair.

"Why are you taking this out on me? You must admit that I am right about this scatterbrain," let out the archduchess, hitting her fists on the emperor's desk.

"No, you are wrong! If only you didn't spend your days pestering her with the slightest thing... I will find my beloved wife and, upon her return, I will ask you to be more understanding towards her. Am I making myself clear?" ordered the monarch, staring at his mother harshly.

He called his best men together and laid out the situation for them. Sissi had to be rescued whatever the cost and wherever she was. The emperor loved her and he had no intention of giving up on finding her. As a first initiative, he sent some soldiers to Bavaria. He wanted to check with Duke Max if his wife hadn't sought refuse at his residence. An armed group galloped to Munich straight away. Franz Joseph, who was in charge of this delicate affair, couldn't sleep all night. The worst scenarios raced through his mind. A kidnapping, an accident, or a murder, all these possibilities played out in his head.

"No! You are alive..." murmured Franz.

The empress stayed with the Bohemians for over a month. She integrated with these people rather easily. The women of the community adopted her as one of their own. Always on the alert, Sissi lived in constant fear of being recognized. If Yourik learned that the wife of the Austrian monarch was among them, she would undoubtedly be used in an exchange. But how much money would they ask for?

To avoid alarming the subjects of Empire, Franz announced that the empress would be staying at the Wittelsbachs for a little while. With the complicity of his father-in law, Franz Joseph considered that it was the best solution to avoid disclosing the secret. If revolutionaries detained the sovereign, they could assassinate her in a fit of panic.

When the winter was coming to an end, the emperor somewhat lost hope. Franz still thought that his wife was of this world, but he was no longer certain that he would see her again one day. Despite that, he demanded that the intensive search be continued.

Each night, Sissi looked up at the star-filled sky lengthily. Away from her husband and her child, she still hoped that she would hold them into her arms again. She was beginning to think that her only chance to be reunited with her people was to tell the truth. If she revealed her true identity and explained that she wasn't responsible for the unforgivable actions of the preceding monarchs, perhaps Yourik would help her return to Vienna.

One early morning, she joined the head of the Bohemians in his caravan. Sissi's vehicle wasn't far from there. It belonged to a fortune-teller, an old woman who was said to be about one hundred years old. She had taken the foreigner under her wing. Since the empress' first day among the nomads, the eldest member of the people who had been hunted down by the

Austrian emperors had offered food and lodging to the unfortunate woman. In compensation, she helped out the community however she could. She cut wood, prepared meals, played with the children, and taught the older ones to read and write. Sissi felt incredibly comfortable among the nomads. She wasn't considered incompetent or scatterbrained. She was respected for her participation in the life of the group.

"Yourik, may I speak to you?" she said by way of introduction, as she walked into his cart.

"Of course! Come in, Elisabeth," answered the man, pouring himself a glass of brandy.

The sovereign sat on a wooden barrel, next to the head of the Bohemians. They were alone and very few members of the group were awake. *This is the perfect time to start a composed conversation with him,* she thought.

The head of the former subjects of the late kingdom of Bohemia was born on April 1st, 1835. The son and descendant of an uninterrupted lineage of leaders lived on the roads of Europe. An only child, he received the heavy task of looking after the fate of his people. From an early age, his people's wise men taught him his future responsibilities. Only four other men bore the same title as him. They had spread across Eastern Austria, Hungary, Bavaria, and Poland. Yourik Bartòk had fallen in love with a woman in the past, but she died when her caravan capsized in a stormy stream. Since that day, he had never given his heart to anyone else. With time, sorrow had toughened him. Life hadn't allowed him to have children, therefore he didn't have any potential successor. According to the legend of the nomads, he was a direct descendant of the last King of Bohemia.

"Tell me, if you were to meet the Emperor of Austria, what would you tell him?" asked Sissi, folding her hands.

The brown-haired man looked straight into her eyes and rubbed the goatee that concealed his prominent chin. For weeks he had been expecting this question. Yourik had even taken the time to prepare an answer.

"My dear friend, I know that Franz Joseph I isn't responsible for the vile actions of his predecessors. But since his coronation, His Majesty has never agreed to some level of inclusion for my people within his empire," he declared with a conciliatory tone.

Sissi wasn't particularly gifted when it came to political matters, and so she didn't understand what the head of the Bohemians meant exactly. On the other hand, she was able to rally the adversaries to a common cause.

"Perhaps the monarch's advisers aren't the best ones at that?" let out the empress.

"In that case, the monarch doesn't have absolute power over his empire. If ill-advised men dictate to him what his thoughts should be, he isn't a great lord," he replied humorously.

"In that case, for the good of your people, why don't you try meeting Franz Joseph in person to explain the situation to him?" suggested Sissi with a provocative voice.

"The reason is simple... If I go before His Majesty, he will order my capture to enslave my people," replied the nomad.

"I see that you have a very bad opinion of him."

"Elisabeth, if you were the monarch or, even better, the empress, what would you do for the Bohemians?" exclaimed the individual, relishing his question.

Fear suddenly overcame Sissi. *He suspects something*, she thought. Her frail hands became wet and her cheeks flushed. She was uncomfortable on her coarse barrel.

"If I were the emperor's wife, I would try to show him that an alliance with your people would benefit both parties," she replied tactfully.

"Interesting! So I can count on you to convince him then," said the leader, bowing his head towards her.

She didn't quite get the meaning of Yourik's words and gesture. Why did he suggest that she speak about it with the monarch and why had he bowed before her? All of a sudden, the empress understood that she was unmasked. The Bohemian knew her true identity.

"I surmise that you know who I am!" declared Sissi, standing up.

"Indeed! You are Elisabeth of Wittelsbach, Empress of Austria," explained the other one solemnly.

"Since when have you known?"

117

"Well, you see, we have spies at the Imperial Court... Two weeks ago, one of them told us that Franz Joseph's wife had gone to Bavaria, but rumour had it that neither the Wittelsbachs nor the Habsburgs had heard from Her Majesty," continued the man.

"Why hasn't anyone from the community said anything to me about it?" asked Sissi, sitting back on the wooden barrel.

"Simply because I'm the only one who knows," he confessed, winking at her.

"Why did you wait until today to tell me?"

"I waited until you got to know my people. Because, unlike what you think, I am a pacifist," let out the head of the nomads.

The sovereign had just come to understand the reason behind her host's silence. She would prove to be an ambassador to the power, in other words, her husband. Sissi would have wanted to be angry with the leader of the Bohemians, but she just couldn't. The nomad considered that, without shedding any blood, he could give a second wind to the hopes of his people.

"Yourik, help me return to Schönbrunn Palace and you will find in me a loyal ally," she said rationally.

"Gladly! At dawn, tomorrow, a four-man escort will guide you to the Austrian capital. Once you've reached the limits of Vienna, they will be on their way and you shall continue alone. You will be safe throughout the journey should problems arise."

A profound feeling overcame Sissi. After a month-long absence, she would finally return to the arms of Franz Joseph.

Her love for him had only increased as the days had passed. She would also be able to hold her child close to her heart, the baby girl she had hardly gotten to know. Too nervous about this highly emotional reunion, she couldn't fall asleep.

As promised, before the crowing of the rooster, five horses were waiting in front of Sissi's caravan. To ensure that she left the premises safely, she had decided not to say goodbye to the members of the nomad community. The empress looked affectionately at the old woman sleeping in her straw bed. She had been a great comfort to her. Sissi left the vehicle without a sound. Wearing the attire she had on the day of the accident, she climbed on the back of the valiant horse. Among the four men that surrounded her, she was amazed to see the head of the Bohemians.

"Are you accompanying me?" she asked.

"Absolutely! It is of the utmost importance to me that you go back to Schönbrunn Palace safe and sound," he replied, smiling kindly.

Sissi, protected by her gallant escort, galloped towards the Austrian capital. She couldn't wait to be reunited with her people. The road, which was hard to maneuver because of the spring thaw, seemed extremely long. The eyes filled with tears, the empress saw the roofs of Vienna's first buildings in the distance. *I'm coming!* she whispered. The four individuals slowed down their mounts since it was out of the question for them to accompany her beyond this point. The sovereign turned around, nodded to Yourik and waved at them. Her adventure with the nomad people was coming to an end. As she crossed the streets of the Empire's most populated city, she was becoming the emperor's wife again. Her say in the mountains had changed her forever. She wasn't the same person. From now on, Sissi knew what she wanted from life. Her two priorities were to take care of her daughter and love her husband.

The black-coated horse of the empress stopped before the imposing gate of Schönbrunn Palace. Behind the cast iron, the imperial residence looked more intimidating than ever to Sissi. Her days spent amid caravans had almost managed to make her forget about the building's majesty.

"Open the doors!" ordered the empress to the guards in uniform posted by the entrance.

The two men, astonished to see their mistress after such a long absence, did not react to Sissi's words. She had to repeat her command a second time for them to let her in.

She walked slowly into the imperial estate and headed to the porch of the Habsburg residence. She gently slid off the horse's flank until her feet touched the wet soil. She rushed inside the Austrian castle. She breathed in the usual scent of the place voraciously, which combined sweet citrus fruits and lilac. Sissi hurried throughout the dark corridors of the palace. She reached her private apartments in only a few minutes. She opened the doors and tiptoed inside. Nothing had changed. She felt like she had only left it the night before. Her hand slithered onto the furniture, the frames and the sculptures. Joyful and sad memories raced through her head. So many events had taken place between these walls. Her first sexual relation with

Franz, the nights she had spent alone, waiting for him, the mandatory rest she had taken due to her frail health and her baby's delivery.

"My daughter!"

She had been looking forward to seeing her offspring again for so many days now. Waiting no further, she ran to her child's room. Located in the apartments of the archduchess, the room lead directly to Sophie. The empress got down to the first floor and walked into her aunt's antechamber. No one was there. She partially opened the door, so she could walk to her newborn. She saw Franz Joseph, sitting in an upholstered armchair, holding their child into his arms. The two most precious beings were only a few steps away from her. Hiding in the half-open door, Sissi gazed admiringly at the soft eyes her husband laid on their little girl. He seemed so tired and yet so happy to be holding the only thing he had left of his wife.

"Your Majesty looks exhausted," declared a woman's voice.

The emperor, who thought he was dreaming, immediately recognized his wife's voice. He stood up, placed the baby in her cradle and walked to the door.

"Sissi, my darling, is that you?" he asked febrilely.

The sovereign showed herself. Overwhelmed by the sight of his beloved, the man fell to his knees before the empress. He wept away all the anxiety he had accumulated throughout the past weeks.

"You are alive! Thank God!" cried the monarch, hysterical.

Sissi, moved by so much love, threw herself on the floor to kiss her husband. Embraced together, they remained speechless. Only their gestures expressed their feelings for one another. The scene, which was highly sentimental, nearly lasted an eternity. The two sweethearts touched each other, looked into each other's eyes and kissed a thousand times.

"Franz, I prayed the Almighty to allow me to show you all my affection once again."

"My better half, I had every village of the Empire and Bavaria combed, looking for you. I was worried to death, and so was your family," continued Franz Joseph.

"An incredible event happened on my journey," she added.

Sitting on the marble patio, she told him every detail of the fantastic adventure she had experienced. Everything was so dreamlike that Sissi found her own story surprising.

"What matters is that you are back among us," marvelled Franz.

On the evening of April 8, 1855, the imperial couple gave a sumptuous banquet at Schönbrunn Palace. To celebrate the return of the empress in Vienna, high officials of the Empire and the monarch's family attended the State event. The emperor and his wife had decided to tell the truth about the absence of Sissi. Now that she was out of danger, she no longer risked retaliation from potential abductors. The event took place in the ballroom, which was oversized and rectangular. In the centre, an incredibly long table was set up to accommodate the many guests. Everyone expected to see the magnificent Sissi at the arm of the monarch.

"Their Majesty, the emperor and the empress," shouted a valet.

At least a dozen trumpets resonated across the palace. The guests stood up to welcome the crowned heads. A round of applause spread throughout the table. Sissi, whose hair was wonderfully styled, was attired in a blue dress with matching gemstones. He, decorated with military medals, was wearing a white and red suit embellished with golden lines.

Amid the hundred men and women gathered for this meal, the archduchess saw her daughter-in-law again for the first time. She examined her from head to toe more than once. Disappointed by the return of this scatterbrain, Sophie pretended that she was cheering for her. Truth be told, she would have given anything to get rid of her. Franz's mother considered that her niece was a growing menace. Although her influence remained indisputable at the Imperial Court, the same couldn't be said with respect to her eldest son. She was aware that the monarch's love for his wife diminished her own power. *I must bring this foolish child under my control*, she promised herself.

Married for a year, the two inseparable lovebirds had sworn that no one would ever tear them apart. Their mutual feelings cemented their union. After a circumstantial separation, the imperial couple was determined more than ever to preserve their marriage. Such was the promise they had made each other.

The event that took place at the Habsburg residence was one of the most memorable of the year 1855. The beauty of the empress and the charisma of her husband blew the audience away. Everyone kept an enduring and touching memory of the Imperial Crown.

After ample discussion, Franz and Sissi decided to bring back the personal effects and the furniture of the young archduchess in their private apartments. She, as a mother, had the privilege of keeping her child by her side. Nevertheless, despite her refusal, the monarch demanded that the archduchess be in charge of the baby's education. According to him, Sophie's background and life experience were invaluable assets when it came to the well-being of his offspring.

Out of respect for the empress, Franz hadn't ordered the child's baptism ceremony. Without the presence of Sissi, the event simply became unacceptable to him. He had temporarily chosen the name Sophie – in honour of his mother – for his daughter. If was now time to announce the celebration of the religious ritual to the Empire.

On the morning of April 12, a short but touching Catholic celebration took place at the chapel of Schönbrunn Palace. For the occasion, Duchess Ludovika and her daughter Helene were invited to stay at the Habsburg residence. Only a handful of privileged guests attended the Christian ceremony.

Holding the child into his hands, the priest raised her to offer her to the Almighty. The parents, who witnessed the scene, shed a few tears. Even the authoritarian archduchess felt some pride overwhelm her. She was after all a grandmother for the first time.

"In the name of God and the Holy Scriptures, I baptise you Sophie Friederike Dorothea Maria Josepha. May the Lord protect and bless you. In the name of the Father, the Son and the Holy Spirit. Amen," uttered the clergyman solemnly.

The first child of the imperial couple officially entered the kingdom of Christ. Being female, she could not be a pretender to the throne of Austria, but she was still becoming a fully-fledged member of the illustrious dynasty of the Habsburgs.

The tumultuous relationship between the archduchess and the empress toned down during the next few months. They had no affinity, but respected each other. The two women, out of love for Franz Joseph, fought very rarely. Sophie looked after the evolution of her granddaughter closely while the sovereign supported the emperor in his official responsibilities. As for the monarch, he tried in vain to be more present for his family.

As per the promise she had made to the head of the Bohemians, a formal meeting was arranged at Hofburg Palace. In early September, a delegation of ten people representing the nomads headed to the capital. Leading this group of emissaries, Yourik Bartòk carried the heavy burden of negotiating the interests of his people. To mark the historical event, the emperor commissioned his wife to welcome the diplomats. She was at the origin of this important rapprochement and, according to Franz, she was the best person to greet the guests. Sissi, who took her mission very seriously, prepared diligently for her upcoming challenge. She looked after the menu of the friendship supper, the interior and exterior decorations along with the entertainment for the evening. As for her attire, she chose a new dress, which she had bought directly from the most renowned Parisian store. It was light pink with a long train. To cover her arms, she selected a white shawl with a floral pattern. The empress, who was known for her sumptuous taste in jewelry, was only wearing a simple golden chain. Was it to express her support for the Bohemians, who were the least prosperous subjects of the Empire? She didn't display any diadem or similar adornment either. Discreet dried flowers were placed randomly in Sissi's hair.

Somewhere in the Austrian mountains, not far from the Bavarian border, the wise men gave some advice to the last King of Bohemia. For centuries their people, driven away from their land, had been hoping to reconquer their stolen territory. Yourik embodied their last hope to recover their dignity.

"Don't be charmed by the words of the Habsburg," declared the eldest of the group.

"Demand formal commitments from the emperor," added another, damning the Imperial Crown.

To address the concern of the Bohemians, the leader convened a popular assembly before his departure. The whole community attended the gathering. Standing before his peers, Yourik explained the situation frankly.

"Brothers and sisters, I feel your anxiety towards the initiative of the monarch. I am neither a messiah nor a hero, but I guarantee that I am loyal to you. As true as I am standing before the community today, the Bohemians will get the upper hand after this meeting," he declared raising his arms to motivate his people.

The head of the nomads and his advisers left the temporary encampment. The journey between their hideout and Vienna was far from easy. They had to cross hazardous roads and resting spots that were frequented by the worst highwaymen. Since Sissi's departure, the caravans had changed location more than once.

"Madam, the Bohemians are waiting for you in the drawing room," announced one of her ladies-in-waiting.

As planned the individuals arrived at the imperial residence, which was located in the heart of the biggest Austrian city. With its great number of buildings and imposing factories, Vienna had no reason to envy the other European capitals. The city had been built in the Roman era, on earlier foundations. From the very beginning, it had been the dwelling place of the royal and imperial power. The greatest sovereigns had reigned over the nation from the castles and palaces scattered across its territory. Everyone recognized the majesty of the city.

The empress, with all her courage, joined the emissaries. She was happy to see her friend from the mountains again. Forgetting the protocol, Yourik laid a delicate kiss on the hand of Sissi. She was uncomfortable with the attention that the head of the Bohemians showed her. In the middle of the room, golden armchairs were placed along a thick and colourful carpet.

"My friend, please allow me, in the name of His Majesty, to welcome you here. As you know, the fate of your people preoccupies us greatly. During my stay in your company, I have witnessed your distress. This is why the emperor, in his great kindness, has asked for an audience. The monarch considers that it is of the utmost importance to discuss the future of the Bohemians with you," explained Sissi tactfully.

"Your Majesty, you can rest assured that we have been waiting for such an event since distant times. Thanks to your intervention, the Imperial Crown has recognised that it was necessary to meet with us here," replied Yourik, smiling to her.

"My husband is expecting you, along with your advisers, in the antechamber. His Majesty is impatient to meet you," added the empress politely.

The men thanked her elegantly and followed the valet to the apartments of Franz. Sissi succeeded eloquently at her task of imperial hostess. She was proud to have contributed to the reconciliation between the two leaders, for the sake of a rejected community. Without her help, the Bohemians would have never had this unique opportunity to sit down with Austria's strong man.

After the customary presentations, Franz Joseph invited the nomads to sit around an oval wooden table. Hidden behind the room's entrance, the archduchess listened to the private conversations between her son and the strangers. Jealous of her daughter-in-law's influence on Franz in this matter, Sophie wanted to be informed of the negotiations. She was ferociously opposed to any peace agreement with the "savages" as the authoritarian woman called them. According to her, negotiating with the Bohemians was a fatal mistake for the hegemony of the Habsburgs.

The discussion between the two parties lasted a good two hours. After mutual concessions, a satisfying agreement was reached by the emperor. It stated that the people of the former Bohemia would acknowledge Franz Joseph I as king and sovereign. His powers would be limited to a symbolic constitution, which would be written by the wise men of the nomad community. It would state the monarch's commitment to allow the leaders of the different groups throughout Europe to enact the laws of the people. In return, the nomads would become loyal subjects of the Austrian Empire. Yearly royalties on the income of the Bohemians would be sent to Vienna, which would solely be used to ensure the smooth running of the Habsburg Crown. Finally since she was the main instigator of this peace, Sissi would receive the title of protector of the people's soul along with that of Queen of Bohemia.

To celebrate solemnly this historical agreement, a sumptuous banquet took place in the evening. Embellished with Austrian and Bohemian coats of arms, the room where the reception was held was crowded with guests. More than three hundred people were talking around a table filled with fresh fruit, juicy vegetables, rare meat and alcoholic beverages. To entertain the visitors, a group of musicians played Viennese pieces and Gipsy songs with the most beautiful instruments. In devoted sovereign, Sissi walked across the room to greet each of the guests. Everyone was impressed by Sissi's thoughtfulness.

Everyone but the archduchess who was angrier than ever. The return of the empress changed radically the balance of power, unrivalled until then, between the two women. More mature and more concerned about her duties towards the Imperial Crown, Sissi was gaining confidence. The growing influence of the empress within the Austrian Court diminished Sophie's. Such an affront profoundly annoyed Franz Joseph's mother.

Later in the evening, alone behind the red velvet curtains, Sissi admired the result of her first mission as empress. Childhood memories came back to her. The words of her governess, the Baroness of Wulfen, resounded in her head. The noblewoman had repeatedly told her that the strength of a woman lied in her freedom. She had just made a step forward in that direction. The success of the agreement between the two sworn enemies proved, at least in her mind, that she no longer was the scatterbrain that her mother-in-law took pleasure in humiliating.

"Your Majesty!" said a voice with a strong accent.

Surprised, she swiftly turned towards the man who was standing beside her. Yourik had been waiting to speak to Sissi in private all evening. He knew fully well that she was his best ally in the reinstatement of this mutual peace. Franz was merely the puppet who manipulated the powerful people of the Empire, in particular the terrible Sophie. The love that she felt for his people was the sole guarantee that the monarch would respect his part in the cause of the Bohemians. The head of the nomads had grasped that since the beginning of Sissi's marriage with the emperor.

"You have fulfilled your promise. My people will never forget the help you gave them," declared the individual.

"When a fair mission is worthy of my attention, I undertake it with conviction. The harm caused to Bohemia during the past centuries had to be repaired," exclaimed Sissi.

As a token of admiration, the emissary of the oppressed community bowed before the empress. He had never done so before a crowned head, much less before a representative of the Austrian authority. Behind the etiquette, budding feelings pushed Yourik to respect Sissi further. She kindled emotions in him that he had only experienced once in his lifetime. Since his wife's death, his heart had been shut. But today, it longed for a romantic life again. The Bohemian understood more than anyone that Sissi had offered her love to one man only. He could not reveal his feelings, for he risked destroying his people's chances. For the time being, the descendant of the last King of Bohemia concealed his true intentions.

To thank his wife, the emperor gave her a priceless present in his eyes. He had a lodge built, a type of secondary residence, at the west entrance of Vienna. Although small, it wasn't without charm. Its sole purpose was to provide Sissi with more freedom. It was called the manor of "Hermesvilla" and was erected on a wooded estate. Franz wished to recreate Bavaria to obliterate the deep sorrow of his beloved.

"When you miss your land, you shall find it only a few steps from Schönbrunn Palace," he had whispered into her ear.

Somewhat like Marie-Antoinette, former Queen of France, the empress would also have a refuge of her own. Only her guests would be allowed inside. Needless to say that the archduchess wouldn't be one of them.

"My darling, how can I show you my gratitude?" she had replied, embracing him.

Nearing the end of the year 1855, the atmosphere within the imperial family was quite harmonious. Sissi, who was eighteen years of age, better fulfilled her duty as imperial wife and mother. She could now count on the Bohemians as allies along with some members of the Austrian nobility. She frequently visited the Wittelsbachs, mostly during the warm season, and she took an active part in the life of the Habsburg Empire.

The happiness of the imperial couple peaked when the doctor told Sissi that she was pregnant again. A second child would soon join the powerful dynasty of the Habsburgs. She was hoping to give Franz Joseph a son by giving birth to a male heir. A boy would further consolidate her position with the monarch and within the Viennese power. Winter was beginning on a joyful note for the empress. She was starting to find her place in this universe so adverse to change.

CHAPTER 5

An Afflicted Sovereign

Schönbrunn Palace
1856-1866

WO-MONTH pregnant, Sissi decided to keep her
physical activities to a minimum. For the baby's sake,
but mostly for her own health, she stopped some of her leisure
activities. Her outdoor strolls along with the trips she took
outside of the Empire were among them. The sovereign also
cut down on her many public appearances. Her objective was
to reduce all unnecessary physical effort on a daily basis.

On his own initiative, the emperor wrote to his aunt to ask
if she could come stay with Sissi. He knew that his wife would
appreciate the support of a member of her family. Her mother
was certainly the best suited person to keep her company. He
spared no expense and sent an escort to bring Ludovika back to
Vienna. The duchess arrived a few days later. She spent more
than a month at Schönbrunn Palace. She made the most of her
stay in Austria by trying to convince her sister to leave the education of the little archduchess to her daughter. As stubborn

as always, Sophie did not want to hear it. She had already lost ground to her daughter-in-law and would not let her gain any more. By staying in control of the monarch's offspring, she made sure that she was involved in the future of the Imperial Crown.

A new conflict broke out in Eastern Europe around mid-March of 1856. This time around, the Emperor of All Russia considered expanding his possessions on the continent. He wanted to increase his access to the sea, so he could establish a naval force. In times of growing commercial exchanges, the safety of water passageways was becoming essential to a country's economy. Acting as the most powerful monarch of Europe, Franz Joseph could not stand idly by. He had to outdistance the enemy troops during their ascent. So, the emperor left the capital for several weeks. While he was away, he temporarily transferred part of his prerogatives to his mother. Sissi, who was in her second month of pregnancy, was not in the right state to take on such responsibilities. She was quite exhausted by her physical condition and could not compete with the archduchess.

Nearly every day, Sissi headed to her refuge before breakfast. Sophie's presence in her entourage was hard to bear. Only her mother accompanied her to the manor of Hermesvilla. Solitude had become one of her most faithful allies. Franz Joseph's frequent absences were starting to damage their relationship more than ever.

"I married a man, not a title!" thundered Sissi in one of their quarrels.

Since the sovereign's birthday, on December 24, the emperor had only spent a total of fifteen days with her. Their second-year anniversary was only a few weeks away, but their marriage was in a bad state. The fact that Sissi was left alone undoubtedly impacted her attitude towards the institution she represented. More than ever, her aunt's obstinate attempts at discrediting her were the real reason for the crumbling of the imperial couple. After a few months of hiatus, Sophie carried on the fight in light of her new responsibilities as temporary regent. She used her position to destroy Sissi's work with the Bohemians. Her first provocative action was to inflate their taxation. In spite of the formal agreement between the Crown of the Habsburgs and the head of the nomads, the archduchess aggravated the situation of the rejected people. Discontent spread among the members of the nomad community.

Lying on a blue fabric sofa, the empress burst out crying in front of Ludovika. The burden of suffering she carried bout oppressed Sissi. She could no longer hide the pain that overwhelmed her.

"My darling, why so many tears?" asked the noblewoman, giving her a white handkerchief.

"Mother, if only you knew about your sister's spitefulness. Since the day I joined the imperial family, she hasn't stopped destroying me," exclaimed the pregnant woman with a trembling voice.

Ludovika knew that her eldest sister wasn't easy to get along with. As a child, she always had to have the upper hand. On more than one occasion, the two siblings spent months without speaking or writing to each other. Sophie's despicable attitude did not by any means facilitate reconciliations.

"Sissi, if you let me, I shall speak to my sister. Perhaps that after a good discussion, she will come to understand how much her words trouble you," suggested Ludovika.

"No! She would only seek revenge if I let you to do that," explained Sissi, anxious.

For her daughter's sake, Ludovika did nothing of the sort. Her mother's heart prevented her from aggravating further the fate of her offspring. She would keep it to herself.

The dreadful war that was raging across Eastern Europe stopped abruptly at the beginning of spring. Russia, after numerous negotiations, managed to obtain some land on the Baltic. With this new access to the sea, the emperor removed his armed troops from bordering countries. Franz, an excellent mediator, had avoided a bloody battle. Since his part was done, he returned to Schönbrunn Palace with the idea of rekindling the flame with Sissi.

In the meantime, the duchess was back on the road to Bavaria to be with her husband. She had been taking care of her daughter for quite some time. Her other children were waiting for her at Ludwigstrasse palace. On her way to Munich, Ludovika shed a few tears. Leaving Sissi in her sister's clutches broke her heart. She had noticed the devastating effect of Sophie's decisions on the mental and physical health of the empress. Her face, which used to light up with a smile, had become the mere reflection of a morose woman. Even her body suffered the consequences. Once well-known for her feminine curves, Sissi had lost a noticeable amount of weight.

Towards the week of April 20, the emperor returned to the Austrian capital. Cheered by his people, he arrived as a true hero in the streets of Vienna. A crowd of countless men and women had gathered along the way, shouting for joy as he passed them. The prestige of the Crown of the Habsburgs reached unequalled summits. The emperor had established his authority over the nobility and his subjects. Nobody cared about the downsides of his success on his wife.

Eager to press her husband against her, Sissi demanded to wait for him in the entrance hall of the imperial residence. Sitting on a chair as straight as a soldier, she was excited about seeing Franz Joseph again. On so many nights, she had cried her eyes out with loneliness. Today, her sweetheart was coming back to her.

The procession suddenly stopped before the porch of Schönbrunn Palace. More than twenty beautifully adorned horses crossed the gate of the estate. The empress jumped up. Her eyes, which had been lifeless for so long, were shining brightly. The man she had been waiting for this whole time had finally returned.

"Franz!" she cried at the sight of her beloved husband.

The monarch, who was delighted to see his wife again, ran to her. They threw themselves into each other's arms. Behind the red velvet curtains of the sitting room, which faced the frontage, Sophie spied on the two sweethearts. When she saw her son and her daughter-in-law embrace, she was overcome with a certain amount of jealousy. She, who had never been madly in love with Franz Joseph's father, had sacrificed her soul for the dynasty of the Habsburgs. The archduchess was fifty-one years old, and she knew all too well what she had based her life on. Since Franz Karl's degenerative disease, she had kept her chin up. The mother of the emperor had given herself the nearly divine mission of sending Franz to the top of Europe's power ladder. The Austrian supremacy owed its position in great part to Sophie's relentless work. Even though she was born a Wittelsbach, Sissi's mother-in-law embodied the image of the Habsburgs better than the Habsburgs themselves.

"My darling, I've never closed my eyes without thinking about your pretty face," said the man, touching his wife's hair lovingly.

"I've missed you so much. Every night, before I fell asleep, I begged God to bring you back to me as soon as possible," said Sissi, pressing her head against her husband's torso.

"How is our little Sophie?"

"She's getting prettier every day."

"Our daughter most certainly takes after her mother…" added the monarch, smiling.

The emperor placed his fingers onto his wife's belly. He gently felt her body's fullness. Franz Joseph wanted to check on Sissi's pregnancy. He was sincerely hoping that a son was growing inside her.

"Has your mother been of pleasant company?" asked Franz, inviting the empress to follow him to their apartments.

"Yes, she proved to be very useful."

"Has your relationship with the archduchess improved?" he continued.

She feared that she would place him in an awkward position if she told him the truth. It was wiser to talk about this issue at a later time.

"I was hardly ever at the castle... The atmosphere at the manor cheers me up quite a bit," said Sissi to her husband to change the subject.

Alone in their room, the two sweethearts lied down next to each another, on the pastel-coloured satin sheets. They spent part of the day cuddling. Franz made love to his wife like he hadn't done so in a very long time. He tenderly caressed the empress's breasts with his manly hands. He noticed that they had grown in volume. Because of her pregnancy, Sissi's body changed temporarily. Despite these physical transformations, the monarch was irrepressibly attracted to the sovereign.

During the weeks that followed, the emperor gradually took back his decision-making prerogatives. He could only sing his mother's praises as to the way she had taken charge of things during his absence. Franz did not know that she had renewed the hostilities with the Bohemians. Keen on the absolute supremacy of Austria upon the nomads, Sophie had also offended the Hungarian nobility by cancelling a meeting between one of their representatives and the monarch's brother. Some threatening dissatisfaction spread across the circles of intellectuals in compliant countries.

The birth of the imperial couple's second child took place on July 12, 1856. Contrarily to their custom, Franz and Sissi did not spend their summer vacation at Ischl Castle. The advanced pregnancy of the empress did not allow her to go to Bavaria. It was too risky to get on the bumpy roads that connected the two countries. Helene, who was eager to see her sister again, headed to Vienna for a few days. She was present during the delivery of Sissi's child. She gave the Crown of the Habsburgs another daughter. The monarch was the happiest father of the royal and imperial courts on the continent. True to herself, Sophie criticized the absence of a male heir to look after the future of the throne.

The new little archduchess was named Gisela Louisa Maria. Plumper than her eldest sibling, the young girl took after the emperor. She had his eyes and his mouth, which proved beyond any doubt that Franz Joseph was indeed the father of the child. The immediate members of the imperial family now included Franz, Sissi and their two daughters, Sophie and Gisela.

In 1856, the monarch and his wife travelled to Rome on official business. A loyal defender of the Catholic faith, Franz was to have an audience with the pope. Pius IX had successively summoned the crowned heads that answered to the Church of Christ. He wished to consolidate the papal presence in the political affairs of Europe.

During their stay in the Papal States, the empress – with the help of her ladies-in-waiting – visited most stores of the Eternal City. A fashion enthusiast, Sissi could not miss such an opportunity. She spent an astronomical amount of money in the city of the seven hills.

Harmony surrounded the nest of the imperial couple once again. The archduchess, who was busy finding the best suitors for her other children, somewhat neglected Franz Joseph. He did not complain about it, and took advantage of this quiet period to get closer to Sissi. As the years passed, the sovereign had less and less time to go to Bavaria. Her functions as empress and mother kept her relentlessly busy. In spite of everything, she often felt lonely in the immensity of Schönbrunn Palace. Some people even said that she wasn't cut out to be the wife of a monarch, a statement which she probably agreed with to some extent. Sissi had never accepted her imperial position. In a different world, she would have probably chosen a simpler life like her mother.

In 1857, misfortune stroke Franz Joseph and the empress with full force. During an official visit in Hungary, their youngest daughter caught a contagious virus. The little Gisela, who was barely ten-months old, contracted measles.

Staying at a private hotel in Budapest, the imperial family was going through some dark times. Lying in a bed, Sissi's child cried constantly. Red patches covered her limbs.

"Gisela, my darling, for the love of God, fight…" thundered the sovereign, squatted down on the edge of the wooden furniture.

Her husband was standing behind her. Despite his power, he could not heal his offspring. The monarch cursed their location that he held responsible for his young daughter's infection.

"If we hadn't set foot in Hungary, our child wouldn't be in this bed," he told whoever was listening.

Desperate for a solution, the archduchess considered that the expertise of Austria was essential. Since she did not have faith in the competence of the Magyars in this field, she demanded the presence of a Viennese doctor at once.

"Franz, demand the services of a doctor from the Empire at once," begged Sophie.

"No! It will be too late if we wait. We are in Budapest, there must certainly be a man of science able to save our daughter?" exclaimed Sissi, raising her voice.

"You're a fool! We are the imperial family, not a Hungarian peasant," replied the archduchess to her daughter-in-law with a baleful look.

Cornered between his mother and his wife, Franz Joseph leaned towards the archduchess. In fact, he shared Sophie's opinion as to the inferiority of this kingdom's inhabitants. His child was a Habsburg, and she had to receive the care of Vienna's most competent practitioners.

"Franz! If our Gisela leaves us, I will hold you responsible until my last breath," promised the empress.

Deaf to Sissi's words, he sent an escort to the Austrian capital. His men had to bring back the most distinguished specialist of the city at full speed.

Miraculously, on the night of May 28 to 29, the youngest child of the imperial couple regained her strength. The serious symptoms seemed to have vanished. Asleep on an armchair, the empress was awaken by the giggles of Gisela, who was playing with her mother's hat. Sissi, moved and overwhelmed with joy, let out a shriek. The noise woke Franz and his mother, who ran to the room of the young Habsburg. As they opened the door, the emperor saw his youngest daughter clapping her hands in her bed. At her side, Sissi was shaking with happiness before the near-resurrection of her offspring.

"My darling! Admire our child who's recovered her health," she rejoiced, bouncing about.

Franz Joseph moved towards Gisela and took her into his arms. He laid a thousand kisses on her sweet little face. He praised the Lord for his divine intervention. Even Sophie, who was of a composed nature, seemed content to see her granddaughter alive and well.

"Franz, God has answered my prayers!" cried the empress in a surge of delight.

For the remainder of the night, the members of the imperial family stayed with the miraculously cured child. The heaviness of the night before gave way to the joy of the moment. All kissed in this time of elation.

Early the next morning, another calamity afflicted the Austrian parents. When the empress was about to rock her eldest child, she noticed that she had the same symptoms. A persistent cough, nasal discharge and cherry red spots on the delicate body of little Sophie. Her radiant face suddenly lost its glow. Sissi knew perfectly well that her eldest daughter was of frailer health than her youngest. Her puny physique would hinder her recovery from such a hardship.

"What's going on?" asked the emperor, about to join the representative of the Hungarians.

"Franz, I think that the Almighty wants to punish us," she declared, crying on an armchair.

The sovereign, sitting with Sophie in her arms, lifted her towards her husband.

"Look! Our daughter is suffering from Gisela's illness," explained Sissi, shutting her eyes.

"What are you telling me?" he replied in shock.

"My dear, we must summon a doctor from the capital at once. Sophie doesn't have the strength of her younger sibling..." declared the mother with an imploring look.

"My darling, the doctor from Vienna should arrive at any time now," replied the emperor gently.

"Enough! Don't you see that your blindness will cost us the life of our offspring? I beseech you to demand the presence..." let out Sissi, interrupted by her aunt.

"Madam, stop this childishness! Franz has given you an answer, period!" said the archduchess drily, frowning.

Confronted with the wall that was rising up before her, Sissi threw in the sponge in desperation. She couldn't outweigh her mother-in-law, who was more intransigent than ever. She could only pray that the cortege heading to Budapest would arrive shortly.

The child's health was deteriorating by the hour. Alone with her aunt, Sissi could not count on her husband to comfort her for he had gone to a meeting with the emissary of the Magyars. The emperor faced an unbearable and unsettling situation. On one part, his eldest daughter was dying, and on the other, the Imperial Crown demanded that he remain collected before the Hungarians.

Suddenly the young Sophie, who was still in her mother's arms, stopped breathing. The atony of the child's muscles caught Sissi's eye. Unsure of the situation, she slowly moved her fingers on the belly of the young archduchess to better understand what was happening. There wasn't any movement. She was struck by a horrifying fit of panic. Terrified, she placed the palm of her hand under the baby's nostrils. Nothing. There wasn't any breath coming from the young girl's nose.

"Sophie! Madam, please come here," she cried with trembling lips.

The emperor's mother indolently walked to her niece in the children's bedroom. When she reached the dark room, she saw the young Habsburg lying, lifeless, in Sissi's arms. At the sight of the scene, the archduchess grasped the extent of the drama. She mechanically snatched the child from the hands of Sissi. Still in shock from the trauma of losing her daughter, the empress did not react to her aunt's rude behaviour. Her brain was functioning in slow motion. Everything around her seemed to have stopped. She did not hear anything and her vision was blurry. The universe had closed in on her.

"Sissi, get a hold of yourself!" thundered the archduchess with tears in her eyes.

After a short while, the empress finally came to her senses. The word "death" resounded in her head. The face of her young girl came back to her.

"Sophie! I want my little Sophie," she demanded, shouting at the top of her voice.

"Quickly! Please inform His Majesty of this terrible event," told the mother of the monarch to one of her ladies-in-waiting.

In a sudden outburst, the empress threw herself on her aunt with all her strength. Surprised by the attack of her daughter-in-law, the archduchess fell on her back. Witnesses to the scene, the favourites of the Imperial Court were rooted to the spot and did not react. Never before in the history of the Habsburgs had two members of the dynasty literally come to blows. Lying on the body of her mother-in-law, Sissi, transformed by rage, was strangling her aunt's wrinkled neck with her bare hands.

"This is all your fault!" cried the assailant, holding her position.

Chocked by her niece, Sophie fought relentlessly to escape the wrath of the empress. The archduchess, whose face was red and whose lips were nearly blue, let out shrieks of pain.

"Let me go!" she said, struggling.

Nothing would do it. Sissi did not hear the words of Franz Joseph's mother. After an endless minute, two rather bulky men pulled the two sworn enemies apart, holding Sissi tightly. She, in a fit of hysteria, spoke coarsely to her mother-in-law. She held her responsible for the death of her child. As for Sophie, shaken by the assault she had just been a victim of, damned the empress. She swore to destroy her before her last breath.

The night of the tragedy, Franz suggested to his wife that she return to Schönbrunn Palace. Her state made him fear the worst. The emperor did not recognize the woman he had married in April 1854. Without wasting any time, the empress hopped into a carriage. Eight men looked after their mistress on the way to Vienna. Alone in the vehicle, she looked at the star-filled sky. She firmly believed that her little archduchess was one of these bright constellations.

"My darling, I will always love you," she whispered, staring at the night.

When the cortege came to a halt before the palace, Sissi headed to her private apartments hurriedly. Away from Sophie, she could mourn peacefully. She was entering a dark period of her existence.

The official funeral of the young archduchess took place on June 1, 1857. After a day in the chapel of rest, the remains of the Habsburg were moved inside the Augustinian church. Several Austrian and European dignitaries walked by the coffin of little Sophie. A handful of white candles lighted up the doleful location. To express their sympathies, the bohemian people offered an imposing funeral wreath, which was placed in front of the bier.

The body of the imperial couple's child was moved between Schönbrunn Palace and the religious building, located in the heart of Vienna, at night, as per the suggestion of the emperor's advisors, in order to avoid moving crowds. Perpendicular to the altar, the coffin of the deceased was covered with the flag of the Empire. Many sprays of white flowers adorned the building's walls. For the occasion, a choir of young Viennese enlivened the ceremony with their angelical hymns. The funeral service was led by a Milanese cardinal, especially assigned by the supreme pontiff. Sissi's family along with the members of the House of the Habsburgs sat in the first rows of the church. The other benches were occupied by the nobility of the Empire, Bavarian sovereigns, Hungarian emissaries and the head of the nomads.

Sitting only a few steps away from her child, the empress, whose face was hidden behind a black veil, couldn't help but cry. Grief had been eaten away at her since the unexpected death of her daughter. This terrible suffering had prevented her from getting any sleep. Sissi had sought refuge in complete silence and did not even speak to her husband anymore. Shaken by the passing of his eldest daughter, Franz Joseph would have wanted to share his sadness with Sissi. But since she was overpowered by an insatiable anger, she refused him access to her heart. According to her, her husband was as guilty as the archduchess, and he did not deserve her compassion.

The only person she agreed to speak with was her sister. The day after the funeral, the mourning mother locked herself into her manor. Helene, who had accompanied her to her private residence, tenderly cared for her younger sibling. Lying on the bed of the imperial wife, the two sisters talked for half a day. As rain was flooding the streets of the capital, Sissi shared her feelings with her confidante.

"My dear friend, Sophie died because of my lack of firmness," she said, saddened, by way of introduction.

"You are mistaken! The only thing that you can blame yourself for is having a diabolical mother-in-law," added the eldest sister, squeezing her hand.

"I hate this woman… She has never stopped hurting me on purpose," continued the empress, grinding her teeth.

"There! If the archduchess was no longer of this world, you would be at peace," went on Helene.

"Do you know what hurts me the most in this tragedy?" asked Sissi.

Helene had her own suspicions as to what the sovereign's answer would be. She had noticed how much Sissi had detached herself from Franz Joseph. Their love, once so strong, was now on the decline, but Helene mostly wondered about the aftermath. What would happen to their relationship as a couple?

"I think that my feelings for Franz evaporated as a result of my little Sophie's passing. If he hadn't followed the instructions of Her Imperial Highness, my child would still be among us today," she confessed.

The two women, who were closer than ever, continued their private conversation. Alone at the manor of Hermesvilla, they could speak freely and share their most secret thoughts.

On many occasions during the year, Helene had paid her favourite sister a visit. Most of the time, the Wittelsbachs sought refuge at the sovereign's Viennese lodge. During the vacation of the imperial couple at Ischl Castle, Sissi couldn't go a day without the company of her eldest sister. The mourning period of the empress had strengthened the – already quite sturdy – ties of the two Bavarians.

The night before her twentieth birthday, Sissi – to ensure her position with Franz Joseph – accepted to spend the night with her husband. Since the death of the young archduchess, she had systematically refused to give herself to Franz. Rumours of repudiation had come to her attention. For fear they might be true, she had no other choice but to fulfill her marital obligations to her husband.

A few months later, during an annual ball given at Schönbrunn Palace, Sissi felt a pain in her abdomen. Accustomed to this type of discomfort, she knew what it meant: she would be giving birth to another child, another daughter? At the end of the day, on August 21, 1858, the imperial couple found out that the child was a boy. Satisfied that she had finally provided the Austrian Crown with an heir, the empress paid little interest to the newborn. Wounded by the loss of her second daughter, she didn't have the strength to grow attached to another child. Truth be told, a slow yet important transformation had begun on that ill-fated month of May of the previous year. Her unfailing love of life and her feelings for the emperor had dangerously faded. The naive Wittelsbach had turned into a dejected woman.

After fighting tooth and nail against her mother-in-law to earn the right to raise her children, she was now relieved to leave it up to the archduchess. She, who had lost a considerable amount of weight, sank into a profound and lengthy depression. She spent months locking herself into her apartments or isolating herself in her private refuge.

In early 1859, extremely worried about the frail health of his wife, Franz Joseph suggested that she get some rest in Bavaria. He had never stopped loving her and to prove it to her one more time, he allowed her to go back to her family. Surrounded by her people, she could only recover and regain her joy of living. Glad to get away from the Imperial Court, she promptly accepted the offer of Franz.

During her stay on her native soil, she grew closer to her parents. The years she had spent at Schönbrunn Palace had pushed Sissi away from her father. He, who hated to travel outside of Bavaria, had only seen his daughter on very rare occasions. The main contact they had had together was when the imperial couple spent their vacation at Ischl Castle. Her father's age – as he was now in his fifties – and rheumatism complicated his movements. The hunting enthusiast couldn't even walk alone in the woods anymore. Before his favourite got married, he frequently went to the forest with her. Today, none of his children accompanied him on the wooden trails. As the years passed, Max befriended alcohol and indulged in it on a regular basis, increasingly so.

Sissi's return gave some energy back to the old duke. The presence of his daughter rejuvenated him, to his family's delight. When spring came, the two former nature lovers strolled in the woods.

"Father, the life of my childhood was far more invigorating than my current life," she confessed to him as they walked under sap-filled buds of different shapes.

The nobleman had never accepted the departure of Sissi for Vienna. What he had dreaded the most for his daughter had come true with time. His ray of sunshine, as he sometimes called her, was nothing more than a wilted flower. Her beauty had remained as dazzling as when she was a child, but her eyes didn't sparkle as they used to. The fire in her had died out, and the duke sensed it a long time ago.

Married to the Prince of Thurn and Taxis, Helene no longer resided in the south of Bavaria since the previous autumn. By marrying a nobleman, she had acquired new responsibilities towards him and their relationship. She, very disciplined in her private life, became even more so towards her husband. In spite of that, Sissi's eldest sister spent a few days with her in the summer of 1859. The two confidantes experienced diametrically opposed situations. The youngest sibling suffered from the heavy load that the imperial title burdened her with, whereas the other one came to life through European aristocracy.

Helene of Wittelsbach, born duchess in Bavaria, accepted the marriage offer of a member of a rich family in the kingdom. The eldest daughter of the ducal couple, who was twenty-four years old, decided to marry the heir of the principality of Thurn and Taxis. She knew him very little, but she got along very well with the man. They had a great number of things in common, starting with the love of children. The religious celebration took place at Possenhofen Castle, in the presence of a hundred guests. Suffering from severe depression, Sissi did not attend her sister's wedding. Since that day, Helene had been living with her husband at his castle, near the Danube River.

After incessant letters from her husband asking her to come back to Austria, the empress agreed to return to Schönbrunn Palace despite her wishes. Nearly ten months passed before the sovereign set foot on the Empire's soil again. During her extended absence, Sissi only received the visit of Franz Joseph on five occasions. The emperor, who was overwhelmed by his responsibilities, could not afford to leave the capital for more than three consecutive days. Even his traditional vacation was cancelled due to a last-minute military conflict.

On October 2, nearing the end of the afternoon, Sissi's carriage crossed the gate of Schönbrunn Palace. A thin layer of snow camouflaged the ground here and there. A chilly wind from the north was blowing on the area. The empress looked out the window of the black coach. What she saw didn't appeal to her. Everything seemed so lifeless. She shivered. So many events, some joyful but most of them unhappy, had taken place in this too vast a building.

"Your Majesty! Welcome home," exclaimed the coachman.

Sissi got off the carriage reluctantly. She walked timidly on the frozen ground. She stopped, like a worried animal, a few metres away from the palace and examined the premises. Someone was spying on her, it was obvious, but she couldn't see who. What she did not know was that her mother-in-law was observing her behind the crimson curtains of her apartments. *The scatterbrain is back among us,* whispered the mother of the monarch. The archduchess, Sissi's formidable enemy, had never forgiven the empress for her abrupt assault upon the death of her grand-daughter. Sophie still wanted to destroy the life of her daughter-in-law.

Sissi walked into the hall of Schönbrunn Palace unwillingly. The typical smell of the vestibule brought back cruel memories. With tears in her eyes, she stood by limply; clearly, she didn't feel at ease among the rich decoration of the palace.

"Madam, we've missed you!" let out a servant politely bowing before her.

The empress could only give a faint smile. It wasn't that she hated the servant, but rather that she wasn't in mood. Each of her steps brought her closer to the lion's den. Despite her long recovery away from the schemes of the Austrian Court, she wasn't as strong as her enemy. Sissi unhurriedly climbed the stairs to the second floor with a vague pout. She headed feverishly to her private quarters. A guard, positioned before her doors, saluted her and gave her access to the antechamber. The man in a black and white uniform closed the door behind her. Nothing had been touched in the room. Even her pearl necklace was still on the small chest in the corner. She continued towards her bedroom. No one had ventured there either. The velvet curtains were still half-opened. Sissi lay down on her bed and stared at the ceiling for a long while. More than five years had passed since her wedding to the Emperor of Austria. From an insignificant duchess in Bavaria, she had become the sovereign of an empire where the sun never went down. So many adventures had taken place in her short existence. An impossible first love with a Prussian count, a grandiose union with Franz Joseph I, a passionate relationship with her husband, a fortuitous encounter with the leader of the Bohemians, and a traumatic death which turned her life upside down. What did fate have in store for her now?

Suddenly, someone knocked on her bedroom door. She stood up promptly, pinching her cheeks.

"Come in!" she said politely.

Franz walked into the room with a smile on his face which showed that he still felt the same way about her. He had been looking forward to this reunion for so many months. The big day had finally arrived. His wife, the mother of his children, had returned to her family.

"Sissi! Your presence is filling me with joy," he declared with conviction.

"My darling, I have returned by your side," replied Sissi opening her arms.

With a happy heart, the emperor got closer to his beloved. She hadn't lost her beauty or her charm. The imperial couple was together again, under the same roof.

Franz lovingly wrapped his arms around the body of the empress. He indisputably felt peace overcome him. He had desperately missed his faithful, everyday ally. With the return of Sissi, the monarch could find the support he so desperately needed.

She did not share her husband's feelings. Of course, she still loved him passionately, but not as much as when they first met. The sufferings she had endured during the past years had partly tarnished her flame. This realization, which she didn't expect, stupefied her.

After meeting with Franz Joseph, the empress paid her children a visit. They were sleeping soundly, lying in their bed, and did not seem to worry about life's hardships. She looked at them tenderly and thanked the Almighty for protecting them. Sissi walked to the cot where Archduchess Gisela was sleeping. The little girl, who was barely three years old, had curly light-brown hair just like Duchess Ludovika. The colour of her eyes was the same as Franz's. The sovereign then turned to her son, the male heir who had been much desired by the imperial couple. The boy, who was a little over one year old, was the spitting image of Archduchess Sophie. His traits were identical to hers. Despite this resemblance, she loved him deeply. These two little angels were her only reason for not breaking her marriage. Without them, she would have left the emperor to return to Bavaria. Notwithstanding the judgment of others, Sissi would have deserted her husband.

The next morning, the empress ate in the company of her husband and children. Reunited around the table in the small dining room, the family was talking freely. At first glance, everything seemed perfect at the Habsburgs. The atmosphere, although joyful, grew tense when the archduchess walked into the room. Wearing a black dress as a sign of mourning since the return of her daughter-in-law, Sophie did not even bother to greet Sissi.

"Mother, show some respect to my wife," let out the monarch.

"Who? This unworthy mother who abandoned her offspring for her own personal pleasure," she thundered.

Furious, Franz Joseph stood up from his chair impetuously. He moved towards the archduchess, vexed.

"You should be more cordial when speaking to the Empress of Austria," replied the man with a ferocious voice.

"You are forgetting that she is only sovereign because you are her husband… And that you are wearing the Imperial Crown because your parents have allowed it," she said, turning her back to him.

The scene thrilled Sissi. Franz, who had forever been subjected to his mother's instructions, had just confronted her. He had never done so in the past. By proving to be a valiant protector, her husband had just given her sheer pleasure. For once, Sissi didn't have to defend herself from the blows of her enemy.

Alone again, the imperial family continued their meal as if nothing had happened. Gisela and Rudolf, who witnessed the altercation between the elders, did not seem affected by the incident.

"Franz, thank you for your standing up for me!" she confessed.

The man did not react to his wife's words. He simply smiled at her. Still under the shock of the confrontation, the emperor had to relax. A busy day was ahead of him, and he could not afford to be distracted by a family discord.

In 1860, a new year started for the crowned heads of Austria. The empress, who was then twenty-three years old and whose health was faltering, decided to go to the snow-clad mountains. Accompanied by her husband, Sissi wanted to stroll down the paths like in the old days. She was unable to stay more than a month at the imperial residence. Even if she frequently went to the manor of Hermesvilla, she desperately missed nature's fresh air. With her children, Sissi had a lot of fun during a complete day. To please his beloved, the emperor rented out an inn and its premises. Despite the wintry cold, the family of the monarch had a nice time.

In the evening, upon mealtime, when a milky moon was rising in the black sky, Sissi suffered from persistent headaches. She believed them to be related to the physical activity she had done throughout the day.

"Franz, please forgive me, but I must lie down for a short while," announced Sissi as she left the table.

Franz stayed with his children and kept them company. The imperial family was escorted by twenty armed men and five devoted servants for the occasion.

Sissi rested in the uncomfortable bed in her room. She was suddenly shaken by a violent cough, which seemed to be come directly from her chest. She could not fall asleep while the illness spread inside her. Soon, her body became wet with perspiration. Her delicate throat swelled up from the inside. It was clear that Sissi wasn't in her normal state.

It was quite late in the evening when the emperor set out to go to the sovereign's room. He wanted to make sure that she was sleeping soundly. He tiptoed inside and leaned over Sissi to kiss her forehead. When his lips touched the skin of the empress, he understood that she wasn't in her usual condition.

"My darling! Do you feel well?" he asked gently.

The empress was shivering and moaning unintelligible words. It was obvious that she needed immediate care.

"Jann! Her Majesty isn't feeling well," yelled out Franz Joseph to the most experienced servant.

The domestics gathered around the sick woman right away. They all busied themselves regulating Sissi's abnormal temperature. Some changed the damp covers. Others dried the forehead, the face and the hands of their mistress. Meanwhile, Franz put their children to bed in their temporary room. All night, the empress suffered from the disease that was raging through her body. At dawn, blood was flowing from her nostrils.

"We are returning to Schönbrunn Palace straight away," ordered the emperor.

Wrapped up in several layers of thick wool blankets, Sissi sat in the poorly insulated carriage. With an incredible swiftness, the monarch, his wife and their children headed back to the capital. In this remote inn, she could not in any way receive the adequate care. She had to return to the residence of the Habsburgs to be treated by the best doctors of Vienna.

After a few hours, the vehicle rode into the castle's entrance at full speed. Without delay, three sturdy men carried the sovereign into her private apartments. Franz was right them behind, tormented by some anxiety. Sissi's frailty may have been known by all, but this time the situation was far more alarming than usual.

"Jann, take care of Their Imperial Highnesses," exclaimed Franz climbing the stairs.

Like a delicate flower, the woman's body was placed on her cosy bed. The servants shut the velvet curtains in the room and brought more blankets. They undressed the empress and slipped her into a nightgown. In the meantime, a valet from the castle visited the surgery of the city's most reputed practitioner. Soon, the specialist arrived in his patient's room.

"Please leave us alone," demanded the old bald man.

Everyone left the room one by one. Even the monarch complied with the request of the man of science.

"You!" said the doctor, looking at the youngest lady-in-waiting. "Please remain here as I will probably need your assistance."

The favourite of the Imperial Court stayed with her mistress during the doctor's examination. Using his instruments, he tried to understand the reason for the empress' feverish health. After a quarter of an hour, while Franz was waiting patiently on an armchair in the antechamber, the practitioner came out of the room.

"Your Majesty! Madam is suffering from tuberculosis," he informed him.

"Is her life in any danger?" asked the monarch with a worried look.

"No, not if the illness is treated early on," replied the other one carrying a small leather case in his hand.

"Where can she get the best care?" asked the husband.

"I suggest Madeira! It's the ideal place to get some fresh air… Moreover, there are excellent healthcare specialists who will be able to take care of Her Majesty," the old man concluded as he left the premises.

On the following days, Sissi headed to Portugal to rest for a little while. Accompanied by three of her ladies-in-waiting and by as many guards, she stayed in one of the king's residences. Under the warm sun, she regained her strength. This sojourn at the other end of Europe kindled in her an interest for travelling. Her appetite for jaunts abroad began during this first long journey outside of the Austrian Empire.

PART II

Out of Sight, Out of Mind

CHAPTER 6

Running Away from the Imperial Court

Many locations throughout Europe
1860-1867

SISSI RETURNED to Schönbrunn Palace towards the month of February, after spending more than three weeks in Madeira. The illness seemed cured, but it wasn't completely out of the way. During her convalescence by the Atlantic Ocean, the empress had given some considerable thought to her future. She was convinced that her health problems were connected to her mother-in-law. *Sophie will eventually kill me,* she thought. Nothing was working between the archduchess and Sissi. They were both obstinately opposed in all their points of view: the education of her own children, the decoration of the Habsburg residences, the outfits that she wore and her public appearances. No, there simply wasn't anything they could both agree on.

On her way back to Vienna, the empress found herself believing that running away would be the only solution to escape from the claws of her enemy. Spending some time in foreign destinations would be a means of enjoying life again for Sissi. She promised herself to reflect on this question lengthily.

Upon her return from Portugal, the empress learned that her husband had gone to Prussia. An imminent war was threatening Europe. Napoleon III had decided to expand his empire towards the east. To oppose his territorial ambitions, Franz went to the location of the armed conflict. Surrounded by several military troops, Franz Joseph commanded his men in the battlefields.

In an effort to participate to her husband's actions in her own way, Sissi temporarily transformed her manor in an infirmary. She cared for injured soldiers who had returned from the war that was raging on the continent. With all her determination, she spent entire days supervising the activities of her hospice to ensure that they ran smoothly. To support her initiative, other members of the imperial family took part in her social commitment. Sophie, true to herself as always, did not encourage the work of her daughter-in-law in any way.

"It is not the role of the Empress of Austria to spend time at the bedside of injured soldiers," merely said the archduchess.

Single-minded, Sissi kept on doing her charitable work for more than two months. She constantly went to the manor of Hermesvilla to check on the situation. Three men joined those who had already been admitted to the small brick lodge. Despite her goodwill, she could no longer be on top of the considerable task which was becoming more and more demanding. Her fatigue had the upper hand on her benevolent intentions.

Exhausted, the sovereign left for days at a time to stroll around the countryside neighbouring the capital. She went horseback riding nearly every day. In the evening, she took care of her children in the privacy of her own apartment. When her off-spring was finally asleep, she finished the evening by writing in her diary. When she still had some energy left, Sissi wrote letters to the emperor. In her messages, which were often painfully long for their recipient, she asked, or rather begged, for Franz's return. She was bored, alone in this lifeless and soulless castle.

Confronted with the extended absence of the monarch, she would throw herself into solitude. Seeking means of freeing herself from it, she would consume tobacco and cigarettes. Several times a day, Sissi would be seen in possession of products that were forbidden by the etiquette of the Imperial Court. Sophie, who fumed over her niece swaggering with her tobacco, lectured her on more than one occasion. But nothing could prevent the sovereign from sinking deeper into her vice.

Acting as a role model for the young ladies of the nobility, she would prove to be a bad example for them. Some of her supporters would follow in her footsteps, much to the dismay of the old generation. Soon, Austria was flooded with cigarette-smoking courtesans. All the European courts were beginning to spread the word about Sissi.

In June of 1860, when summer came, Franz Joseph still hadn't returned from the battlefield. Relentless, the French sovereign had no intention of submitting to the rest of the continent. He kept on fighting fiercely on many fronts at a time. Forced to remain on-site, the emperor could only apologize to his beloved with handwritten letters.

My darling,

For going on five month now, I have been waking up in the morning thinking about the day I shall be able to hold you against me. So many reasons encourage me to believe that my love for you will never die. You are the one and only woman in my heart.

Your faithful friend,

Franz

Despite all this correspondence, Sissi gradually detached herself from her husband. She became someone else. An image that she would cultivate through time to protect herself from the cruelty of the outside world.

During the same period, the empress became obsessed with her body's beauty. She hardly ate anything and rarely drank alcoholic beverages. In a short amount of time, she lost a lot of weight. She was under the constant supervision of a doctor. During one of his visits to Schönbrunn Palace, the man of science diagnosed his patient with severe anorexia. Everything was simply falling apart for Sissi.

It never rained but it poured in the existence of Sissi, and so an annoying rival came to the Imperial Court. One of the brothers of Franz, Archduke Ferdinand Maximilian, married a dazzling Belgian princess. Daughter to King Leopold I, this woman was indisputably one of the most courted royal dignities in Europe. Her outstanding beauty made her a radiant and unique individual. Soon, she moved into Schönbrunn Palace with her husband. Very quickly, Sophie held the archduchess in high esteem. Ambitious and intelligent, she had all the assets that the mother of the emperor was looking for in her daughters-in-law.

During a ball given by the empress, one summer evening, the two adversaries had their first stormy discussion. In front of the archduchess, Charlotte appeared wearing a magnificent white and scarlet dress. A diamond necklace belonging to her late mother adorned the elegant and slender neck of the proud woman. A few steps away from her, Sissi was speaking with one of her ladies-in-waiting. Her hair was tied back in plaits. The empress seemed to experience some slight discomfort in her stomach, and she pressed on her abdomen strongly.

"Your Majesty isn't feeling well?" asked the Belgian.

Sissi turned towards the two women and began speaking.

"Fear not… It's just one of my body's whims," she replied smiling.

"Perhaps it is telling you to eat properly," replied the rival looking for the reaction of her mother-in-law from the corner of her eye.

Insulted by the words of her sister-in-law, Sissi was simmering with rage. She was sick and tired of Sophie's reproaches, and now this insolent woman was joining in. She had already experienced too many tensions with her aunt, and she certainly couldn't bear any more.

"My dear friend, I can see that you probably finish my plates," let out the empress on the defensive.

In truth, Charlotte of Belgium had no reason to envy the other women of the Imperial Court. Her silhouette and her clothing were both perfect. It was becoming more difficult for Sissi to fight her enemy on equal terms.

Princess Charlotte of Belgium was born on June 7, 1840, about three years after Sissi. A member of one of the most coveted dynasties in Europe, the young woman was a relative of the late King Louis Philippe I, French sovereign, and the very popular Queen Victoria of Great Britain and Ireland. Withdrawn into herself as a child, she would come out of her shell after marrying Archduke Ferdinand Maximilian. She felt some sorrow for losing her mother when she was barely ten years old. Constantly courted by the noblemen of the continent, she would finally go for the House of Habsburg. Having become Vicereine of Lombardy–Venetia through her union in 1858, the Belgian would only meet her sister-in-law in 1860.

In the beginning of autumn, the emperor would finally return to Schönbrunn Palace, completely defeated. After losing the battle against France, he would become slightly depressed. Locked up in his office at Hofburg Palace, Franz Joseph didn't take his humiliation very well. He had so often been known for his military power. Today, he embodied the shame of the imperial family. Even his mother, Sophie, would reproach him for his lack of judgement in the conflict with Bonaparte.

The relationship with his wife had become a mere reflection of a debilitated union. The empress had changed so much that Franz did not recognize her. There was an ocean between the two crowned heads. Franz would start seeing his former mistresses regularly. Scattered across the four corners of Austria, they would take up a fair amount of his time.

Abandoned by her husband, Sissi would seek a way to escape this infernal situation. In the meantime, her illness would sink her into an endless cycle of physical aches. She spent the last weeks of that year confined to bed. Surrounded by an army of doctors, she thought that she was about to breathe her last. She was nothing but a shadow of her former self. Neither her own family, nor her friends understood the sovereign.

On December 24, 1860, her birthday, Sissi decided to retreat to Bavaria. She spent more than a month at Ischl Castle without her husband by her side. She had learned to tame the solitude of snowy days. Isolated in the woods, she frequently took walks in the forest of the Habsburg estate. The empress, away from the worries of Vienna, was particularly fond of the place's tranquility. Tens of domestics were at her service at the imperial residence. The monarch had granted her a private guard of ten highly armed men. When she didn't stroll in the sleeping forest surrounding the ownership of the Habsburgs, she visited her sister, in the northern part of the kingdom. Once reunited, the two confidantes spent their time spending extravagant amounts of money in Nuremberg's luxury stores.

A few weeks later, the empress received the unexpected visit of an old friend from the past. Yourik, who had been informed of Sissi's presence nearby, set out to see her. Under a dazzling snow, he asked for an audience with her. He waited patiently in the entrance hall of the palace.

"Madam, a man named Yourik Bartòk wishes to meet you," announced Léopoldine with a nasal voice due to a cold.

Upon hearing the words of the forty-year-old servant, the empress jumped out of her bed. Her body was still warm from the covers. The name of the visitor gave her some energy back. She put on a comfortable dress with a floral pattern and styled her hair hastily.

"Am I decent?" she asked looking at her domestic.

"Absolutely, Madam!"

"Please bring the individual into the sitting room. I shall meet him there shortly," ordered Sissi kindly.

As Léopoldine obeyed, the empress paced around the room. "Why was he here?" she murmured. Sissi was happy to know that the head of the Bohemians was inside the castle. She was hoping that he hadn't been sent by Franz Joseph to convince her to return to Vienna. Going back to Austria was absolutely out of the question.

"Yourik! What a wonderful surprise!" she exclaimed as she walked into the sitting room wearing a crown.

The nomad slowly turned to Sissi. Standing before his queen made him feel slightly uncomfortable. Sovereign of Bohemia since the signature of the agreement between Franz and him, she was a token of his reign's success as leader of the nomads.

"Your Majesty! When I was informed of your stay in this kingdom, I had to give you my regards in person," he said bowing sincerely.

Sissi showed her guest to a seat on the sofa. Alone in the poorly lighted room, the two friends exchanged customary formalities. As the conversation went on, their discussion was becoming less official. A familiarity grew between them. Seated near him, the empress listened to the latest news about his people with interest.

"In this period of winter, the community has preferred to retreat to the valley. The wind from the north is too piercing on top of the mountains," explained Yourik, drinking a cup of hot chocolate mixed with a spoonful of strong coffee beans.

"Why not settle down on the outskirts of Vienna? In case of illness, you could more easily seek the help of doctors," suggested Sissi smiling.

The man admitted that the idea was interesting and that he would take the time to consider it seriously. During the cold season, elderly people and young infants did die more often than usual. The head of the Bohemians truly cared about the needs and the well-being of his people.

The meeting, although very pleasant, did not go on past noon. Despite the invitation to stay for lunch, the individual declined the offer because he needed to leave Ischl Castle to get back on the road. He was expected in Paris to attend a huge gathering of nomads. Just like every year, the heads of the communities met in the French capital. During their three-day meeting, they stated the guidelines that ensured the future of their group. The road between Bavaria and the heart of the Seine River was still perilous, especially on the snowy paths of Europe.

"Your Majesty, I hope that you will be glowing with happiness again..." said Yourik as he left the sitting room.

Worried to see his friend in such a pitiful state, the descendant of the last King of Bohemia was heavy-hearted at the thought of leaving Sissi alone with herself. His eloquent sadness could not conceal the suffering that oppressed him.

The imperial couple was together once again as the first buds started to appear. The white ground gradually gave way to verdant colours. The birds that had gone south were chirruping again on Austrian soil.

At a supper given in the honour of the King of Poland, who was on an official visit in the capital, Sissi seemed more lively and dynamic than usual. The fresh air of Bavaria had restored

some unhoped-for energy into her. She attended several charitable activities in neighbouring cities and in other parts of the
Empire. Everyone was delighted to see their empress in such
good shape. Even Franz, who had become a regular at brothels
which he visited on the sly, congratulated his wife on her dedication towards her role as sovereign.

"My dear, the people appreciate your presence beside their
monarch," he had mentioned to her during an evening at the
opera of Vienna.

For several months now, the wedded couple no longer
had intercourse. Sissi had given a daughter and an heir to the
dynasty of the Habsburgs. Her duty to the Imperial Crown had
therefore been fulfilled. Even during her rare presence beside
the emperor, she no longer shared his bed. It was common
knowledge that the only bond that remained between Franz
Joseph and Sissi was their act of marriage. Nevertheless, they
still had feelings for each another. Was their passion truly
extinguished?

The following year, she returned to Madeira for an inde-
terminate amount of time. Her health, which had been excellent for the past months, let her down again. It was impossible
for her to stay at Schönbrunn Palace for more than six months.
Beyond this period of time, her body reacted in an alarming
way. What seemed, in the beginning, like an internal illness
quickly became a physical reaction to her helplessness towards
fulfilling her role as wife and sovereign. The difficult life at the
Imperial Court was eating away the strength of the empress
slowly.

The night before her departure for Portugal, she received the undesired visit of her terrible mother-in-law. Together in Sissi's antechamber, they talked nonsense as usual. Standing before her daughter-in-law, Sophie disapproved of her several retreats out of the country.

"You're leaving again!" let out the aunt with a menacing look.

"Stop harassing me! If you hadn't made my life a living hell, Franz and I would be with each another constantly," replied Sissi angrily.

"It's always somebody else's fault and never your own."

"How dare you speak these words to me? Since the first day of my marriage with His Majesty, you have tried everything to humiliate and discredit me in the eyes of my husband, and everyone else involved," cried the empress hysterically.

"You brutally assaulted me in Hungary. Have you already forgotten?" reprimanded the other woman.

"Fear not... If the guard hadn't come between us, Your Imperial Highness would no longer be here to lecture me," replied Sissi staring into the eyes of her sworn enemy.

Scandalized by these words, the archduchess left the apartments of her niece straight away. Purple with rage, she hurried into the dark corridors of Schönbrunn Palace. Sophie did not accept to be opposed, much less so by this scatterbrain of a Wittelsbach.

This last confrontation had gone too far according to the sovereign. She didn't have the physical strength, and she wasn't in the mood to endure these occasional attacks. The empress had her luggage prepared for another journey at the other end of the continent. This time around, she did not consider returning to Austria before a long while.

Prior to vanishing under her silky sheets, Sissi went to her children's bedroom. They were all deeply asleep. Looking at them, a stream of tears slid down her pale cheeks. The mother loved her offspring deeply and utterly. For nothing in the world she would have wished misfortune upon her daughter and son. If the empress constantly ran away from the Imperial Court, it certainly wasn't because of the young Sophie and Rudolf. On the contrary, there wasn't anything in it for her children should she persist in staying in Vienna. They would feel the pain of Sissi and would suffer the adverse consequences. No, for their future's sake, she had to get away from Schönbrunn Palace. Before shutting the door, she kissed their foreheads one last time.

"May God watch over you!" the woman whispered as she returned to her room.

At six o'clock sharp, the carriage of the empress was waiting before the sturdy doors of the imperial residence. Sissi's personal effects were piled up on the roof and the coachman was patiently waiting for his passenger. A five-man cavalry was to escort the sovereign to her destination.

Sissi walked down the main staircase towards the ground floor. She nodded at the domestics as she crossed the corridors of the huge building. Neither Franz Joseph nor the archduchess bid the sovereign farewell. She didn't take offense, quite the contrary, since it would have been an obnoxious comedy.

The endless journey between Vienna and Madeira did not tire Sissi at all. She greatly enjoyed the travels since they allowed her to gaze admiringly at the scenery of the different countries she came across. The month of April was the perfect time of the year to get on the roads of Europe. The snow, which was almost completely melted, gave way to breathtaking scenes. After months of limited sunlight, the fresh and sparkling colours of spring filled her with some joy of living again. Sissi did a brief stopover at Ludwigstrasse Palace to kiss her parents.

Alone since the departure of their children, the ducal couple spent their time attending soirées held by the high society. Max hated these outings vehemently, but they were his sole occupation since he could no longer enjoy the presence of his children. Days seemed longer and less interesting when he locked himself inside his residence. With fifty-four years of age, Max had a frailer health than before. Strolls in the forest had become scarce and hunting nearly impossible.

Sissi arrived in Portugal after a few weeks on the road. The sovereign's cortege crossed Austria, Bavaria, Switzerland, France, Spain and Portugal. The long journey went smoothly.

Madeira, Sissi's favourite resting place, was a small archipelago composed of several islands. A Portuguese Crown dependency, the island was located in the Atlantic Ocean, nearly halfway between Europe and Africa. The place was well-known for its mild climate and sandy beaches. There were few inhabitants, and they were always very welcoming with tourists. Every man of science recommended that their patients stay in this breathtaking location. The empress was no exception, and she went whenever she could.

Once she arrived at the harbour of the main island, she was relieved to leave the continent. She loved being among the islanders because no one knew her identity. Sissi could easily pass for a rich woman without any imperial title. She stayed at a private hotel, where she lived in a luxurious suite. Apart from the two ladies-in-waiting who accompanied her, she didn't see any familiar faces from Schönbrunn Palace.

Three days after setting foot in Madeira, Sissi attended a French theatrical performance. Written by the famous Molière, the play had been praised for more than two hundred years. It had been ordered by King Louis XIV in the seventeenth century. Among the actors, a man named Henri Leteigne played the main character. He had undeniable charisma and a keen intelligence that far exceeded that of his stage colleagues. The thirty-something man piqued the empress' curiosity as soon as she noticed him in his eccentric part. She asked Georgina, the eldest favourite, to find out more about this mysterious individual. The woman carried out her mistress' directive within the hour. After hearing the information gathered by her servant, Sissi considered meeting the Frenchman. Her wish was fulfilled that very evening, during a meal in her private quarters.

For the occasion, the empress gave her two ladies-in-waiting the night off along with three of her five guards. To look after her safety, only two armed men were allowed to watch the premises. The other ones attended the activities held in the great hall of the hotel where they were staying. Sissi had asked that a table be set up on the narrow patio. She loved sunsets and wanted to share her interest with the artist.

Henri arrived at the requested time as per the instructions of the sovereign's favourite. Wearing a white suit, he was kindly welcomed by his hostess around 7 pm. As for Sissi, she was dressed with a blue sundress and a delicate gold chain. The man, intimidated to find himself in the company of a crowned head, mumbled his first few sentences.

"Sir, your performance on stage impressed me," declared the empress to make him feel more at ease.

"Your Majesty is much too kind," replied the guest, lowering his head.

"Where does this passion for *la comédie française* come from?"

"My mother, God bless her soul, was a Molière enthusiast. She attended every single performance by this great author before she died. The woman inspired me to portray the different characters written by the literary genius," explained the man sipping a glass of alcoholic beverage.

The last time that Sissi had spent such a pleasant evening was at a tête-à-tête dinner with Franz Joseph. A few years had gone by since this memorable event. Today, she was nearly twenty-five years old, eight of which she had spent at the Imperial Court. A quarter of a century from her life had passed. Apart from her childhood and her first year of marriage with the emperor, she could not boast about the most beautiful years of her existence.

The actor, somewhat light-hearted because of the alcohol, rested a short while on the sofa in the living room. Divided into small same-size rooms, the sovereign's suite looked a lot like a luxurious residence in the heart of Lisbon. Portuguese architecture allowed Sissi to get away from the formal appearance of Schönbrunn Palace. After five minutes, she walked inside her quarters. Intrigued by the extended absence of her guest, she headed where the individual was seated. She was surprised to find Henri squatting on the couch. He was sleeping peacefully, without worrying about the etiquette. Sissi found the physique of the Frenchman attractive. Although he didn't have the most beautiful face, he could easily compete with potential rivals. Despite the carnal desire that he awoke in her, the empress did not want to cross the forbidden line. On the one hand, her social status could expose her to formal repudiation and, on the other hand, she still had romantic feelings for Franz in the bottom of her heart. Sissi quickly came to the conclusion that it was wiser to ask one of her guards to carry the artist in another room of the private hotel. Out of principle, she would cover the charge.

The next morning, the actor woke up in an unknown bed. He tried to remember what had happened the night before. Some fresh images suddenly came back to him. Henri felt immeasurably ashamed.

"I must ask the sovereign to forgive me," he told himself aloud.

He went to the suite of the empress hoping to meet her. Only too late. She, who was a morning person, had left her apartments an hour earlier. The man asked where Sissi had gone, but the guards didn't say much. He hurried outside the building speedily.

"Where could a sovereign be on this island?" whispered the actor looking for such a place.

He thought that the best thing to do was to head where she had seen him for the first time. Without wasting any time, Henri ran across the streets of the city, which overflowed with activity in this busy period. He went to the small theatre where he played the night before. Despite a thorough search, Henri saw no face like that of Sissi. He went on searching elsewhere in the surroundings. She wasn't at the Catholic Church or the most frequented beach either. It was difficult for him to look for the sovereign since he did not know anything about her interests.

After a frantic race throughout the city, the artist considered returning to the establishment where the theatre company was staying. He was convinced that she would not want to speak to him again after his inappropriate behaviour the night before. The Frenchman was about to head in the direction of his hotel when Georgina appeared in front of him.

"Miss!" cried the actor as he got nearer the lady-in-waiting.

The favourite immediately recognized Henri. She stopped so he would be able to reach her on the porch of a local restaurant.

"Mister Leteigne, how are you this morning?" she asked politely.

"Very well! Please forgive me, but would it be possible for me to exchange a few words with Her Majesty?" declared the man energetically.

"The empress is currently in the company of her doctors. If you wish, I can give her your request as soon as possible?" suggested the woman, smiling.

Obviously, he had no other choice but to accept the offer of the lady-in-waiting. This way, the artist would be able to find out Sissi's opinion of him. If she refused to meet him, he would know for certain.

"Thank you! If Madam agrees to see me again, you can leave me a message at the reception of this hotel," he said, specifying the location in question.

The favourite headed back to the private hotel of the empress. Before her mistress returned, she had to tidy up her suite since Sissi hated living in a mess.

On that same evening, the sovereign accepted to see her guest again. This time, she demanded that her lady-in-waiting be present.

"Georgina, I want you to stay by my side for this meeting."

As he had done the previous evening, the man returned to the suite of the empress. Inside, Sissi and her favourite Austrian were waiting for him. Alone with the two women, Henri Leteigne was less nervous than the night before. If one of them intimidated him because of her imperial rank, the other one was more accessible.

Throughout the meal, she noticed that the actor's gaze was often fixed on her protégée. She quickly grasped the underlying meaning of this gesture. If she, a crowned head, could not give in to love, perhaps her lady-in-waiting could. A brilliant idea suddenly crossed her mind. A wedding... It had been such a long time since the empress organized an activity of some kind. Yes, she would push her favourite into the arms of the Frenchman. *Now that's a stimulating mission*, thought Sissi.

"Tell me Henri, have you been in love?" she asked smoking a cigarette.

Sissi knew that smoking was utterly unacceptable at the Court of the Habsburgs, but she took advantage of her get-aways abroad to indulge in her favourite vice. No member of the imperial family was seen in public mouthing a cigarette. As usual, she couldn't care less about the judgement of others. If she craved something, she satisfied her craving by all means possible.

"Only once, it was a long time ago," replied the guest playing with a piece of toffee.

Sitting around the table, the three friends ate a delicious meal that included poultry, vegetables and different cheeses.

This was without question the empress' recipe of choice. She loved chicken-based dishes. In her childhood, the domestics of Possenhofen Castle regularly prepared such meals for her. All her life, Sissi would cherish her passion for this type of food.

"Don't be shy. Tell us your story," she suggested winking teasingly.

"When I was still a boy, my father owned a shoe store. He inherited the shop from his uncle who had died without descendants. As new storekeeper, he decided to expand the business. Unfortunately, he did not have the financial resources to see his project through. So he decided to set his dream aside until he made enough money. Years passed and he died without realizing his dream," said the man lowering his head.

He had never told his secret to anyone, much less to two perfect strangers. And yet, that evening, he felt comfortable with them.

"Then, I took over my father's business to earn a living. I quickly noticed that I wasn't cut out for the job. I despised the endless hours I spent making shoes. An incredible waste of time, in my opinion. I had to sell the business. After speaking about it with some friends, one of them offered to buy the shop for a reasonable price. As I was free to fulfil my ambitions, I decided to go to an audition. The passion for the theatre that my mother passed down to me had grown over the years," he continued before shedding a tear in her memory.

The story that Henri was telling them moved the lady-in-waiting. She hung on every word the stranger said. She was intrigued by it all. Sissi, who witnessed the reaction of her favourite, was elated inside. *Perhaps this will be easier than I imagined?* she thought to herself.

"At an audition, a well-known actress watched in the shadows my debut on the stage. Caroline, her name was Caroline. She was a pretty young woman with curly hair. Her face was out of this world. As soon as I laid eyes on her, my heart was overwhelmed by her bewitching beauty. She was two years younger than me. After my performance in front of the members of the managing team, she invited me to her place. I was instantly attracted to her home, which was as charming as her. In a rather hasty manner, I set out to ask her hand in marriage. She accepted with so much conviction that I thought I had found a rare gem. But, the next day, her body was found in front of her doorstep. A thief had murdered her for a necklace of little value. I haven't opened my heart to another woman since," he concluded with a shaky voice.

"What a tragic story. Losing the love of your life in such circumstances," exclaimed Georgina weeping.

"Do you think that one day you will be able to offer yourself to another woman again?" asked the empress, hoping for a positive answer.

The actor was speechless for a few seconds. He looked at the sovereign's question from different angles. Henri had never really considered finding such a genuine love again.

"Yes!" he declared with an honest voice.

Although the word may have been short, it was enough for the empress to pursue her mission. Such a sensitive man could only be the perfect husband for her protégée. She had to reveal her intentions discreetly, so she wouldn't scare off the actor.

"Tomorrow, we are going to a small island located nearby; we've been told that a colony of rare birds has found shelter there. Would you accompany us?" suggested Sissi winking at the other woman.

"I would like to, but I'm performing on stage in the evening. My company and I have one last show to do before we return to Paris, next week," replied the artist bitterly.

"If I promise that we will be back before the opening of your play..." swore Sissi hoping that he would accept.

"Why not! Count me in," asserted the guest raising his glass of wine.

The three friends spent another hour talking about their respective lives. More discreet, the empress let her lady-in-waiting and Henri get acquainted. As the conversation developed, some affinity manifested between them. The ploy of the empress seemed to be working.

Around ten o'clock, under a glorious sun, the sovereign and her two ladies-in-waiting headed to the harbour. Accompanied by only one armed man, Sissi wanted for this day to unfold as normally as possible. It wasn't for her sake, but rather to see her wedding project blossom. The idea of having the Frenchman and her protégée fall in love had grown to another level, so much so that she now saw them joining their lives before God. If all went well, she considered freeing Georgina from her obligation towards the Imperial Crown.

"Mister Leteigne!" exclaimed Sissi when she saw him heading towards the boat.

"Your Majesty!" said the artist walking towards the group.

He climbed on board and placed himself right beside the favourite. This gesture, although trivial, did not go unnoticed by Sissi. She even smiled faintly, only to reveal her noble intentions.

The captain of the boat started the engines. On the deck, everyone looked at the city moving away from the coastline. When she was on water, Sissi felt as free as a bird. She even proclaimed herself seagull of the oceans. Like these birds, the empress enjoyed seeing new horizons.

"My brave man, don't you think that Georgina is dazzling in this blue dress? She could easily be mistaken for one of these mysterious mermaids," she said.

The man spontaneously agreed with the statement of Sissi. The lady-in-waiting, who had a delicate waist, was frequently complimented by men.

The favourite of the empress began serving Sissi the very next day of her imperial wedding. Born in 1835, in a suburb of Vienna, she came from an Austrian family of lower nobility. Her father was a supervisor to the army of the Habsburgs. Her mother, who was the daughter of a baron from the southern part of the country, was a close friend of the archduchess. Despite her close ties with Sophie, Georgina von

Salburg did not think highly of the woman. She had witnessed her spiteful behaviour towards the empress time and again. Also, the protégée of the sovereign quickly formed a bad opinion of the archduchess. Blessed with feline grace, she had everything to appeal to men. Only one thing wasn't in her favour and that was some elocution problems. Despite the diligent care of specialists, she had never been able to correct the situation.

After fifteen minutes on the sea, the captain moored the boat to the coast of the wild island. With birds unknown to the continent for sole inhabitants, the isle seemed as idyllic as the earthly paradise described in the Holy Scriptures. Millions of odoriferous flowers of different shapes and colours adorned its vegetation. No road or property had been built on this virgin land.

Sissi, followed by her two ladies-in-waiting, trod on the sand of the island for the first time. The group marvelled at the bucolic scene that was unfolding before their very eyes. The landscape was even more fantastic than they had been told by the employees of the hotel. Fruit-bearing trees sat proudly on top of a cliff.

"My friends, wouldn't you agree that there is no place as magnificent as this anywhere in Europe?" let out the empress holding on to her hat to prevent it from being blown away by the wind.

Everyone agreed unanimously. They couldn't take their eyes away from the sublime scenery of this part of the archipelago.

"Georgina, would you find us a spot in the shade. Henri, would you mind accompanying my protégée in case she encountered some wild animal?" asked the empress with a friendly voice.

The duo immediately left in search of the ideal location for Sissi. After a short while, the lady-in-waiting found a small rock under a huge, luxuriant tree. Sunrays could barely pierce through its green foliage. When the servant turned around to go back where she came from, a grey reptile was in her way. With a body of equal length to a human being, the four-legged creature had razor sharp claws on each paw. The lizard laid motionless on the burning sand; inside its open maw a collection of knifelike teeth lined up. An endless red tongue fell to the ground. A stupefying fear prevented Georgina from moving or screaming.

"Stay calm! Do not move because the animal could react badly," said Henri moving behind the threatening creature.

With a light step, the actor slowly moved towards the obstacle. To defend himself, he held on to a huge tree branch. Frightened, the favourite of the Austrian empress feared for her life, but also for her Good Samaritan's.

With a fatal blow, the Frenchman cracked open the skull of the reptile before he had time to retaliate. To make sure that it was truly dead, the artist hit its head several times. A pool of blood spurted out from the body of the rough-skinned victim.

"Sir, you've just saved my life," cried the woman, throwing herself into Henri's arms.

"Miss, I would never leave you in a situation that put you in jeopardy," he declared, pressing her against him.

This mishap definitely brought them closer together. When they returned to Sissi, her protégée told her all about the feat of the brave man.

"My dear, I think that he is fond of you," declared the empress looking at the face of the actor.

Throughout this sunny day, Georgina and her courageous rescuer talked alone. Away from the group, they spent hours discussing their lives. At the sight of the lovebirds, Sissi found herself thinking about the good times of her couple. She and Franz had also experienced unforgettable moments of intimacy. She had been so enamoured with the monarch in earlier times... She would have followed him to the end of the world if the emperor had asked her to. In fact, she had done so by accepting to marry him. Sophie was the person who had destroyed their relationship. The archduchess, with her repeated plots and squalid spitefulness, had managed to break the powerful bond that united them. That added to the maliciousness of her husband's mother, and the highly demanding duties of the Imperial Court. Because of his title, Franz Joseph was never by the side of his better half. Always busy serving Austria as his responsibilities required of him, he had severely neglected the empress. The years had passed, and Sissi's heart had closed up slowly. His repeated absences from Schönbrunn Palace were the cause of all the suffering she had accumulated over time. As she reminisced about these happy days, a tear fell down Sissi's cheek. *It's too late for regrets,* she convinced herself.

As planned by the empress, the boat returned to the harbour of Madeira's main island. Henri, who was going to perform in the evening, was expected by his theatre company. For one last time, he would be portraying the same character as in the previous shows. Sitting in the audience, the sovereign and her lady-in-waiting applauded the actor vigorously. The artist had demonstrated his skills more than once throughout his career, but this time he had outdone himself. Even his stage colleagues noticed that his emotion transcended his performance. Henri wasn't working, but rather unveiling the human being that was hidden inside him.

"Bravo!" cried Georgina leaping up.

Henri had recognized the voice of the woman for whom his heart skipped a beat. That very instant, Sissi understood that she had won her bet hands down. They had fallen in love with one another, as if by magic. Was it fate or the sovereign who had brought them together for life?

The night before his departure for France, Henri Leteigne asked for a final audience with Sissi. The request was immediately granted. The actor went to the empress' suite with a clear objective. She was aware of it and had lengthily prepared herself for this last meeting.

"Your Majesty, since the first time I laid eyes on your lady-in-waiting, my heart has been pining for her. May I ask for your permission to marry Georgina von Salburg?" begged the artist, on his knees before the empress.

Sissi, standing up proudly, was relishing her victory. Her mission hadn't been as difficult as she had anticipated. Obviously, she would give him the hand of her favourite.

"I give you my permission, as long as my protégée accepts your offer," she replied with a sense of accomplishment.

With the blessing of the empress, the man officially asked the lady-in-waiting to marry him. Before he finished his sentence, her answer was already written on her face. The servant was in love with the Frenchman and she wanted to spend the rest of her life with him.

Georgina and Sissi mutually agreed that the favourite would remain in the service of the empress until the end of the month. On the calendar, there was only a week and a half left. The protégée had the intention of enjoying her last days with the sovereign. The years she had spent at Schönbrunn Palace had provided many occasions for her to travel in the company of the empress. With time, they had become very good friends. Sissi saw a loyal confidante in her.

On September 30, 1862, around ten o'clock, Sissi's craft was waiting for her at the harbour of Madeira's main island. Under a light rain, she exchanged a few words of farewell with her lady-in-waiting. Near them, the other favourite was holding a pink umbrella above their heads.

"My dear Georgina, live life to the fullest... Don't repeat my mistakes. You are fortunate enough not to be restrained by responsibilities as is my case," declared the empress caressing her cheek with the palm of her hand.

"Madam, I shall live each day as if it were my last," replied the other, weeping a fountain of tears.

Before boarding the boat, Sissi gave her friend a present. It was a gold ring topped with a magnificent ruby. This jewel had belonged to her mother, the duchess of Bavaria. She had given it to her on the day of her wedding with Franz Joseph. It hadn't brought her any kind of protection during all these years, but perhaps it would bring Georgina some satisfaction.

"Your Majesty is much too kind with me. I have nothing comparable with this jewel to give you," claimed the lady-in-waiting, holding the precious object in her frail hand.

"Your devotion to me was a beautiful token of fidelity. Be happy, my dear friend," the empress concluded as she climbed on the bridge that lead to her craft.

The boat slowly moved away from the harbour while the fiancée energetically waved at her former mistress. Soon, the island of Madeira disappeared from Sissi's field of view. Her stay on the Portuguese archipelago had just come to an end. Her return to Vienna was inescapable. She had to get back to the imperial family to ensure that her marriage remained legal according to the laws of the Church of Rome. It was with a heavy heart that Sissi headed back to Austria.

In her cabin, sitting on a wooden chair, the empress inked a page in her diary.

On this thirtieth day of the year eighteen sixty-two, I am regretfully on my way back to my misery. Beautifully scented days of joyful Madeira, you shall be missed. Warm midday sun, you shall no longer embellish my otherwise gloomy existence. There, my worst enemy and the pains of a position I never wanted await. My sole comfort lies in the infinite joy that pressing my offspring against my body shall bring me.

Sissi

Through these few handwritten lines, jotted down with a trembling hand, she had just revealed what was tormenting her. When she put her quill back in the inkwell, she felt a surge of anxiety spread inside her. Knowing that her mother-in-law was waiting for her resolutely caused her aches in the abdomen. It was clear that her illness wasn't merely physical. The idea of returning to the capital upset her completely. After such pains, Sissi promised herself she wouldn't stay at the imperial residence more than a few months. She was already thinking about her next trip under the sun. This time around, she was considering leaving Austria for several months, perhaps even for an entire year. She had absolutely no intention of listening to the sarcastic comments of the archduchess or spending endless nights waiting for the return of the emperor, Franz Joseph.

CHAPTER 7

A Hungarian Entourage

Budapest
1863-1866

IN EARLY 1863, the father of the empress fell
seriously ill. After a long stroll near a small lake
around Possenhofen Castle, he stumbled on a pebble hidden
under a thin layer of snow. The man, known for his plump
body, fell face down into the water. With great difficulty,
he managed to find his way out of the pond. A lone wolf, the
duke wasn't accompanied during his mishap. Therefore, he
could only count on himself to get out of this unfortunate
situation.

On the following days, Max's health declined to a critical condition. Confined to bed, he saw a delegation of doctors
from the Bavarian capital. Their opinion was unanimous: Max
suffered from a severe pneumonia. Worried about her husband,
Ludovika wrote a letter to her daughter to let her know about
the situation. The mother asked the empress to send the most
competent practitioners of Vienna at her father's bedside. She

swallowed her pride and begged the sovereign to do everything in her power to save the duke.

As soon as Sissi received her mother's message, she demanded that the best Austrian men of science accompany her to see Maximilian. Out of love for his wife, Franz Joseph promised that the bill would be covered by the Treasury of the Imperial Court.

"You make me the happiest woman of the Empire," she told her husband.

The day after she received Ludovika's letter, a cortege left Schönbrunn Palace. On board the black coach, Sissi prayed the Almighty to spare the head of the household.

"Lord, I beg you to protect my father."

After a few days, Sissi and the healthcare specialists arrived at the residence of the ducal couple. Impatient to see Max, she got off the vehicle in a flash. Without greeting the duchess, who was standing in the entrance hall, she hurried to his bedroom. The duke was sleeping soundly on the old wooden furniture. She tiptoed to his bed. Her saddened and worried eyes fixed upon the face of Sissi, which was significantly thinner than usual. She was upset to see him lying there, nearly motionless. In a compassionate manner, she gently leaned over her father's ear.

"Please come back to us!" she whispered.

A few steps behind the empress, the duchess burst out crying. Throughout the years, she and her husband had built a respectful relationship. Although love wasn't part of the equation, some level of affinity had grown between them. Without him, Ludovika's life would never have the same meaning. Selfishly, she did not want to become a widow for the rest of her life.

"Sissi… Is that you?" asked the sick man feebly, with his eyes closed.

"Yes father! I'm here!" she replied with a warm and gentle voice.

The empress brought her ear towards Max's mouth. She wanted to hear his words, but the man, exhausted by his condition, had a great deal of difficulty speaking.

"My daughter… I prayed God to send you to me… My life isn't as stur… sturdy as it used to be…" he continued with determination.

"Don't say such sad things," interrupted his favourite, wiping her face.

"Sissi, forgive me for… leaving you in Sophie's claws," added the duke with his pale trembling lips.

Max, despite the distance between Vienna and Munich, frequently received news from the Imperial Court. They came from the letters that the archduchess sent to his wife or from gossip that spread across the circles of the Bavarian nobility. The duke had always regretted the day he had agreed to marry his daughter to the emperor. He respected his nephew, Franz Joseph, but had always known about the influence that his terrible sister-in-law had over him. The father had accumulated a great deal of remorse during all these years. Today, as he felt his end near, he wanted the forgiveness of his favourite.

"You've done nothing wrong. I accepted to marry Franz... and I, alone, is responsible for my own fate," she continued, caressing his chalky white face.

Tired by the discussion, he stopped conversing with Sissi. His mind did not allow him to remain awake from lengthy periods of time.

She left the room, biting her lower lip. Her mother followed, shutting the door gently. They headed to the first living room on the ground floor. The doctors that accompanied the sovereign were waiting for them there, seated on sofas.

"Gentlemen, the duke's condition is alarming. I ask that, no, I demand that you save him," declared the empress looking at each and every one of them.

Without wasting any time, the men of science went to the upper floor where the bedridden patient was sleeping. Sissi had ordered them to cure Max, and they intended on fulfilling her wish.

Despondent, the two women hugged each other for a long while. The ties of suffering united them. Alone amongst the furniture, mother and daughter could no longer hold back tears.

"Sissi, you are the kindest child the Earth has ever seen," exclaimed Ludovika in tears.

For more than twelve hours, the practitioners were hard at work, improving Maximilian's condition. Some busied themselves with bloodletting on the arms, while others gave him injections. They analyzed his symptoms, suggested solutions and rejected the less plausible possibilities.

At noon on the following day, the empress, overwrought, stormed into her father's bedroom. Surprised by her unexpected presence, the men of science left the room. She walked towards the duke. His eyes were still shut and his face pale. Desperation overwhelmed her. Sissi fell to her knees on the flooring. She was crushed by circumstances; she pressed her head against the blankets. Suddenly, a manly hand brushed her hair. She looked up towards the patient's body. Her disappointment vanished, and she smiled broadly. Under the sheets, the man was trying to move slowly.

"Father! Father!" she cried nervously.

Restless, Sissi bounced up and ran to the adjoining room.

"Come! The duke is back among us!" shouted the empress hopping across the hallway.

The doctors immediately rushed to Sissi's room. They examined him meticulously and confirmed his recovery. Their interventions had brought the duke out of his nearly comatose state. A few minutes later, the duchess arrived at her spouse's beside. She had raced up the stairs to see the miraculously cured man with her own eyes.

"Max! My dear husband, you gave me a terrible fright," she said, flustered.

Everyone was delighted about the recovery of the duke, particularly Sissi since her father represented the happiest moments of her life. By disappearing, he would rob her of the few joyful memories she had left.

The empress stayed with her parents for a week. In the meantime, the practitioners returned to the capital Austrian.

They had fulfilled the difficult task of bringing the sovereign's father back to life, a true exploit to their credit. Upon her return to Schönbrunn Palace, Sissi had the intention of rewarding them for their dedication. She would donate a generous scholarship to their department, at the prestigious University of Vienna.

Halfway through her stay in Bavaria, Sissi's brothers and sisters paid the duke and duchess a visit. Eager to see their famous sister, they spoke about her life at the Imperial Court. With great kindness, she told them all about the intrigues of the Habsburg residence. She purposely omitted to reveal the darker side of her existence.

On the night of January 17, when the moon dazzled a starry sky, Sissi went outside Possenhofen Castle. She wanted to breathe the fresh air of her native land before heading back to Austria. She knew fully well that the archduchess would reproach her for demanding the presence of the most renowned doctors of Vienna in Bavaria. She would even tell her that Franz didn't have to pay their fees. Sophie would gladly criticize the lifestyle of her brother-in-law. It was clear in Sissi's mind that she had to get away from the members of the House of Habsburg as soon as possible.

Helene took advantage of her brothers' chess tournament to join her younger sister. Wrapped up in a fur coat, she wanted to speak with her childhood confidante.

"Sissi, what are you doing, alone in the snow?"

"My dear, I'm gazing at the moon," she replied smiling.

Despite the cold wintry night, they stayed outside for a quarter of an hour. During their childhood, the Wittelsbachs often spent entire evenings walking on the snowy ground of the family estate. Their most intimate conversations had taken place precisely where they were.

"Why do you return to your husband if you are so unhappy?" asked Helene.

"I don't have other options. I still love Franz… At least I think so!" replied Sissi.

"You think so!? Are you sure about that?"

Truth be told, the empress knew that she was lying to her sister. Her feelings weren't as strong today as they once had been. On the other hand, Sissi deeply respected the monarch. He had never injured her physically or harmed her intentionally. The emperor wasn't a great husband because his responsibilities towards the Empire overburdened him on a daily basis. She didn't reproach him his repeated absences on a whim, to the contrary. For years, Sissi had tried to save her union with her husband. Unfortunately, time had worn out their relationship.

"Helene, the person responsible for the destruction of my marriage with His Majesty is in fact called Sophie. You know our aunt as well as I do…" added Sissi.

"Of course! She would do anything to control Europe and the rest of the world," let out the eldest sister ironically.

Upon these words, the two sisters burst out laughing. Images of the archduchess came to mind. When they were little girls, their mother's sister introduced herself to the Prince of Liechtenstein. The man, who was visiting Bavaria, attended a banquet given in his honour at the royal residence.

Invited to the event, Sophie was chosen by her brother to sit near the prince. When she raised her glass to greet the wife of the foreign sovereign, she spilled the alcoholic beverage on the woman's dress. Max, who was also present that evening, had told the story of the archduchess' faux pas over and over again. When the mother of the emperor stayed at Ischl Castle and invited Ludovika's family to official meals, the two Wittelsbachs always thought of this famous reception. Even their perfect aunt wasn't flawless in her official life.

After a short absence, the empress returned to Vienna as planned. As usual, her mother-in-law gladly lectured her about her lack of judgement.

"How can you neglect your husband and your children so frequently?" declared the archduchess before the other members of the imperial family.

Once again, the emperor didn't take his wife's side. The more frequent Sissi's absences became, the more estranged the two spouses grew. She felt alone, even when they were in the same room.

"I'm letting you know that I'm leaving for Corfu Island. My carriage is leaving Vienna in two days," announced the empress heading to her apartments.

The journey between the Austrian capital and Greece was perilous for any traveller who dared venture on it. Mercantile convoys were frequently ambushed by nomad thieves. It was not uncommon for the vehicle's driver to perish in the trap. Despite the sizeable obstacle, the sovereign did not back down on her decision.

Sissi's cortege crossed the Balkans without a hitch. The road was truly magnificent according to the empress. Used to refined architecture, she admired with curiosity houses and other like buildings. After several days, the black coach of the empress arrived in the south of Bulgaria. Entirely devastated by the Ottoman wars, this region displayed a surprising poverty. She had never witnessed such atrocious scenes. The corpses of children lay here and there on the roadsides. Sissi's eyes were flooded with tears as a result of these disturbing images. Mothers, in rags, were carrying the small bodies to a mass grave.

"This is a nightmare!" she told herself in a soft voice.

The further the carriage went towards the south, the more ravaged the villages were. Suddenly, for no reason, the vehicle stopped abruptly. Intrigued, she looked outside. She turned pale when she saw about ten armed men blocking the way. One of them, who was chubbier, aimed his rifle at the coachman. The swindler mumbled a few words in a foreign language that Sissi did not know. Since he didn't understand what his aggressor was saying, the driver did not react. Impatient, the foreigner shot him in the head. The cavalry of the empress, made up of five guards, responded violently. A merciless battle followed between the two enemy sides. Petrified, she, still stuck to her leather seat, prayed the Almighty to intervene in her favour.

After a short-lived confrontation, a heavy silence surrounded the carriage. Sissi, still in shock after the brutal murder of her coachman, refused to go outside. She shut her eyes and waited a short while. Nothing. No noise. Forced to find out about the state of the situation, she hesitantly got off the vehicle. When the sovereign saw the soldiers lying in a pool of blood, she let out a terrible scream. A few steps away from this gruesome scene, the thieves had suffered the same cruel fate. She was suddenly worried about her own destiny. What would become of her, now that she found herself alone in a hostile country?

"Madam, I don't think that this scene is suitable for a woman of your rank," exclaimed a manly voice.

Frightened, she headed unsteadily towards the stranger.

"Gentleman, I don't know you, but please do not harm me," begged Sissi shaking like a leaf.

"Fear not, I am not that kind of a man," replied the individual sitting on his mount.

"What do you want with me, then?" she asked with a conciliatory voice.

"I'm going to Corfu Island… I could probably help you get back on the road," suggested the stranger, smiling.

"Your offer is much appreciated! If you could find me a trustworthy coachman, I would be very happy," she explained.

"Where are you heading exactly?"

"Forgive me! I'm going to the same place as you," she admitted timidly.

"Excellent! I'll hire a coachman and we can continue the journey together in your carriage. What do you say?"

"I gladly accept!" said the empress, thanking the man for his offer.

The traveller swiftly found a young local to carry on the journey south. Sissi sat inside the coach and was accompanied by her saviour. Intimidated by the physical appearance of the stranger, she did not look at him for a long while.

"Madam, am I so repulsive?" he asked, winking at her.

"Absolutely not! To the contrary..." she replied without thinking about the embarrassment she put herself into.

Sissi had just revealed that she was attracted to the man, and her spontaneous words made her blush.

"Please forgive my rudeness. I am Gyula Andràssy," said the foreigner lifting his brown hat as a sign of respect for the empress.

"Pleased to meet you! I am Elisabeth..." she declared without finishing her sentence.

The empress, in a surge of enthusiasm, forgot that she couldn't reveal her true identity. It was extremely risky, even imprudent, for a crowned head to make herself known without a guard to protect her. By disclosing her title, she would become the perfect target for anyone with harmful intentions.

"Elisabeth Possen," said Sissi in reference to her family's castle.

"Tell me, my dear friend, for what reason are you heading to Corfu Island?" asked the stranger with curiosity.

"I'm suffering from an illness that only this climate can ease," she replied, not very far from the truth.

They continued their conversation en route to their destination. Nothing they were saying was compromising for either one of them. They were merely exchanging trivial information about their taste in food or about the sauciest rumours concerning the royal dignities of Europe. Sissi made sure not to give away too many details about such gossip. She did not want the stranger to suspect her identity in any way.

The carriage finally arrived at Sarrandë, a small village not far from where they were heading. The two travellers had to go to the harbour to catch a craft to Corfu Island. Unfortunately, night was fast-approaching and no boat sailed as soon as there was a hint of darkness in the sky. The first one available was leaving around five o'clock the next morning.

"Madam, I think that we will have to find a hotel for the night," asserted the individual, looking around the harbour to see if there was such an establishment nearby.

"I think so too!" she said smiling.

After asking around about accommodations, Andràssy found a tiny inn, conveniently located at a reasonable distance of the boats. The building solely had three rooms, but only one of them was available.

"I'm afraid that we will be forced to share the same room," he declared, opening the door.

At a glance, Sissi saw the small bed and was surprised that she would have to spend the night in it. It was out of the question that she should share it with any man other than her husband.

"A blanket on the floor will be perfect," exclaimed the foreigner who had perceived the perplexed look of the empress.

"Sir, forgive me for subjecting you to such discomfort," she apologized, somewhat confused by the situation.

"It's nothing! I'm leaving briefly… so that you can change in private," suggested the man kindly.

Once she had found her way under the thick, silky blankets, the stranger did the same on the damp floor of the room. After their eventful day, they fell asleep rather quickly.

Awake before the sovereign, the traveller went to the reception desk to pay the bill. When she opened her eyes, Sissi noticed that she was alone. Worried, she jumped out of bed and looked for Andràssy. Nothing. He seemed to have left. Disappointed, she found reassurance in the thought that she wasn't very far from Corfu Island. She set out to get dressed and start the day. She put on a flimsy, light red dress with a matching hat.

When Sissi left the room to head to the counter of the inn, she was surprised to see the man, sitting at a table at the end of the corridor. He had been waiting patiently on a chair for quite some time.

"Are you ready?" asked the stranger walking towards her.

"Of course!" she replied politely.

The two travellers went to the harbour of the village with the carriage. The man negotiated two one-way tickets to their destination. Meanwhile, Sissi had her luggage carried on the boat. They got on board the craft and sat on two wooden seats on the deck. Andràssy and Sissi were the only two passengers on board.

The boat sailed on the blue waters of the Mediterranean Sea. The empress, happy to find herself at sea, decided to eat the two oranges that she had bought from a merchant at the harbour.

"Don't tell me that these fruits will be your meal?"

"Why not? I eat like a bird, my dear!" she said, peeling the orange.

They both fell silent for half of the ferry crossing. In the meantime, she savoured the juice of her fruits while he looked at the birds flying in the sky that morning. They only knew each other for a day. Nevertheless, Sissi was completely comfortable with the foreigner. She even felt safe.

"You've asked me the reason for my journey to Corfu Island, but you haven't given me yours," she said, breaking the tranquility of the moment.

"Business! I have some contacts in this region, and I must meet with them," explained Andràssy.

"Tell me, where are you from exactly?" asked Sissi looking him in the eye.

"Budapest!" he exclaimed, putting his hat back on to protect himself from the sun.

Upon hearing the name of this Hungarian city, she jumped on her chair. The last time she had gone to the capital of the Magyars was in 1857, the year her eldest daughter had passed away. Budapest had a negative connotation for her. And so a few tears fell down her smooth cheeks. From the corner of his eye, the stranger noticed the teary eyes of the woman.

"Why are you crying?" asked the foreigner, offering her the handkerchief that he always carried in his pockets.

"It's nothing! I'm rather emotional," lied Sissi.

The traveller knew that she wasn't telling the truth, but, out of respect, he did not ask further questions.

The boat finally berthed early in the afternoon. The two travelling companions disembarked, thanking the captain. They took a vehicle to Parelioi, one of the most densely populated cities of the island. It was an idyllic location for both its magnificent vegetation and marvellous architecture. Although she was used to travelling, Sissi considered it to be her favourite destination. Everything seemed so warm and welcoming. When the carriage arrived at the heart of the locality, the empress got off the vehicle. She gave an amount of money to the domestic of Kérkyra Hotel, where she would be staying during her trip.

"Sir, I wish you a pleasant stay," she said to the Hungarian, smiling to him kindly.

"Madam, would you accept to see me again?" he exclaimed, walking to the sovereign.

Unsure of her answer, Sissi remained silent for an instant.

The presence of a familiar face could only make for more enjoyable days. Alone amid a foreign island, she considered the offer as some kind of security. Should a problem arise, she could count on Andràssy's help.

"Excellent idea! I'll be expecting you tomorrow morning, around eight o'clock, for breakfast," she suggested.

Satisfied with the answer of the empress, he returned inside the carriage. He waved at her and ordered the driver to be on his way.

Without revealing her name and her social rank, Sissi met the Hungarian traveller on a few occasions. The first two weeks went wonderfully well for the empress. She was seen by her doctors on a daily basis and entertained herself in the company of Andràssy. Days went by quickly since Sissi enjoyed his presence.

Around February 5, 1863, he left Corfu Island to return to Budapest. He spent the evening before his departure with the empress. Alone on the patio of the hotel where she was staying, the man and Sissi were speaking together for the last time, drinking a local beverage.

"Sir, you shall be missed!" she assured, smiling to the stranger.

"I will miss you even more!" he replied, looking at her tenderly.

As time went by, feelings had blossomed between them. Even if they weren't in love, they were definitely attracted to each other. She was particularly fond of Andràssy's brown eyes, square shaped face and sturdy stature. What titillated her the most was how intently he listened to her.

"My dear, I must tell you my true identity," she ventured to say.

Intrigued, the individual put his glass down and looked into the eyes of Sissi with a fierce curiosity.

"If you are from Hungary, you must certainly know the Emperor of Austria?"

"Absolutely! I've even met His Majesty on a few occasions," he admitted sincerely.

"For what reason?" she enquired with interest.

"I am the count of a small eastern region in my country. My family has been affiliated to the history of the Magyars for centuries," explained the stranger precisely.

The more information he gave her, the more Sissi was starting to dread the rest. She had often heard her husband speak of a Hungarian nobleman who was defying him. This duel was the reason behind the constant conflicts between his people and the imperial authority.

"I'm the leader of the resistance movement against the supremacy of the Habsburgs on our lands," declared the man.

"Your words trouble me deeply… Then you know who I am?" she exclaimed.

"No! I don't," replied the man holding her arm gently.

"Elisabeth of Wittelsbach, Empress of Austria and Queen of Bohemia," she confessed, lowering her eyes.

Stunned to find himself before the wife of his enemy, he moved back a few steps. The Hungarian had never met this woman before because the empress hadn't set foot in Budapest since the death of the young archduchess. He now understood the wealth that she seemed to possess. How could he have been taken with Franz Joseph's wife?

"Your Majesty, forgive me, but I must leave you immediately," let out the nobleman before he vanished.

Sissi, who was abandoned anew, burst out crying for she was shaken by Andràssy's reaction. She had been so joyful in his company. Once again, her rank prevented her from getting the little happiness that she could hope for. The empress spent the night weeping over her misfortune.

The next morning, at dawn, the leader of the resistance boarded a boat. He returned to Greece to continue his journey to the most important city of his country. On his way there, he reminisced about the special moments he had had with the sovereign.

After spending more than a month on Corfu Island, Sissi gladly welcomed the presence of one of her ladies-in-waiting. Solitude weighed on her a little less after the arrival of her favourite.

"What's going on at the Imperial Court?" had asked the empress.

"His Majesty continues his domination of Europe," had answered Mirka, smiling.

Mirka Wilfen was born in 1840, near Bern, in Switzerland. Her parents, travelling circus artists, had abandoned her in an orphanage for young girls. She was raised by strict and compassionless women. It wasn't uncommon for them to hit her repeatedly for no reason. After working as a domestic for a noble family in Vienna, she received an offer to work at Schönbrunn Palace. One thing led to another and she obtained the coved position of lady-in-waiting for the empress. She had been in the service of her mistress for three years.

Sissi stayed on Corfu Island for about two consecutive years. Despite her husband's several letters asking her to return to Vienna, she remained impassive. She had never felt so good in her entire life. She could do as she pleased without any intervention from anyone. She visited Corfu, attended theatrical performances, concerts, and enjoyed the extraordinary climate of the region. Unfortunately, since she was out of money, she had to return to the Austrian capital. Insulted by the extended absence of his wife, Franz had stopped providing her with the necessary amounts to cover her expenses. Penniless, she had no other choice but to pack up and resume her position at Schönbrunn Palace.

In the spring of 1865, the cortege of the sovereign stopped before the doors of the imperial residence. Once again, Sissi walked inside the building without trying to conceal her bitterness. Her children, Gisela and Rudolf, were nine and seven years old respectively. They could hardly recognize their mother since she had left them so frequently. Sophie, always true to herself, expressed her ceaseless reproach to her daughter-in-law. As for Franz, he wasn't any more available than before her departure. The illness and usual sufferings of Sissi returned very quickly.

Two years after her return from Corfu, the unexpected visit of a Hungarian delegation would change the situation at the Imperial Court. A war between Austria and the Magyar people had just broken out. In order to find a solution to this political issue, the emperor had summoned Budapest emissaries. He had expressly asked the empress to look after the guests. She had accepted with some reservations, knowing that Count Andràssy would be among them.

Surrounded by competent advisers, Sissi proved to be creative when preparing the menus. The dishes were all made up of foods that Hungarians were fond of: tomatoes, sweet peppers, onions, black pepper, paprika, and sour cream. For their entertainment, the sovereign decided to organize three activities: a ball, a theatrical performance and a masked soirée. The guests would be staying on the third floor of Schönbrunn Palace.

A total of ten diplomats appeared in the Austrian capital on May 1: seven men and three women. Their cortege arrived with pomp and circumstance at the imperial residence. Everyone got off the vehicle with some apprehension. Rumours had it that a trap was awaiting them upon their arrival. In truth, there was no such thing.

"Be vigilant! We mustn't trust these Habsburgs," warned the leader of the group.

As a good hostess, Sissi welcomed the guests outside. For the occasion, she was wearing a lime green dress adorned with white lace, and a beautiful diadem was laid on her head.

"Milords, miladies, His Majesty joins me in welcoming you. I am Empress Elisabeth," she said by way of introduction.

Despite the two years that had passed since they bid each other farewell, Andràssy immediately recognized the mysterious traveller. After spending great moments in her company, he had abandoned her with an explanation. Today, the nobleman found himself before her. He felt somewhat uncomfortable, but concealed it rather well.

"Madam, allow me to thank you for your welcome," he replied with a neutral voice.

Without conferring beforehand, they both pretended not to know each other. For their mutual safety, it was wiser to act in such a way. The empress, followed by the Hungarians, walked inside the impressive building. She led them to the drawing room. Once there, Sissi showed them to their seats.

"His Majesty shouldn't be long," she announced politely.

The representatives sat on the sofas while waiting for the arrival of the emperor. As for Sissi, she took a seat on a small bench, in front of the ivory piano. She set out to entertain the guests by playing some known melodies. The instrument reverberated throughout the room thanks to the agile hands of the empress.

The magical moment and the soft music that filled the space shook Andràssy. He had never heard Mozart being played so skillfully. The feelings he had had for Sissi began to stir him again. The charm and the beauty of the empress agitated the man.

Suddenly, Franz Joseph entered the room in the company of his mother. Interrupted by their presence, Sissi removed her slender hands from the keyboard. She stood up gracefully and joined her husband and the archduchess. They Magyars stood up and bowed briefly before the leader of the Empire.

"Count Andràssy, I am happy to see you again," exclaimed the monarch as he walked to the emissary.

"The pleasure is all mine!" replied the other one, shaking the hand of his host.

"You've met my wife?" declared the monarch, inviting the foreigner to place a light customary kiss on her hand.

"Pleased to meet you, Madam," said the nobleman smiling to Sissi.

"Here is my mother, Archduchess Sophie," continued the emperor.

After the introductions, Franz invited the diplomats to another room. A rectangular table sat in the middle of the second living room. Austrian advisers were already seated on one side while the chairs intended for the Hungarians remained vacant. The aunt and her niece offered their final salutations and resumed their activities.

For more than four hours, advisers and diplomats discussed means of restoring peace between the two countries. More arrogant, Austrians had a hard time negotiating with the representatives of a nation that they clearly considered inferior to them.

"Your Majesty, you cannot destroy Hungary simply because you own it," thundered the count angrily.

"Historically, Budapest has always answered to Vienna in one way or another," replied the emperor firmly.

"That's false! Magyars have never submitted to anyone, much less to Austrians," let out the man straightening up.

Outraged by the words of the monarch, Andràssy left the premises hastily. Habsburg or not, he wasn't going to endure the insults of his enemy. Enraged, he headed outside Schönbrunn Palace, passing by Sissi swiftly. Intrigued by his violent mood, she followed him to the doors of the imperial residence. She felt comfortable speaking to him there.

"Why did you abandon me in such a cavalier manner?" asked the sovereign making sure that no one was listening to their conversation.

"How should I have reacted, according to you? See for yourself… you are the wife of our invader," he replied pointing at the building.

"You should have explained it to me. I am no fool, you know… I would have understood!" exclaimed the empress with a disappointed-filled voice.

"Indeed! Forgive me!"

"Why did you just leave the living room so hastily?"

"The emperor never stops insulting my people. His Majesty believes that he can crush the pride of the Magyars without any reaction from me," decried Andràssy.

She walked to him and took his hand kindly. Saddened by the situation, Sissi wished to comfort the nobleman.

"I want to help you!" she told him, looking into his eyes.

"How could you do that?" asked the other, pensive.

"If you had an ally to convince the emperor…" offered Sissi winking at him.

"Why would you do that for us?" asked the diplomat politely.

"If a nation needs my help, why would I stand idly by?"

Gyula Andràssy was one of the most influential politicians in Hungary. Born on March 3, 1823, he studied law at university.

Early on, the individual took an active part in the independence movement of his country. He was found guilty of treason against the Imperial authority of Austria. The Magyar lived in exile for a few years in Paris. From the French capital, he would maintain an extensive correspondence with his allies in Budapest. In 1857, the count – a title he had inherited from his father – would return among his people. Andràssy would then get elected at the Hungarian Parliament and would occupy several essential positions in government.

That same evening, a sumptuous banquet was given in honour of the Hungarian delegates. Meticulously planned by the sovereign, the meal gathered together more than two hundred guests at the castle of the Habsburgs, including the Magyars living in Austria, the business owners of Vienna and a few Bohemians. Part of the nomads lived on the periphery of the Hungarian capital.

"Your evening is a magnificent success," whispered the head of the emissaries in Sissi's ear.

After the royal feast, musicians played their instrument to entertain the guests. Domestics removed the table from the middle of the room so that everyone could dance freely. As per the etiquette, the ball was opened by the imperial couple. The emperor and his wife waltzed in front of curious onlookers. Among them, Count Andràssy admired the graceful movements of the empress.

"A true butterfly!" he said to one of his compatriots.

At the end of the first dance, Franz Joseph asked the prettiest Hungarian woman to accompany him in the middle. The head of the Magyars did the same by inviting Sissi. They spun along the joyful music. Nothing would have prevented them from enjoying this magical moment.

"Madam, I have dreamed about this instant since the first time I laid eyes on you," said the Hungarian sincerely.

"Andràssy, we must be careful… We are being watched!" whispered the empress.

Later in the evening, Sissi took leave of the guests to rest in her apartments. She had fulfilled the mission that the emperor had given her. Exhausted, she had to relax for a while to regain her strength. Her rather frail health did not help in any way her physical capacity. She lay down on her huge bed and shut her eyes. Suddenly she heard a sound not far from her room. The noise caught her attention. Sissi got up slowly and walked to the antechamber. The poorly lighted area did not help her already blurred vision because of fatigue.

"Who is it?" she whispered with trembling lips. "Make yourself known or I will call the guards."

"Please do not!" replied a manly voice.

The head of the Magyars finally appeared in the candlelight. He had followed Sissi to her private quarters. The man wished to speak to her away from the eavesdropping guests.

"Andràssy! What are you doing here? If someone finds you in my apartments, you will be punished by my husband."

"I'm willing to take the risk! Madam, my heart suffers when you are away from me," confessed the nobleman without difficulty.

Surprised by this declaration, she remained speechless more than an instant. Andràssy revealed his feelings, knowing fully well that the emperor was nearby. His courageous, or completely rash, action made Sissi smile. She walked to the diplomat and placed a discreet kiss on his cheek. Content with the sovereign's demonstration, he kissed her with an intense passion. Madly enamoured with him, she let the Hungarian fondle her. The two lovers showed each other their mutual love through affectionate gestures while Franz Joseph danced with the most charming woman of the evening.

"Sissi, I love you!" said the diplomat feeling the empress.

"Me too!"

In a fit of frenzied passion, they headed to the bed in Sissi's room. The emissary then slowly undressed the empress. In the process, he savoured each part of Franz's wife's body. She was so beautiful that he was mesmerized by her naked flesh. Alone under the thick, silky blankets, the two lovers caressed each other sensually.

"Andràssy... I feel so good in your arms," she confessed.

Attracted by the burning body of the empress, the Magyar let his male member inside her inner thighs. Sissi immediately felt a long forgotten pleasure. Lying on her back, she completely abandoned herself to her lover's motions. She relished these ongoing movements which made her moan with ecstasy. He kissed her on the mouth to muffle them. Their excitement allowed them to experience sexual intercourse in perfect harmony. After an hour of pleasure, they both felt asleep on the unmade bed.

In the middle of the night, the count woke up with a start. The man was naked beside the sovereign, so he gently got out of bed, swiftly put his clothes back on and placed a kiss on his lover's forehead. The head of the delegation discreetly walked to the floor intended for the Hungarians. Sissi's unfaithfulness was unnoticed by the domestics of Schönbrunn Palace.

The next afternoon, discussions between the two sides continued around the same table as the night before. Once again, Franz Joseph made offensive remarks about the enemy nation. Determined to find a lasting solution for his people, Andràssy disregarded the insolence of Franz. The matter at hand was much too important for him to give in to an escalating series of uncalled-for insults.

"Your Majesty! If you were at the head of Hungary, what would you do for the good of my country?" asked the count as an argument.

"I would make sure that the Magyar people is as powerful as the people of my empire," assured the monarch.

Pleasantly surprised by what he had just heard, the nobleman was then convinced that all was not lost for Hungary. They were far from reaching a fair comprise for Budapest, but there was hope. With Sissi's support, Andràssy was beginning to see the light at the end of the tunnel.

A few days later, the delegation returned to the neighbouring capital. The emissaries had managed to negotiate with the emperor, but no formal agreement had been reached. Nevertheless, the once palpable tension had decreased.

The night before, the two lovers had bid each other farewell in a woody pathway of Schönbrunn Palace. On the spur of the moment, they had exchanged a passionate kiss in front of Sissi's lady-in-waiting. Mirka had sworn to keep quiet about this matter of easy morals. The sovereign had full confidence in her favourite.

"Honey, promise me that you will write to me as often as possible," demanded Sissi.

The attitude of the empress slightly improved after the departure of the Hungarian diplomats. Everyone wondered where this resurgence of energy came from. Each had their own theory, but no one found the real reason. Only the protégée of Sissi knew the origin of this new behaviour.

The imperial couple headed to Warsaw in June 1866 to meet the Polish sovereign. The two spouses had been invited to attend the festivities surrounding the ascent to the throne of the monarch. The grandson of the late leader of the royal family had inherited the crown of this Eastern European country. Since it was affiliated to the House of Habsburg, it was unavoidable that Franz Joseph and his wife be present at the ceremony.

During the journey that brought them to the other capital, the two passengers maintained a shallow conversation made up of nothing more than a few trivial words here and there. Their relationship certainly had improved, but not to the point of resuming their former discussions.

Their stay with the newly crowned head went rather well. In front of the public, they appeared to be a strong and united couple. Nevertheless, within intellectual circles, rumours had it that they were both drifting apart. Obviously, the emperor and his wife pushed aside this gossip by playing the part of the happy couple.

Franz Joseph and Sissi mutually agreed to try and set an example as a strong family. They decided to go to Ischl Castle with the children and the archduchess. As in the past, they stayed in the imperial residence in Bavaria. The two months unfolded smoothly. The empress took advantage of her presence near her parents to visit them daily. Even Helene spent a few days at the family estate of Possenhofen. When the Habsburgs returned to Vienna, harmony was among them.

During the year 1866, Sissi did not travel on her own. She remained in Austria to take care of her children and fulfill her responsibilities towards the Imperial Crown. The only trip she did without her husband was an official visit in Hungary.

Following the negotiations undertaken with the Magyars since 1865, the emperor sent the sovereign to represent him. As he was busy solving a European conflict, he could not go to Budapest to attend a formal meeting with the representatives of the people. When the monarch offered the mission to Sissi, she accepted gladly. Being part of an historical event was a dream objective for anyone with a minimum of ambition. Indeed, this mattered to Sissi, but the personal reason behind it was as important. Seeing her lover again, Count Andràssy, even if it meant reliving the painful memories of her daughter Sophie's passing.

Sissi was welcomed in a dignified manner by the Hungarians, who were known for their hospitality. When she travelled the streets of Budapest in her coach, crowds gathered along the way. Everyone was curious to catch a glimpse of the Austrian emperor's wife. Children ran behind the carriage after its passage among them. She was surprised to find so much sympathy from a nation that she did not know. The anxiety she felt from returning to the location of her eldest daughter's death faded quickly.

"Long live Erzsébet!" shouted the Magyars in her presence.

She finally arrived in front of the royal palace, a charming though not very luxurious building in comparison to Schönbrunn. On the porch of the residence of ancient Hungarian kings, Count Andràssy was waiting for his lover. With him, a handful of local leaders applauded the arrival of the empress.

"Welcome to the kingdom of Hungary," exclaimed the nobleman bowing earnestly.

"In the name of His Majesty the Emperor, thank you for welcoming me in your lovely capital," she said by way of introduction.

After waving at the crowd gathered before them, the two lovers walked inside the palace. The representatives of the people followed them to a room on the ground floor. Everyone sat at a round wooden table. Once seated, Sissi admired the paintings that were hung on the walls. They portrayed sceneries of the Hungarian countryside. She, who was fond of nature, was impressed by these images.

"We are gathered here today to reach an official agreement with the Emperor of Austria," declared the leader of the Magyars straight away.

Following the opening of the assembly, some proposals were presented by the Hungarians. They would accept to give Franz Joseph the Royal Crown if he ensured full prosperity for their people. After some modifications formally requested by the two parties, Sissi signed the document rendering the concluded agreement tangible.

"I feel very privileged to sign this document," she said sincerely.

The incessant conflict between the two nations had just been solved officially. Decades of relentless confrontation were now part of the past. Franz became the new King of Hungary from then on. It had been decided by the emissaries of the Magyars that the coronation would take place in early summer. Once again, Sissi had successfully reconciled the enemies of Austria with the Empire. This gesture would make the empress even more popular in Europe.

CHAPTER 8

The Queen of Hungary

Kingdom of Hungary
1867

*T*HE EMPRESS of Austria would spend more and
more time in the Hungarian capital. She would truly
feel at ease among the Magyars. Passionate about this people,
Sissi would do her best to learn its language and find out more
about its diverse culture. She would continually travel between
Schönbrunn Palace, to take care of her children, and the private residence of Count Andràssy. Enthusiastic about seeing
his wife blossom through her new responsibilities as future
queen of that country, the emperor would support all of Sissi's
reformatory initiatives. She would be surrounded by competent advisers to help her take care of the kingdom's financial
situation. Critically in debt, Hungary was the poor relation
of the European continent. Never had the sovereign gotten so
involved in political affairs. Having lost interest in her role as
wife of the head of State, she readily identified with her new
task, protector of this fresh land.

Sissi would travel outside of the Austro-Hungarian Empire only once in March 1867. She would go to Paris for the funeral of her former lady-in-waiting. Georgina had passed away from an illness. The domestic had caught gout during one of her trips in Northern Africa. She was pregnant, but she had lost the child as a result of the sickness. Despite the diligent care of the doctors, which Sissi paid for, the sovereign's friend did not live longer than two weeks.

During her short stay in France, she went to the opera for a concert. Since she was a child, she had always dreamed of visiting the country of the legendary Joan of Arc. Today, from her seat, Sissi let her gaze wander throughout the room, curious to see the members of the audience. From her box, she felt many inquisitive eyes on her. Everyone had heard about her tense relationship with the archduchess. The craziest rumours about their perpetual confrontation spread across the aristocratic circles of the continent. More open-minded, the younger generations saw Sissi as a woman of her time. Her thirst for freedom was a source of jealousy for many noblewomen subjected to the restrictions of the etiquette.

Walking down the steps of the building after the concert, Sissi headed to her carriage. When she was about to take a seat inside the vehicle, an armed man threw himself on her. The aggressor threw her off balance, and she fell on the stony ground. Her black fur hat was propelled far from her. The incident happened so fast that even the coachman froze.

"Give me your jewels!" yelled the individual, threatening her with a knife.

"Let go of me!" she thundered, struggling.

He violently hit her face to prevent her from being rescued. She felt unbearable pain in her nose. Touching her nostrils, she noticed that a viscous liquid was falling down her chin.

"Take them!" begged the empress.

The stranger snatched her diamond necklace and gold earrings then disappeared in a dark alley. Shaken, Sissi remained motionless on the ground several minutes.

"Madam, are you alright?" asked a feminine voice.

Not far from there, a damsel had witnessed the scene. She wanted to help the victim, but the thief was already gone. She sought out some assistance inside the building. Three men ran down the steps and rushed to Sissi. Extremely gently, they carried the empress to a known doctor.

After four days of convalescence, she headed back to Vienna. She kept a bitter memory of her stay in the French capital and promised herself never to return.

The day of Franz Joseph's and his wife's coronation was fast approaching. Since she had been living at Schönbrunn Palace, the empress had never been so excited about an event of this scale. For Sissi, her responsibilities towards the House of Habsburg were ordinarily considered to be moments of torture. This time around, she had fully participated in the preparation of this consecration.

The imperial family, having obtained its royal title on Hungarian soil, arrived in Budapest on June 1, 1867. For the occasion, Franz and the sovereign stayed at the castle of the last Magyar kings. The very same place where she had signed – in the name of the monarch – the agreement that ended the bloody wars which had been going on since ancient times.

On the days before the coronation, Sissi met her lover in secret many times. Using the organization of the event as an excuse, she found herself in Andràssy's arms. Was Franz Joseph aware of his wife's infidelities? If so, Franz did not mention it. For the sake of the couple's stability, perhaps he preferred to let it slide.

When the sun was rising on Budapest, the long awaited day finally arrived. On June 8, the royal couple left the residence of the ancient Magyar monarchs to head to the place of coronation. A cortege of twenty horsemen preceded the carriage. A cavalry counting as many guards followed the vehicle. Inside the white coach, the future King and Queen of Hungary waved at their new subjects. More than one hundred thousand onlookers had gathered along the itinerary of the convoy. Everyone cheered, not for the monarch, but for their beloved Erzsébet. It wasn't the son of the archduchess that the people wanted to see, but Sissi. In their eyes, she embodied the future of their country. Her strength of character was known by most Magyars. She was a testament to the prosperity of their kingdom.

"Do you hear! Your subjects love you!" declared Franz Joseph looking at the mother of his children.

She knew that her husband's words were justified. On more than one occasion, Sissi had witnessed the affections of the Hungarian people. Wasn't the person who represented them during negotiations with the Imperial Crown the lover of their new sovereign?

The vehicle with the royal couple on board rode to the Catholic cathedral of the capital. The religious temple, a magnificent architectural building, had been chosen by Count Andràssy as the place of coronation. For generations, all Hungarian monarchs had received their crown before the altar of this church. In order to continue the more than one-hundred-year-old tradition, Franz and his wife also had to receive the object of power from the hands of the cardinal.

"Sissi! Without you, this day probably would have never happened," he asserted before getting off the carriage.

"Thank you, my dear husband," she replied, smiling sincerely.

They disembarked from the vehicle gracefully and walked on the red carpet that had been unrolled to welcome them. On both sides of the finely crafted fabric, men wearing chestnut uniforms played the trumpet. The atmosphere was more than pleasant for Sissi and the people alike. They entered the imposing cathedral. Floral arrangements and ribbons of different colours adorned the premises. The main aisle, which was made of white marble, showed the way to the altar. The audience counted more than five hundred guests, mostly from Hungary. Among them, a few foreigners sat on their wooden bench. The Archduchess of Austria, some members of the House of Habsburg and the King of Poland were present.

Kneeling on a stool upholstered in red material, the two sovereigns were waiting feverishly for the prelate to speak.

Franz was wearing walnut clothes along with a fur cape on his right shoulder. Sissi, more stylish, had put on a white dress with a long black veil attached to her hair and a mink tippet.

"Today is a great day for the kingdom of Hungary. Before God and the Holy Scriptures, we hand over the Royal Crown to our new rulers," began the old man with a grey beard. He raised his arms towards the sky and uttered a ritual prayer aloud. "Our Father who art in heaven, hallowed be thy name, thy kingdom come, thy will be done on earth as it is in heaven. Forgive us our trespasses, as we forgive those who trespass against us, and lead us not into temptation. Give us this day our daily bread. Amen!"

After angelical hymns and music resonated in the cathedral, Franz Joseph stood up gently. He walked to the clergyman and kneeled down before him. The man skillfully laid the crown on the emperor's head. In turn, the monarch did the same to Sissi. Once crowned, she stood up and placed herself beside her husband. The members of the audience did likewise and clapped their hands for the new monarchs. The kingdom of Hungary had found a king and queen once again after many years of confrontation.

Franz and his wife left the cathedral for the Parliament. The huge building, located near the Danube River, had housed the assembly of the members of parliament since the establishment of some kind of aristocratic democracy. Upon their arrival, they were glorified by a great number of subjects just as they had been at the place of coronation.

"Long live the king! Long live the queen!"

After about ten minutes, the carriage of the royal couple came to a halt before the doors of the building. It had been decided that two ceremonies would officially celebrate the ascent of Franz to the Hungarian throne: a religious celebration, according to the catholic tradition, and another before the country's seat of power. Standing in front of the gathered people, Franz delivered a symbolic speech.

"I, Franz Joseph I, Emperor of Austria and King of Hungary, am here before you to swear allegiance to the Magyars, to its history and its traditions. I promise to do my best to protect the kingdom of Hungary and my subjects. So help me God!"

Cries of joy echoed across the four corners of the capital. The words of the monarch marked the beginning of a flourishing era. Near him, Sissi applauded the commitment that her husband had just sealed aloud. The war between the two countries was now a thing of the past.

As a token of their appreciation, the people – through the Parliament – gave the sovereigns an estate in a suburb of Budapest. Built on a wooded land, Gödöllö Castle would become the seat of royal authority in Hungary.

On the night of the accession of the royal couple, Sissi met her lover at his private residence. As for Franz, he returned to Vienna to be with his children, who hadn't attended the coronation. Alone with Andràssy, she abandoned herself to him completely all night long. They had fulfilled their plan to put Sissi on the Hungarian throne.

"My dear, you are now the Queen of the Magyars. And I am a Magyar myself," said Andràssy kissing her passionately.

"Indeed! You are my subject…" exclaimed the woman laughing.

"Your most loyal and devoted subject, Your Majesty," specified the man ironically bowing to her immoderately.

The empress only came back to Schönbrunn Palace two days later. If she got back on the road to the Austrian capital so quickly, it was to appease the rumours of infidelity that existed about her. Also, she decided to spend the summer vacation with her family. They stayed, along with Sophie, two full months in Bavaria. At thirty years of age, she was more comfortable than ever in her role as sovereign.

During their stay at the residence of the Habsburgs, Franz Joseph tried to get closer the woman he had so deeply loved. For the good of their children and the image of the Empire, he considered it essential to rekindle a passionate relationship with Sissi.

One morning, when the sun was shining particularly brightly, the monarch went to the apartments of the empress. He tiptoed inside the room of Sissi, hoping to surprise her. But as soon as he opened the door, he noticed that his wife had left the premises, probably to go for a stroll in the woods. He had a good idea where she could be. Wasting no time, he left outside Ischl Castle. Despite his thirty-seven years of age, he had kept an excellent physical condition. He moved quickly on the pathways of the forest and arrived where everything had all begun. The cabin, damaged by the bad weather, was nothing more than a pile of worn-out wood. The monarch, convinced to see Sissi, was bitterly disappointed not to find her there.

"Where is Her Majesty?" he asked himself looking around him.

Dismayed by Sissi's absence, he retraced his steps to return to the palace. When he was about to come out of the forest, the emperor saw his wife sitting alone on a bench. Wearing light but decent clothing, she was writing in her diary.

> *Today, without the presence of my count, life is tedious. Although I manage to find ways to enjoy my stay, it would be much more enjoyable if you were close to me. If my arms were wings, I would fly out in the sky to be with you. May my heart cherish you until my last breath.*
>
> *Your Erzsébet*

Franz headed to Sissi in the hope of spending happy moments together. Absorbed in her thoughts, she did not noticed her husband.

"My dear, I am happy to see you so radiant this morning," he said gallantly.

"My friend! You scared me…" she exclaimed, shutting her notebook.

"Please forgive me. I didn't know that you hadn't seen me arrive," he apologized, somewhat bitter by the lack of enthusiasm of his wife.

"It's nothing! The children are alright?"

"Absolutely! Would you care to pay your parents a visit in our company?" offered Franz.

Pensive, she took about fifteen seconds to answer. Truth be told, Sissi was planning on heading to Possenhofen Castle in the afternoon. Normally, she was supposed to go alone. *Why not?* she thought.

"You make me the most privileged husband of Europe," exclaimed the emperor.

Content with the turn of events, he returned inside the palace. The monarch, with a joyful look, asked the domestics to get Gisela and Rudolf ready. As for Franz Joseph, he headed to his private apartments. He had to find suitable clothes that the empress would like.

"Franz!" declared the archduchess knocking on his door.

"What is it, mother?" replied Franz opening the door to his room.

"Is it true that you are bringing the children to see Sissi's parents?" asked Sophie.

"It's true indeed! Do you have any objection?" he continued, worrying little about the approval of the archduchess.

"Excellent idea! I will accompany you!" she suggested.

This assertion disconcerted Franz Joseph. He knew fully well that the sovereign would be angry about the presence of her enemy. Could he prevent her from following them to see the duke and duchess?

"Mother, if you come, do you think that you can manage not to fight with Sissi?" he said looking her in the eye.

"Son! The fact that you're judging me in such a way saddens me."

She promised him that everything would go smoothly if her daughter-in-law also made an effort.

Around noon, an ebony carriage was waiting before the imposing doors of the imperial residence. Escorted by four guards, the vehicle was ready to head to the estate of Possenhofen. Franz Joseph and the two children were the first to sit on the leather benches. Sissi followed them a few minutes later.

"We are ready! Let's go!" ordered the empress to the coachman.

"No, wait! Her Imperial Highness is accompanying us," added the emperor, anticipating Sissi's negative reaction.

Indeed, her face changed radically after her husband's declaration. She did not agree at all with this decision.

"Franz! Are you serious?" she asked with a dissatisfied voice.

"My darling! My mother promised that everything would go beautifully," declared the monarch in a conciliatory manner.

"No! I refuse that Sophie be present... The archduchess hasn't stopped destroying me for as long as I can remember..." thundered Sissi.

In the meantime, the interested party walked to the carriage. She had partly heard her daughter-in-law's words.

"As you can see, Her Majesty loathes me," said Sophie.

"Madam, you know fully well that I have all the reasons in the world to detest you," let out Sissi, purple with rage.

Frightened by the fight, the children wept and wept. They didn't like to see their mother and their grandmother insult each other.

"Stop this squabble! Sissi, do you accept that the archduchess accompanies us or not?" asked Franz bluntly.

"No!" she replied forthrightly.

"Perfect! In that case, mother, please forgive us, but we must do without your presence," exclaimed the emperor looking at Sophie.

Both the archduchess and the empress were surprised by Franz Joseph's cutting decision. Rare, nearly nonexistent even, were the instances when he had contradicted or hurt the old woman. The emperor wished to get closer to his wife and would not back down under any circumstances in order for his project to come true.

"As you wish, Your Majesty," she replied, taken aback.

Sophie returned inside Ischl Castle. Sissi, impressed by attitude of Franz, smiled at him pleasantly. The coachman immediately whipped the horses to get to the residence of the sovereign's parents. The journey lasted less than an hour.

"Here's grandfather!" cried Rudolf when he saw him in the distance.

The Archduke heir of Austria adored Duke Max because he took him fishing regularly. Every summer, he accompanied Max to the lakeside at the back of the estate. The boy, madly enamoured with this pastime, could spend hours beside Sissi's father.

"Rudolf, be careful with the duke. You know that his health isn't as strong as it used to be," warned the emperor.

The carriage had barely stopped near Possenhofen Castle when Sissi's son jumped to the ground and started running towards Max. He threw himself into the arms of the old man, weakened by the passage of time.

"Grandfather! I want to go to the lake," begged the young Habsburg.

"I was about to suggest it," he lied kindly.

Ludovika had heard her grandson speak and ran to the unexpected visitors. She got outside and headed to her daughter with open arms.

"Sissi, you are radiant! Franz, thank you for your presence. My sweet Gisela, you are becoming a true damsel. And you, Rudolf, you look just like your father," exclaimed the duchess with a joyful voice.

After a few customary greetings, the group walked inside the ducal residence. Only the duke and the young archduke stayed under the sun. Max, to make his grandson happy, accompanied him fishing.

In the main living room, the three adults began speaking about the new responsibilities of the imperial couple in the kingdom of Hungary. The sovereign enthusiastically explained in detail the day of the royal coronation. She was so happy about her role as Queen of the Magyars that she talked about it with fervent conviction.

"Mother, if you had been present by our side throughout the official ceremonies, you would have been astounded by the sumptuousness of the events," declared Sissi, the eyes sparkling with joy.

"It is true that the Hungarian people know how to welcome their guests. In my opinion, the organization of this memorable day was incredible," said the monarch smiling to Sissi.

Everyone knew that the main person responsible for the success of the coronation was Sissi. Since the beginning of the negotiations with the emissaries, she had taken on this affair masterfully. She had taken care of the smallest to the most important detail and had made sure that the interests of both parties were protected. The emperor was proud of his wife.

"Are you planning on having any more children? I'm asking because the empress is not getting any younger," asked Ludovika without thinking.

The man and the woman looked at each other in surprise, without really knowing the answer.

"My aunt, I must admit that we haven't thought about it," asserted the monarch not to displease Sissi.

Later in the afternoon, the duke and his grandson joined the rest of the family. They had caught three big fish in the lake. In truth, it was Max who had caught them, but he gave Rudolf the credit.

"Father, look at these huge fish," rejoiced the young archduke showing his treasure.

Franz, his wife and their children spent the evening with the ducal couple. The empress repeated to her father in close detail the story she had told earlier about the coronation. Exhausted, he hadn't gone to Budapest to attend this grand event. The duke had nonetheless heard about it in European newspapers.

Around eight o'clock, the imperial family returned to Ischl Castle with a smile. The day had unfolded beautifully and some harmony had returned between Franz Joseph and his wife.

"Thank you for such a pleasant day," declared Sissi, speaking to the monarch.

"Your words fill my heart with joy," he replied with a spark of hope in the eyes.

When they arrived at the imperial residence, the children were deeply asleep on the bench of the carriage. The day they had spent in the company of their grandparents had exhausted them completely. Franz ordered two manservants to carry Gisela and Rudolf in their respective rooms. As for the parents, they headed to the living room on the ground floor.

Sitting on a sofa, near one of the room's windows, Sophie was patiently waiting for the return of her son and her daughter-in-law. After her humiliation, her foul mood hadn't budged since noon.

"Franz! I must speak to you in private," exclaimed the archduchess when the emperor had barely set foot on the living room carpet.

Sissi, who did not want to fight with her mother-in-law in any way, decided to head to her apartments. She knew the reason behind this conversation. After spending such an extraordinary day, it was out of the question that she would let her aunt destroy her happiness once again.

Indeed, the old woman lectured the monarch for his offensive behaviour towards her. As was her custom, she tried to put the blame on the empress and turn Franz against her. Determined to mend things with Sissi, he brushed off his mother's nonsense.

A terrible tragedy hit the imperial family head-on, more particularly Sophie. Around June 30, a messenger brought some dreadful news to the Archduchess of Austria. Her other son, Ferdinand Maximilian, had just been assassinated by Mexican republicans. Named Emperor of Mexico by Napoleon III of France, he governed the country rather clumsily. Many of his subjects did not recognize him as their sovereign. During a civil uprising, he was shot by some rebels. He died on the morning of June 19, 1867.

"No!" thundered the archduchess falling on the flooring of the entrance hall.

The news of the Habsburg's murder shook the authoritarian Sophie strongly. She was incapable of hiding her dismay despite her reserved temperament.

"Damn this Frenchman. This is all his fault! He abandoned Ferdinand Maximilian at the hands of these savages," she let out in a fit of profound hysteria.

A witness to the sad scene, Sissi felt some pity, even compassion, for her mother-in-law. She had never seen her in such a dejected state. All the sufferings she had endured because of her aunt just faded. In 1857, the empress had lost her eldest daughter. She could understand the distress that Sophie was experiencing. Losing a child was certainly the worst hardship that a mother could go through. In a spontaneous fashion, Sissi walked to the archduchess. She leaned down towards the old woman and helped her back up.

"Sophie, come sit down. I understand your pain and, believe me, I share it," said Sissi benevolently.

"Why are you so kind to me?" asked the other with tears in her eyes.

"Madam, I never wanted to become your enemy. You are my aunt and my mother-in-law... so I hold you in high esteem," confessed the empress.

"They killed my son! Why?" stammered the archduchess.

"Ferdinand Maximilian has been a good sovereign. It was circumstances that played against him," explained Sissi to comfort Sophie.

The emperor decided to repatriate his brother's body to the Austrian capital. An official funeral service was to take place at the imperial chapel of Schönbrunn Palace. To avenge the death of the monarch, the House of Habsburg refused to correspond with Napoleon III of France. He had abandoned his Mexican counterpart cowardly when he needed his military help. The funeral attracted a crowd of countless people. They all gathered before the gate of the imperial residence. As for the widow of the archduchess' son, she returned to her family in Belgium. Charlotte had been fortunate enough to leave Mexico two weeks prior to the terrible tragedy.

Following the death of Ferdinand Maximilian, Sophie's attitude changed radically. She was no longer the same woman after such a dreadful event. The mother of the emperor did not go out of her way to fight with her daughter-in-law anymore, not even to take part in the political affairs of the Empire. She locked herself into her private apartments for entire days.

For the other members of the imperial family, life went on as usual. The relationship between Franz Joseph and Sissi continued to progress slowly. They attended ceremonies and banquets together more frequently. The empress even sold the manor of Hermesvilla, for it had become useless.

In spite of it all, her love for Count Andràssy remained unchanged. She went to Budapest regularly. Passionate about Hungary, the empress hired two Magyars to fill the positions of lady-in-waiting. As queen of the country, she attended the charitable events held in the countryside. It wasn't uncommon to see her in orphanages or hospitals, speaking with her subjects. Sissi thought that it was of the utmost importance to maintain an excellent relationship with the members of Parliament. And so she received them as often as possible at Gödöllö Castle for all kinds of receptions.

Everything seemed to be going well in the life of the empress. The Magyar people adored her, the Austrians respected her and the Bohemians idolized her. Her mother-in-law, the terrifying Sophie, was no longer a threat, and her relationship with her husband had greatly improved. As for her children, they were growing closer to their mother with age.

In early autumn of 1867, Sissi considered becoming pregnant again. She wanted to give a son to the Royal Crown, so he could reign over Hungary. The sovereign wished to offer a distinct monarch to the throne of the Magyars. Rudolf, being the heir of Austria, could not lay claim to this title. So she decided to share Franz Joseph's bed again, at least a few nights per month. In the meantime, she kept seeing and having sexual intercourse with her lover. Her attraction for Gyula Andràssy was so strong that Sissi was unable to stop seeing him in secret.

CHAPTER 9

The Descent into Hell

Everywhere in Europe
1868-1898

ISSI'S STEEP collapse started in the year 1868. The empress, whose health was already frail, was struck by illness again although it was initially under control. Anaemia was gradually destroying her immune system. Some claimed that Sissi was partly responsible for her health problems since she did not eat properly. She only drank water or poultry broth and, to feed herself, she solely ate oranges. Doctors were constantly called to the patient's bedside. She was becoming weaker by the day. Her critical state worried the members of the imperial family, particularly Franz Joseph.

In the meantime, she learned that she was expecting another child. Pregnant again, she could only strengthen the dynasty of the Habsburgs. Some scandalmongers attributed paternity to the Hungarian and not to the emperor. Truth be told, Sissi herself did not know the identity of the father. It didn't matter for she would keep this secret to herself.

Bedridden, the empress would not go to Hungary frequently between January and April. Her condition worsened in such a way that some practitioners were beginning to think that she would not live through the year.

One evening of March, after a short stroll in the corridors of Schönbrunn Palace, Sissi fell into a prolonged state of unconsciousness. Carried to her apartments, the sovereign was unresponsive to the medication administered by the men of science.

"Father, is mother going to die?" had asked the young Sophie.

"Let's pray the Almighty and ask him to watch over the empress," was Franz's sole answer.

Day and night, health specialists did everything in their power to help her. Finally, she returned to the world of the living. It wasn't the first and certainly wouldn't be the last time she collapsed.

When she had recovered, Sissi hurried to Gödöllö Castle. For weeks now she hadn't pressed her lover against her. When she was reunited with the Magyar, she threw herself on him. They kissed tenderly for a long while.

The empress would finally give birth towards mid-April. Surrounded by her husband and her sister Helene, she would bring a beautiful baby girl into the world, without any difficulty. Happy about having a new daughter, she was nonetheless a little disappointed that it wasn't a boy. This would be the first child that she would be allowed to keep by her side. After her three previous deliveries, the archduchess had demanded to take care of the education of the imperial couple's offspring. Now harmless, Sophie was no longer an obstacle in the eyes of the mother.

The infant's baptism took place a month after its birth. Organized by the empress, the religious ceremony would be performed at the cathedral of Budapest. The event, presided by the cardinal of the capital, was very private since only the members of Franz Joseph's and Sissi's families were allowed to attend.

"In the name of our Lord, I baptize you Marie Valerie of Habsburg," had said the prelate as he raised the child.

Sissi had chosen this name in honour of the Hungarian region where the child had been born.

From her birth on, the little archduchess became the favourite of the empress. Sissi fulfilled her role of mother with some agility. The attention that she would give the young Marie Valerie wouldn't be welcomed positively by the two other children. Even the monarch expressed some apprehensions about this excessive love. Was it because the young girl was the count's that Sissi loved her so much? Only the sovereign knew the reason for this powerful feeling.

For more than two consecutive years, she dedicated herself unfailingly to the education of the young archduchess. And yet she did not forget about her responsibilities towards the Austrian and Hungarian Crowns. Sissi had even become a true member of the House of Habsburg. Everyone accepted her and worshiped all of her actions for the Empire and the kingdom.

In 1870, illness afflicted her once again. Suffering from physical pains more than ever, the empress returned to Madeira for several weeks. On the archipelago, her condition would be monitored by men of science who came especially from France. Known as the country's most competent doctors, they were mandated to cure Sissi. They would succeed in helping her through the ups and downs of her frail state at best.

She would return to Schönbrunn Palace halfway through the same year. Sissi would go back to her life of mother, wife and sovereign upon her return. She would take on her duties brilliantly and prove to scandalmongers that her health didn't prevent her from seeing her commitments through. She would attend all the activities of the Empire of Austria and the kingdom of Hungary. Gossip about her would soon vanish.

At the end of 1870, all the imperial family went to Gödöllö Castle to spend the Christmas festivities. Sissi had decided to start a new tradition by spending the last month of the year in Budapest. Her husband encouraged her actions towards the Hungarian people. It was the first birthday that she celebrated on the soil of the Magyars. The Parliament had a statue built at the effigy of their queen on the main square of the capital.

Everything went perfectly well at the Imperial Court for about two years. Sissi's health even seemed to remain stable for a while. The happiness that she had longed for so desperately had finally settled into her life. Nevertheless, she still felt some sort of loneliness. How could she feel alone when so many people surrounded her?

One day, a tragic event would shake up the members of the imperial family. On May 28, 1872, at the age of sixty-seven, Archduchess Sophie of Austria passed away in her sleep of natural causes. Upon her departure she would not leave anyone indifferent. The first person to sing her praises among the long list of people who spoke at her funeral was the Empress Sissi. They had been the worst enemies that the Earth had ever seen and yet the passing of the emperor's mother left a big empty space in the life of the sovereign. The woman who had been her aunt and mother-in-law had taught her to stand up for herself, no matter what life put in her way.

"Farewell, Madam!" she said at the official funeral service.

After the death of the archduchess, Franz Joseph was confronted with despair. By losing his mother, he had lost the cornerstone of his own life. She had always protected him in a motherly fashion. Today, the monarch had to take responsibility for his decisions alone. The loss of Sophie would encourage him to seek comfort with his wife.

Incapable to stand still, she would begin a series of journeys throughout Europe. In 1873, she would travel to the south of France for nearly five months. Near Marseille, the empress would find inner peace. She would meet some woman named Louise of Savoie, countess of Toulouse. The two would become great friends. They had several points in common, starting with their taste for adventure. She would even put the countess up when she was passing through the port city during Sissi's extended stay.

The Frenchwoman, native of Poitiers, was born on December 20, 1837 in a family of the old nobility. Her ancestors had acquired their title and their land through King Louis IX. Loyal marshals, they had served the kingdom for centuries. Today, Louise of Savoie's parents no longer had any position in the new French Republic. In 1855, she had married the count of Toulouse. Turned widow five years after her wedding, she would never remarry. She spent her time visiting Europe and Northern Africa. On more than one occasion, wealthy men courted her without success.

When Sissi had returned to Austria, Louise of Savoie drowned after attempting to swim across the Seine River. The empress cried the loss of her new friend who had died much too soon.

Abandoned by his wife, Franz Joseph would reproach the sovereign for her endless trips away from the Empire. She would blame herself to a point where Sissi would finally push her husband into the arms of another woman. After attending a theatrical performance in Vienna, she would meet one of the actresses in private.

"You were dazzling on stage," said Sissi by way of introduction, when she walked into the dressing room of the artist.

"Thank you! May I know who I am speaking to?" asked Katharina Schratt lighting up a cigarette.

"Of course! I am the woman who will offer you to become the Emperor of Austria's mistress," exclaimed Sissi.

"Really! What's your offer," let out the other one, removing her fake eyelashes.

"I am the empress. My husband needs the presence of a woman and I thought of you."

Intrigued, the stranger listened carefully to the words of the sovereign. The presence of Sissi amused her a little since she was looking for a woman for her husband.

"Why do you wish to push His Majesty into my arms? Isn't that dangerous for you since you could face repudiation?" said the actress smiling.

"I know exactly what I'm doing! Are you interested in my proposition or not?" asked the empress, losing her patience.

"The offer is very interesting!"

Sissi invited the potential mistress of the emperor to a meal at Schönbrunn Palace. She would take advantage of her presence to throw her into the arms of Franz.

Katharina Schratt was born in 1853, in a Viennese brothel. She had never known her parents. She wasn't even sure of the day and month of her birth. When she was very young, she would get up on a wooden box on the edge of a street located in the heart of Vienna. To earn a few pennies, the young girl recited excerpts of theatrical plays. One day, when she was about eighteen years old, a man from the artistic community noticed her during one of her public performances. He offered that she join his company in exchange for a basic salary. With time, she began an interesting career on the boards of Austria.

One week later, the actress arrived at the imperial residence as planned. She was welcomed by the empress, in the ground floor living room.

"Do you still accept my offer?" checked Sissi to reassure herself.

"If I am here tonight, it's because I haven't changed my mind," replied Katharina with her usual arrogant demeanour.

During the meal, she left the table to allow for a tête-à-tête between her husband and the woman. She had had the courage to find the actress, but she didn't have the strength to watch the beginning of a relationship between them. The empress headed to her private apartments. A tear fell down her cheek, but she was still convinced, regardless, that this was a necessity.

"I don't have a choice. If I cannot offer His Majesty some comfort, I must make sure that someone else gives it to him," she convinced herself, pacing around her room.

The next morning, at breakfast, Sissi asked the emperor about his meeting with the artist. He let her know that everything had gone perfectly. Franz Joseph even said that they were going to see each other again in the near future.

And so a third person was added to the imperial couple from then on. He had his actress, and the empress her count. The two spouses never spoke about the intimate affairs of the other.

After turning the monarch down, Sissi lost one of her daughters at the end of the year. Gisela, who was barely sixteen years old, married a distant cousin of the Wittelsbach dynasty. Prince Leopold of Bavaria had been promised to the Austrian archduchess for several years. The child of the imperial couple left Schönbrunn Palace to live in Munich.

Facing solitude, Sissi decided to spend several weeks in Corfu Island. With time, she had grown to be a true follower of this country's culture. She even bought a villa that she expanded into a magnificent palace. It was obvious that sovereign had no intention of staying in Vienna for years at a time. Travelling throughout Europe was now her sole preoccupation.

The seagull of the oceans headed to Rome in 1880. With this final pilgrimage to St. Peter's Basilica, the empress wanted to get closer to the Almighty. For more than a year, fortune tellers had been telling her that she would die assassinated. Sissi wanted to meet with the pope to ask for the protection of Christ.

"His Holiness will see you in the morning," announced the priest.

Sitting in the antechamber of the Holy Father's apartments, Sissi was dressed in black from head to toe. She had successfully received permission to be blessed by Leo XIII. A devout Catholic, the empress sincerely believed that the clergyman could ward off the bad omen that awaited her.

"My child!" said the head of the Church of Rome as he walked into the room.

Sissi, as a sign of submission to the supreme pontiff's authority, kissed his ring.

"Your Holiness! I've come from Vienna to receive your holy blessing."

"In the name of Christ and the Almighty, I bless you," uttered Leo XIII making the sign of the cross on the woman's forehead.

After the Christian ritual, they exchanged information about religion in Austria and Hungary. The Holy Father took advantage of this opportunity to convey a written message to the monarch. He stated the main ideas behind some reforms that were initiated by the Roman Curia.

Upon her return from her stay with the head of God's followers, Sissi understood that she had to spread the word of the Lord everywhere in her empire and her kingdom. She spoke of it with Franz Joseph, who approved of her decision to provide her people with a greater access to the bible.

In 1881, another hardship would torment the eventful life of the empress. Her only son, heir to the throne of Austria, wedded Stephanie of Belgium. Now married to a member of the Belgian royal family, Archduke Rudolf left Schönbrunn Palace. Contrarily to his elder sister, he stayed in Austria with his wife. This departure would leave her more alone than ever at the residence of the Habsburgs.

The following years were disastrous for the empress. A series of deaths in her entourage damaged her. In 1886, one of her favourite cousins with whom she exchanged affectionate letters was found lifeless in a lake. The marginal yet cultured King Louis II of Bavaria had always had a soft spot for Max's favourite.

In the spring of 1888, the father of the empress fell seriously ill again. This time, he had a tumour on the lungs. Sissi left hastily to be by his side. Lying in his bed, the man could hardly breathe. He was surrounded by his wife and his two daughters.

"Sissi! After my death, promise me that you will take care of your mother?" asked Max.

"Father, stop saying such things… You will be among us for many more years," replied Sissi with tears in her eyes.

Unfortunately, the duke died in the following weeks. The loss of Maximilian would hit Sissi hard. She had always been his favourite, and he too had abandoned her. She would spend long days locked up in her room.

A few months later, in 1889, Archduke Rudolf committed suicide in a hunting camp. Exhausted by the responsibilities linked to his rank and the weight of his inner suffering, he would take his own life. The tragedy was only worsened by some false rumours, which claimed that the heir of the Austrian throne was killed by mercenaries. Upset by her child's demise, Sissi would suffer from severe depression and would sink into mental and physical illness.

The next year, Gyula Andràssy passed away. Her lover left this world before she did. The man she had loved so dearly during the past years died of old age. For a year, she would visit his grave on a weekly basis.

Her favourite daughter, Marie Valerie, would also leave Schönbrunn Palace in 1890. The twenty-five-year-old archduchess would marry one of her cousins, Archduke Franz Salvator of Habsburg-Tuscany. She would move outside of the Austrian capital. Losing her last child and finding herself without any youngsters around her would make her age prematurely.

Two years after her youngest daughter got married, her mother, Duchess Ludovika, also died. Awfully saddened by the loss of her husband, she could not survive much longer without him. Even more affected by her passing, Sissi was on the verge of insanity.

In 1897, during a summer vacation at Ischl Castle, Sissi would learn about the death of one of her sisters. Sophie Charlotte, who had become Duchess of Alençon, would perish in a fire at a charity event held in Paris. More than two hundred people, including her sister, would be burned alive.

The empress, who had fallen prey to a nervous breakdown, had to get away from the capital to be alone with herself for a while. She went to Roquebrune-Cap-Martin, France. For about five months, she stayed in the region located by the sea. Her mental health had never reached such a state. She had completely isolated herself from others and lived in a world of her own creation. Sissi no longer spoke with her husband, who was too busy with his mistress, or with her brothers and sisters, who were in mourning themselves, inconsolably so.

During her stay on French soil, she escaped her golden cage by attending, nearly every night, an opera or a play. Reading popular authors was also one of her passions. Before going to sleep, she would spend hours gazing at the starry sky. The empress was convinced that all the people that she had loved were somewhere among these celestial bodies.

"Father, wherever you are up there, protect me from the suffering that is tormenting me. I feel so much pain inside that I sometimes think about putting an end to my excruciating existence. Watch over your daughter," she would say on some nights before falling asleep.

She returned to Vienna in the spring of 1898. The sovereign was merely passing through and left for Berlin to receive medical treatments. Her constant travelling, contrarily to what she thought, did not by any means help her regain her strength. Her body, which was exhausted through and through, would grow weaker from so much back and forth on the road.

CHAPTER 10

Dying by Chance

Geneva
1898

*I*N BERLIN, Sissi would be closely monitored by a team of practitioners from a German university. Following new studies performed by some researchers, the empress wanted to try out the new remedies that hadn't been tested yet. Given her more or less blooming condition, she considered that every occasion was a unique opportunity to be cured once and for all. After more than 40 years of suffering, Sissi was fed up with her precarious health. As she got older, her body increasingly betrayed her. Even if the result of the medical treatments was not guaranteed, she still wanted to give it a chance.

For more than a week, she was isolated from the rest of the world, locked up in a modest room of the establishment. According to the men of science, any contact with the outside could alter the data of the process. Amid the white walls, she read her favourite books. She also spent several hours a day writing in her diary, jotting down her every thoughts. Through writing, Sissi freed herself from her fears and her states of mind.

One evening, after a rare outing in the garden of the hospital, she looked back on her life over the past sixty years. So many things had happened throughout her long and eventful existence. Granddaughter of a Bavarian king, she had known wealth from her very first days. The child had learned about the protocol of high society early on. Her parents, Max and Ludovika, had given her the best education possible. Under the wing of the Baroness of Wulfen, she had experienced her first travels through her teachings. Among her most cherished memories, she would never forget her unshakeable bond with her eldest sister. Helene was her main confidante and had remained so years after they had chosen a different path.

Alone in her bed, the empress carried on with the course of her life. Sissi's first love had been a Prussian count. Despite her young age, she had been disappointed quickly. She would experience this feeling again a few years later when her cousin, Franz Joseph, reappeared in her life. After saving him from certain death, a powerful relationship blossomed between them. In turn, it would bring her to marry the monarch. On the night of their religious union, the empress would face physical pain. This would mark the beginning of an endless series of disappointments and sufferings. Constantly harassed by her mother-in-law, she would isolate herself into a profound sadness. For about twenty years, that is to say until 1872, the archduchess, this remorseless aunt, would destroy her. Another terrible blow would be the passing of her eldest daughter. The death of little Sophie had had harmful consequences on the sovereign's mental state.

"My sweet child!" whispered Sissi when she saw this image pass through her mind.

A few other happy episodes surfaced in her blurry memory: the birth of Archduchess Gisela and the heir Rudolf of Austria; her beloved children that she didn't have the privilege to raise as she saw fit; her meeting with Count Gyula Andràssy, the handsome Hungarian – enamoured with her lover, she would manage to have her husband crowned King of the Magyars; her increasingly great number of trips throughout Europe – with these getaways, Sissi would avoid incessant fights with her aunt Sophie; the coming into the world of Marie Valerie of Habsburg, her favourite daughter. She would have the chance to take care of her personally. A few reassuring recollections that were spoiled by the loss of her loved ones.

The empress closed her diary and lay down in her bed, the eyes flooded with tears. Seeing her life pass before her eyes had broken her heart. She could only conclude that both her marriage and her role as crowned head had ended in failure. More than ever, Sissi was convinced that she shouldn't have married her cousin. If she had wed a man of inferior rank, she would have probably been happier.

Due to her stay in Berlin, Sissi would not attend the celebration of the fiftieth anniversary of her husband's ascent to the throne. Franz Joseph I would mark his position as Emperor of Austria in a rather troubled atmosphere. The Hungarian people were a lot less enthusiastic than they had been in 1867 at their coronation. The country's economy was far from glorious and the representatives of the Magyars blamed the Empire, which had become too centralizing. With Andràssy's death, Sissi wasn't as eager to go to Gödöllö Castle as she once had been. The fate of Hungary, which had always been so important to her, now came second. In spite of it all, she would remain deeply attached to her subjects.

On June 13, 1898, after spending two months testing out some treatments, Sissi decided to go to Bavaria. She missed her native land terribly since her parents had died. As she felt old age grow nearer, she wished to take advantage of her physical capacity while she still could. And so the wife of the emperor headed to Ischl Castle alone to revitalize herself.

The imperial residence, birthplace of the romantic feelings of Sissi for the monarch, seemed isolated without the nearby presence of the sovereign's family. In the old days, she could go to the estate of Possenhofen to meet her relatives. Today, the duke and duchess had passed away and the other members of the Wittelsbach dynasty were scattered throughout Europe. Apart from the roughly twenty domestics and as many guards, the empress found herself alone in the middle of the Bavarian forest.

The next day, she would receive an unexpected visitor. One of her living friends would stop by Ischl Castle. Yourik, the head of the Bohemians, arrived in the morning.

"Madam, a nomad is asking for an audience with Your Majesty," announced the eldest servant.

Sitting in a blue armchair, Sissi wasn't expecting anyone during her stay in Bavaria. She was surprised by his presence in the entrance hall.

"Please show him upstairs," she replied, standing up clumsily.

She wanted to welcome the foreigner in a position worthy of her social status. If she was standing up, he would have to bow dignifiedly.

After a brief moment, the stranger walked into the drawing room on the ground floor. He was dressed in black and was wearing a hat that looked familiar to the empress. When Sissi set eyes on his face, she instantly recognized her friend's features.

"Yourik!" she exclaimed, smiling sincerely.

Without delay, the man walked to the woman attired in a black dress.

"Your Majesty! So many years have passed since we last met," he said by way of introduction, bowing deeply.

"My dear, come sit down on this sofa," she said to him, pointing to the piece of furniture.

Sissi sat on her armchair again and invited her guest to do the same. After several years, the two friends finally met again. Constantly absent from Vienna, she wasn't the easiest person to meet in private.

"Tell me, to what do I owe the pleasure of this unexpected presence?" enquired the empress.

"Madam, I'm worried about your situation. At the festivities held for His Majesty, you weren't by his side. If I may, I would like to know why?" asked the nomad politely.

"Well you see, Yourik, I was in Berlin to receive medical treatments. My health isn't as good as it used to be," she replied lowering her head.

He had perceived some discomfort in her gesture. He knew fully well, just like the rest of Europe, that the relationship of the imperial couple was merely hanging by a thread.

"Why don't you join the emperor at Schönbrunn Palace then?" he continued, trying not to offend Sissi.

"My dear, you're worrying me with all these questions…" replied the empress staring into his eyes.

"Please forgive me… I am saddened to see Your Majesty so far from her husband," confessed Yourik.

Indisposed, she stood up from her armchair slowly. She headed to one of the huge windows that bathed in a crystalline light. She did not want to share her emotions with anyone, even with this old friend. Sissi had always been reserved about showing her feelings in public. It wasn't now, at her age, that she would start being an open book. Nevertheless, she needed to pour her heart out to vent the unbearable pain that had been tormenting her for decades.

"Would you like to go for a stroll in the gardens," she suggested looking outside.

"Excellent idea!" asserted the Bohemian also standing up.

Followed by the visitor, the empress walked to the flower bed of Ischl Castle. A vast array of rustic plants of different colours covered the ground. Under a white parasol, Sissi moved with difficulty beside the man who was clearly sturdier than her. She loved finding herself in nature, but her tired body prevented her from enjoying this pleasure as often as she had in the past.

"Yourik, why didn't you fall in love with a woman again after your beloved passed?" asked the mistress of the premises.

"But I did... My heart was enamoured with a pretty lady in the past," he confessed, rubbing the tip of his nose.

"Really? You've never told me this story," she replied with curiosity.

"And yet you were in the first row when this happened," said the nomad smiling.

She could not see what woman he was referring to. Sissi had only seen the head of the Bohemians on very rare occasions. Who was it?

"Please continue."

"In the mid-1850's, a Bavarian came to live in the mountain with our community for a while..." explained Yourik.

"I see!" she interrupted.

She had just grasped what her friend had meant. During all these years, he had kept the secret hidden in his heart. Why confess it to her now?

"I am sorry to have put you in such a delicate position. Forgive me!" exclaimed the man who noted that Sissi was ill at ease.

"It's nothing! I'm surprised that I only found out about your feelings for me today," said Sissi, stopping before a small fruit-bearing tree.

"Madam, believe me… I have always respected your rank within the Empire of Austria. If I'm telling you how I feel about you, it is solely to free myself from a secret that I have been keeping for much too long," he declared, trying to minimize the impact of this revelation.

The empress looked into the eyes of the Bohemian with some curiosity. Although she had never been in love with the nomad, she did not feel indifferent about him either. From the first time they had met, she had felt some carnal desire for this virile nomad. There was a powerful masculinity about him, which every woman dreamed to find by their naked body. And Sissi was no exception.

"Fear not! Your words haven't offended me in any way… To the contrary, deep down, I find them quite comforting," she confessed, smiling to him tenderly.

They did not pursue the discussion further and immediately changed the subject. It was impossible for a crowned head, married to the powerful Emperor of Austria, to have a public affair with a man. The Hungarian count may have played the part of her lover during several years, but she could use her mandatory presence in Budapest as an excuse to see her sweetheart in secret. This scenario was not possible with the Bohemian. Furthermore, Sissi's old age did not allow her to take part in the game of seduction.

On July 10, 1898, Franz Joseph would go to Ischl Castle for a short stay. As busy as always with his responsibilities towards the Imperial Crown, he would only remain in Bavaria for a few days. After spending months apart, the two spouses came together again on the premises where their love was born, a lifetime ago.

"His Majesty has arrived," told one of the servants from the Habsburg residence.

"Good! Please get the meal ready," ordered Sissi.

Knowing that her husband had just travelled a long distance, she wanted to make sure that he ate properly. Despite her repeated absences, she hadn't forgotten good manners.

The monarch walked into the dining room after a short nap. With age – he was now sixty-eight years old –, travelling was becoming more and more difficult for his aging body. Alone around the endlessly long, brown wooden table, they did not speak or look at each other. Time had managed to dull the bond that once united them. He, being absorbed in his imperial function, did not want to bother the sovereign with what was going on in Vienna. As for Sissi, she had no intention of revealing the state of her health to Franz. In this dismal silence, they savoured the food that the castle's cooks had prepared. The atmosphere was so heavy that even the domestics did not stay in the room.

For a long week, the same scene repeated itself night after night. The empress, affected by this constant awkwardness, dreaded supper time for it was unbearable to her. Franz's presence had become a burden for Sissi. She couldn't wait for him to return to the Austrian capital.

The night before his departure, the emperor demanded that his wife walk with him in the gardens. The two spouses hadn't been alone together in nature, in the middle of fragrant plants, for an eternity. Somewhat nostalgic about the times when the two darlings used to run away in the woods, she accepted the invitation of the emperor.

"Sissi, when will you return to Schönbrunn Palace?" he asked.

"I cannot answer that at present. Of course, I will try to come back before fall," she asserted, holding a lily-coloured parasol above her head to protect herself from the sunrays.

Truth be told, she knew the answer to that question, but she obstinately refused to tell him. Franz Joseph would have been very disappointed to learn that Sissi did not plan on setting foot in Austria before several months. She was determined to flee the Imperial Court for the rest of her life.

"You know, the people is asking for its sovereign," he added, hoping that the empress would give in.

Nothing would do it. She wasn't going to give him a specific date, even if she risked making him or the subjects of the Empire angry.

"I know that Your Majesty is eager to know the day of my return, but, for the time being, I cannot be more specific," concluded Sissi heading towards a pebbled pathway.

The next morning, around nine o'clock, the emperor travelled back to Vienna. He bid Sissi farewell and vanished in the thick dust lifted by the wheels of the carriage. That very instant, she felt a light pinch in her belly. A precursory sign, so to speak, of an imminent tragedy.

Before she departed for Switzerland, the empress decided to stop in Bad Nauheim for a short stay. Located in Hesse, this region was well-known for its thermal baths. Taking advantage of these salted waters would help her relieve her aching body. The woman spent three days and three nights in the west of the German Empire.

On August 1, Sissi boarded a train to Geneva. Throughout the journey, she was preoccupied with a vision of the White Lady. This transparent shape, lacking human form, was known to foreshadow death. For generations, its apparition had warned the dynasty of the Habsburgs of imminent catastrophic events, which proved to be true and included a number of lost wars and deaths.

Sitting in her compartment, the empress could not stand still any longer. She got out and paced the carriage's corridor back and forth. Having witnessed the scene, the two ladies-in-waiting who accompanied her were worried about the behaviour of their mistress. Something obviously troubled Sissi.

"Madam, are you feeling well?" asked Countess Sztaray, joining the empress.

"Don't worry! I am fine!" lied Sissi, faking a relaxed smile.

Irma knew very well that it was false. Could she contradict her mistress? Without insisting further, she returned inside her compartment.

Sissi's main lady-in-waiting was in the service of the sovereign since the death of Count Andràssy. Loyal to the Hungarian, she had wanted to follow her master's last love. To remember the man that she had loved so dearly, Sissi accepted her offer. Born on July 10, 1864, Irma Sztaray was nearly thirty years younger than the empress. The daughter of a more or less poor nobleman of Budapest was forced to become a favourite rather quickly. Determined, she would go up the ladder with some ease.

As planned, Sissi finally arrived in Geneva. She would stay – with her retinue – at the Grand Hotel of Caux, nearby Lake Geneva. Located in a magnificent area beyond compare, the building had earned a reputation that spread outside of the country's borders. Aristocrats to European and American businesspeople visited it regularly. She, who was no exception, intended on staying there while she sought treatment with the most renowned Swiss doctors. As ill as always, Sissi constantly went from practitioner to practitioner across the continent. She had often wanted to put an end to these medical trips, but her health prevented her from doing so.

Two weeks after the beginning of her treatments in Geneva, the empress received the unexpected visit of her daughter.

Marie Valerie, standing in front of her room number, knocked gently on her mother's door. After a few seconds, the lady-in-waiting let her in. Sissi, sitting in an armchair, burst into tears when she saw her child's face. More than a year had passed since they last met at Schönbrunn Palace, when she was passing through the Austrian capital.

"My darling!" were the first words of Sissi, choked with emotion.

Moved by the warm welcome of the woman who had brought her into the world, the archduchess threw herself at the feet of the empress. Tears fell down her pinky cheeks. Marie Valerie, who looked just like her mother, couldn't help giving way to her feelings. She was saddened to find Sissi in such a state. Emaciated by the physical suffering, the empress no longer exhibited as much as beauty as she had in the past. Anyone who looked at the face of the old woman would quickly noticed her inner as well as outer pain.

"Mother, I am so happy to be by your side."

The child of the imperial couple was thirty years old. Since her wedding, she had been living in a castle in a suburb of Vienna. The archduchess had given birth to four children so far.

"My daughter, stand up!" said Sissi holding the chin of the young woman into the palm of her hand.

Marie Valerie sat on the sofa and spoke with the empress. So many things had happened in their respective lives. The younger of the two, a wife and devoted mother, had started getting involved in the arts and culture. The other, who was older, had never stopped travelling in different places.

"Madam, I've written a play for a Viennese company," said the daughter.

"Really? What a beautiful initiative!"

They spent two hours talking about subjects that they held dear. Sissi, who felt connected to Marie Valerie, shared her states of mind with her without reservation. She could only trust her offspring now since everyone that she had ever loved had either left her from illness or old age.

"My dear, would you go for a stroll around the lake? It's such a charming place!" declared Sissi.

Without hesitation, the archduchess accompanied her mother to the stretch of water. The blazing sun reflected off the peaceful surface of the lake. Alone on the lakeside trail, they walked hand in hand. Sissi, who was possessed by her memories, took advantage of her daughter's presence to reminisce about her youth.

"Marie Valerie, when I was a child, my father brought me in the forest of Possenhofen regularly," she said with sparkling eyes.

"I know that grandfather loved you very much," said the daughter to comfort her mother.

"My child, are you happy in your marriage with the Archduke of Austria-Tuscany?"

"Of course! He fills me with joy…" she replied avoiding her mother's glance.

Sissi knew fully well that this statement was false. She, who had suffered from her relationship with the emperor, understood the attitude of Marie Valerie.

"Why are you lying to me?" asked the empress holding on to the arm of the archduchess.

"I am unhappy! He never stops courting other women... My heart never stops crying because of it," she finally admitted.

"My darling, don't follow in my footsteps. I have loved His Majesty from the bottom of my soul. But an imperial marriage wasn't right for a Bavarian like me," confessed Sissi.

"Madam, was it the union with my father or the presence of Archduchess Sophie that was the real problem?" asked the child of the monarch.

"Indeed, your grandmother was a mean creature, but my life with the emperor did not suit me. I was often left alone for entire days," she explained.

As she confided in Marie Valerie, Sissi felt a sharp tension strangle her heart. When she reached a small wooden bench, she flopped down on it. Thinking back to these memories was very gruelling for her.

Mother and daughter carried on their discussion with great sincerity. When it was time to eat, the lady-in-waiting met them, a basket filled with tasty food under the arm. Sitting on a straw yellow tablecloth, the three ladies savoured the dishes skillfully prepared for them.

"Do you fear death?" she asked when they were walking back to the Grand Hotel of Caux.

"I long for death, I do not fear it, for I cannot believe that there could be a Power so cruel as to add to the sufferings of this life and keep on tormenting the soul once it has left the body," answered Sissi frankly.

At sunset, the archduchess bid the empress farewell. Never before had they been so close to each other. The mother, standing in the entrance hall of her hotel, kissed her offspring tenderly on both cheeks.

"Madam, let's promise that we will see each other more frequently."

"I swear!" exclaimed Sissi smiling lovingly to her youngest daughter.

On the following days, the empress went to the surgery of the Swiss doctors daily. Her aches, as frequent as before, were destroying her slowly. The men of science gave her the best care possible, but nothing seemed to relieve her pain. Her inner suffering increased each morning when she woke up. More than ever, her body had become a heavy burden. Her hands were swollen, her face had grown pale and her joints were becoming less flexible. Soon, she needed to lean on a cane during her long walks in Geneva.

On the morning of September 8, 1898, on her way out from her usual visit with the practitioners who treated her, Sissi rested on a bench. With her favourite, she peeled a ripe peach. At this hour, there were very few people walking through Brunswick Park, where a flock of birds were chirping. Suddenly, a black raven narrowly brushed the sovereign's wide-brimmed hat. Shaken by this aggression, she dropped her juicy fruit on the ground. It rolled down the street, not far from them, and was crushed by the hooves of a horse pulling a wooden cart.

"A crow isn't a good omen, it always announces misfortune in our house," exclaimed the empress.

Sissi's words made the blood of Countess Sztaray run cold. The tone that her mistress used indicated that she was ready to give in to death. *Has she reached a point of no return?* thought the lady-in-waiting.

After this mishap, the empress returned to her hotel to rest her legs. She gave the day off to her favourite, much to her pleasure. Sissi took advantage of her solitude to write in her diary. For a number of decades now, she had been inking the pages of her notebooks almost daily. These books were piled up in a drawer, in her antechamber at Schönbrunn Palace. Leaning on her writing desk, she thought about the words that she wished to immortalize.

My dearest daughter,

Around ten o'clock, a bird of evil omen warned me about the difficult fate that awaits me. I cannot know whether God wants me to return to him or not. Is that a fatal sign? If the Almighty were thinking of taking me from this world, I am asking you, my child, to allow me to leave it with a peaceful mind. If you could carry out my last wishes, I beg you to leave an opening above my grave so that I can see a bit of sunshine and greenery. If I am so allowed, I shall be able to hear the birds sing upon the arrival of spring. Never forget that I will watch over you and your sister. May the Christ protect you.

Your loving mother,

Sissi

When the empress signed her name at the bottom of the page, she wept a flood of tears and a few drops fell on the wet ink. She had the premonition that she was about to experience a tragedy.

That very evening, after the return of her lady-in-waiting, Sissi started a discussion about death. Each of them, sitting on their favourite armchair, explained their point of view on the subject.

"I am convinced that the end of life brings felicity and peace to the soul," asserted Countess Sztaray.

"Where did you hear that? No one has ever returned!" replied the sovereign bitterly without looking at her favourite.

Her comment brought the conversation to an end abruptly. It was out of the question for the woman to contradict her mistress. Everyone knew how stubborn Sissi could be, despite her usually gentle temperament.

After she received the invitation of a friend — the Baroness of Rothschild — to eat breakfast at her residence, located in a suburb of Geneva, the empress set out to get there. Even if the noblewoman had offered her a passage on a ship, Sissi decided to use her favourite means of transportation. Known for her independence, she wanted to get on board a steamboat. The distance between her and her destination wasn't very long and a thirty-minute journey was all she needed to reach the other shore.

Before she arrived at the castle of the aristocrat, Sissi had some shopping to do in the sumptuous stores of Geneva. It was out of the question that she attend this meeting without wearing one of the most beautiful dresses. Even when she was away from her throne, she remained a crowned head. She would never go out in high society without looking distinctively elegant. After about an hour, she found the ideal attire for her figure. The outfit displayed a palette of pink shades, assorted to a hat of the same colour.

"Her Majesty will be the prettiest lady sitting around the table of the baroness," exclaimed the lady-in-waiting gazing at Sissi.

Content with her find, the old woman left the shop in the company of her protégée. They both headed to the quayside to board the boat.

"Madam, we must speed up because we will be late for the departure," she declared looking at the sovereign.

Leaning on her cane, the empress hurried as best as she could. Trotting ahead of her, Countess Sztaray encouraged her to keep her pace up. Sissi walked along Lake Geneva speedily, despite her old age. Suddenly a man, coming towards her from the opposite direction, hit her violently in the stomach with his fist. Aware of what he had just done, the stranger fled straight away. On the spur of the moment, she was convinced that the individual had tried to rob one of her precious jewels. A witness to the jostle, the attendant rushed to her mistress.

"Madam, are you alright?" she asked with a concerned voice.

"It's nothing... Only a miscreant... We should be on our way if we don't want the boat to leave without us," asserted the sovereign, hyped up on adrenaline.

The lady-in-waiting obeyed the instructions of Sissi and helped her mistress get on board the small boat. Confronted with unbearable pain, the empress fell face down on the ground. Unconscious, she remained motionless when people gathered around her. Irma, who was frightened when she saw Sissi, shrieked with panic.

"Please... help me!"

A man in the crowd offered her his services. A doctor from the Swiss capital, he was visiting the area. When he removed the coat that covered the dress of the empress, the man of science noticed a red stain near the heart. He immediately understood that the woman was injured. Countess Sztaray knew that the wound hadn't happened randomly. The aggressor she had met a few minutes earlier had stabbed her with a sharp object. Upset by Sissi's uncertain state, the lady-in-waiting was unable to hold back her tears. What would become of the sovereign?

Should she inform her husband? All things considered, she decided to disclose the identity of Sissi.

"This is Her Majesty the Empress of Austria. Save her!" cried the attendant hitting the ground with her hands.

After the practitioner heard this new piece of information, he was overcome with nervousness. It was becoming extremely urgent to operate on Sissi in order to stop the bleeding. The doctor ordered that she be transported to her hotel. There, with the intervention of other colleagues, he could tend to the empress.

Five foreigner carried Sissi's blood-soaked body to Beau-Rivage Hotel. Very early that morning, she had had her personal effects moved there. Closer to the downtown area, its location was more convenient given the physical condition of the old woman.

Lying in her bed, the empress feebly regained consciousness. She was in a state of complete confusion. Sissi was much weakened by her open wound. She had lost a considerable amount of blood from the stranger's fatal blow. Surrounded by doctors, she looked for her lady-in-waiting.

"Irma!" she uttered with difficulty.

Standing by the furniture, the favourite heard her name from the mouth of her mistress. She moved towards the body covered in the deadly red liquid.

"Madam!" she exclaimed with a distressed voice from seeing Sissi in such an alarming state.

"Countess, I must... I must give you... a message," continued the victim stammering.

She brought her ear closer to the face of the sovereign. The people moving about her mistress' bed caused a racket, which did not help the attendant hear her feeble voice.

"When my soul... shall lea... ve my bo... dy... I want you to... return to Vienna to an... nounce what I am a... bout to tell you," she added with much difficulty.

The lady-in-waiting did not grasp the words of Sissi in their entirety; she listened to her carefully in spite of that.

"Tell His... Majesty that my love for him... has never died... Pain may have... come between us with time, but my feelings for him... have never died," revealed Sissi sheding a few tears.

"You can rest assured! The emperor will receive your message... Madam, His Majesty knows your heart and all the affection that you have for him," declared Countess Sztaray.

"I regret!"

After this final effort, the sovereign shut her eyes. Exhausted by the suffering that her injury caused her, she took her last breath on September 10, 1898, around 2:40 pm. At sixty, Elisabeth of Wittelsbach, known as Sissi, died from the murderous stabbing of a deranged fanatic. Lying on blankets stained with her own blood, the Empress of Austria, also Queen of Bohemia and Hungary, left the world that had made her cry so often. Only death succeeded in releasing her from her tragic solitude.

Kneeling down by her side, Irma Sztaray would be overwhelmed with an incurable sadness. She had just lost her mistress, but also her friend. The act of a lunatic had taken the life of Sissi.

Two hours after the gratuitous murder of the sovereign, the aggressor was captured by the law-enforcement authorities of Geneva. The twenty-five-year-old man had stabbed Sissi with a sharp file. Luigi Luccheni was an Italian who had come to work on a construction site in Lausanne. The bricklayer, who was passing through the Swiss region, was an anarchist. He wanted to target European leaders to show the dissatisfaction of workers on the continent. After his arrest, he confessed to the crime, stating that he had acted alone. In truth, the investigators would learn that a secret meeting, which he had attended, had deliberately voted for the death of the empress. Informed of her presence in Switzerland, the libertarians had worked out a stratagem to eliminate this woman. They didn't have anything against Sissi, but rather against the imperial power that she embodied. He would also admit that if she hadn't been present on that day, he would have assassinated the Duke of Orléans, his initial target. Happily for the French nobleman, he hadn't been seen in Geneva. The accused, condemned to life imprisonment, would hang himself in his cell on the morning of October 19, 1910, namely twelve years after the demise of the empress.

At the end of the day, a messenger showed up at Schönbrunn Palace hastily. He was brought to the antechamber of the emperor, who was working on his political files. When the valets opened the doors, the man walked into the richly adorned room.

"Your Majesty! I have to tell you the most urgent news," said the individual by way of introduction, bowing to the monarch.

Franz Joseph raised his head, holding pieces of paper in his hands. He was concentrated on their complex content.

"Go ahead!" said the emperor.

"I regret to inform you that I have some dreadful information about Her Majesty the Empress."

Intrigued by the words "regret" and "dreadful", he dropped his documents on his writing desk. He was overwhelmed with a bad feeling. As if he suspected something, the monarch shed a tear, which fell down his cheek.

"The sovereign has been assassinated on this very day," specified the man, making an effort to control his sorrow.

Crushed by the words of his herald, Franz flopped down on his white fabric armchair. He could not believe his ears. The monarch brought his right hand to his heart. The pain was so sharp that it was piercing through his vital organ. He could hardly breathe for the shock was brutal. Shaken by his master's reaction, the messenger ran to the domestics for help. A few seconds later, tens of servants rushed to Franz. They hurriedly offered the emperor some assistance; one of the women untied his collar, another sponged his forehead with water from a glass carafe. The guards immediately asked the doctor to see the old man on the spot. The man of science entered Franz's room and tried to relieve his suffering. Unfortunately, the discomfort that overpowered the monarch was not physical, but rather emotional. After about thirty minutes, Franz Joseph felt more stable. At the age of sixty-eight, the newly widowed man had been distressed by the news of his wife's death. He spent the night pacing his apartments.

"Why? Sissi, come back to me!" cried the monarch, falling to his knees on the floor of his room.

Despite the years that had torn them apart, the two spouses had never stopped loving each other tenderly. Neither the many stays of Sissi outside of Vienna nor the emperor's mistress had shaken their feelings.

At dawn, Archduchess Marie Valerie headed to Schönbrunn Palace to console her father. Informed of her mother's death by the imperial residence, she did not want to be alone with her sorrow. During this cruel hardship, the daughter of Franz wished to share her sadness with her relatives.

"Father! Do not abandon me too," she said when she walked into Franz Joseph's apartments.

Saddened by their loss, the two Austrians hugged each other. The emotion was palpable and the pain nearly indescribable. Franz Joseph had never shown her so much affection.

A few hours later, the second daughter of the monarch arrived. Gisela, the eldest child, had heard the upsetting news through one of her uncles on the Wittelsbach side of the family. Upon his words, the wife of the Prince of Bavaria had gone to Vienna swiftly. In her carriage, along the way, she had wept and wept for the loss of the empress. Even if she hadn't known her mother as well as her younger sibling, she was still very affected by her passing.

Sissi's body left Geneva on September 14, four days after her assassination. In the train carrying the remains of the sovereign, the lady-in-waiting, distraught by the demise of Sissi, looked after her mistress. Sitting on a wooden chair, she stared at the coffin of the empress. Being the last person to have shared moments with the deceased, she was anxious about Franz's reaction. *Would he blame her for not protecting his beloved adequately?* wondered Countess Sztaray.

"Lord, please welcome the soul of Her Majesty. She suffered so much in her lifetime," whispered the favourite, begging the Almighty.

The next day, after an unending itinerary by train, the convoy finally arrived in the Austrian capital. Four sturdy men lifted the coffin of the empress. They walked along the corridor until they reached the last carriage. Irma, covered with a black veil, followed the procession closely. With an unsteady pace, she shed a flood of tears. She was unable to hide the sorrow that weighed on her. Suddenly, while the pall-bearers were getting off the train carrying Sissi's body, deafening cries were heard. Surprised by this racket, the lady-in-waiting looked outside through the frame where she had come to a halt. At the sight of the spectacle her mouth dropped open: a huge crowd, the eyes wet with tears, had come to welcome their empress. More than two thousand subjects from the Empire of Austria were waiting to see the coffin of their Sissi. People from all social classes had gathered on this heartbreaking day of mourning.

Even some children were hoping that the pall-bearers would walk near them.

The favourite, moved by the presence of the people, kept on following the procession. Before her mistress had died, she had promised that she would fulfill her duties until the last minute. For Irma, this meant that her task continued even after the death of Sissi. Her loyalty exceeded earthly life. Her commitment, according to her, went beyond the lifetime of the sovereign.

The emperor had ordered that a chapel of rest be set up for the bier of his wife. It was planned that the members of the imperial family and the Wittelsbach dynasty would engage in private prayer at Hofburg Palace. Located in the heart of the city, the building was more readily accessible to the bereaved guests. Truth be told, Franz Joseph wanted to go through his sorrow without any disturbances from anyone. The estate of Schönbrunn was the perfect location to isolate himself from inquisitive eyes. This way, Franz would be able to cry freely.

Placed in the middle of the room, Sissi's coffin was covered with a flag adorned with the imperial coat of arms. Lily-coloured floral arrangements surrounded the rectangular object where rested the corpse of Sissi, rendering more official the doleful atmosphere. Out of respect for her rank as sovereign, an escort of twenty men wearing white uniforms kept guard. Only a handful of candles lighted up the dark location. In front of the wooden coffin, a Latin inscription was displayed: *Elisabetha Imperatrix Austriae Regina Hungariae.*

For two days, hundreds of people walked before the remains of the empress. Well-known beyond the borders of Austria, Sissi attracted followers from most European countries, but also from Northern Africa. All wanted to show their love for the woman who had taken upon herself the responsibilities of the Imperial Crown.

On September 17, 1898, one week had gone by since the sad day of Sissi's murder. On this day, the official funeral of the late wife of Franz Joseph took place at the church of the Capuchins. The priest presided over the religious ceremony before an audience of one hundred people. In the first row, the emperor and his daughters listened to the Catholic homily. Banners of white flowers, directly from Hungary, adorned the interior of the sacred temple. Painted canvases with Archduchess Sophie and Archduke Rudolf accompanied their mother's coffin.

"My dearest brothers, my dearest sisters, we are here, before God, to honour the death of Her Majesty the Empress."

The churchman, moved by his own words, remained silent a short instant. The sadness that he felt deep inside him had dried up his throat.

"Our beloved sovereign has joined the Almighty. May she find eternal rest. Amen," he said staring at the audience.

The Christian ritual went on for more than an hour. Sitting on a bench in the last rows, Countess Sztaray could not hold back her tears for her pain was excruciating. For seven nights, she hadn't sleep at all. Remorse was eating away at her. She was convinced that she had failed in her mission because of the tragic way her mistress had died. If the lady-in-waiting hadn't hurried up that day, Sissi wouldn't have been lagging behind. At the side of the old woman, she would have been able to protect the empress, risking her own life if necessary.

After the funeral service, a procession of Hungarian hussars carried Sissi's body to a cast iron gate on the left end of the nave. Under the teary eyes of the imperial family, the coffin was moved to its final resting place. One of the men wearing a grey uniform spoke to a monk who was standing behind the railings.

"Who are you? Who asks to enter?" questioned the clergyman wearing brown clothes.

"I am Her Majesty the Empress of Austria and Queen of Hungary," replied the Magyar holding the front of the coffin.

"I do not know of this sovereign. I repeat: Who asks to enter this sacred site?" said the old man again.

"Elisabeth of Wittelsbach."

"I do not know this person," exclaimed the clergyman again.

"I am a poor sinner who implores you to let me in for the mercy of God," declared the guard.

"My child, you may enter the gate," replied the Catholic, satisfied with the words of humility expressed by the pall-bearer.

This tradition dated back to several generations and even the crowned heads had to respect the ritual. In order to have access to the kingdom of Christ, the deceased had to ask permission from the Capuchin gatekeeper. If he granted the request, the bier of the dead could be placed in the imperial crypt.

The procession moved Sissi's coffin to the location where hundreds of members of the illustrious Habsburg dynasty rested. Among them, there were Austrian emperors from previous reigns. As per Franz Joseph's decision, the men put Sissi's body near Archduke Rudolf, the late heir of the Empire. Mother and son were finally reunited in death.

When the audience left the church of the Capuchins, the emperor and the two archduchesses headed to the imperial crypt. In private, they would address their final farewell to Elisabeth of Wittelsbach. Under a dim light, the monarch cried his heart out. Never had Gisela and Marie Valerie seen their father in such a state. He was utterly debilitated by the loss of his beloved. He, who was normally so strong, seemed so fragile that very instant.

"Your Majesty, don't be so sad. Madam will watch over us from where she is now," let out the youngest sibling of the imperial family.

Upon hearing Marie Valerie's words, the monarch dried his face up with the sleeve of his black uniform. He had to inspire strength in his daughters because they needed him. He knew it fully well and swore to fulfill his task of single parent.

"My darlings, your mother was the most admirable woman of the Empire and even beyond the borders of the continent," he said to comfort them.

Before heading back to Schönbrunn Palace, Franz ordered one of his guards to have Sissi's name in Hungarian engraved on her coffin. He knew that his wife had always loved this country. Out of respect for her, Franz would carry out this symbolic gesture.

That very evening, alone in his room, the widower reminisced about the first years of marriage with Sissi. So many recollections rushed through his aging memory. He did not want to forget the one who had stolen his heart. Despite the distance between the two spouses, love had never really vanished.

"Sissi! You shall forever be in my heart," whispered Franz Joseph I of Austria looking out the window in his dark room.

The emperor remained a widower until his last breath, but he continued to maintain a carnal relationship with the actress Katharina Schratt. He would never fall in love with her. The feelings he had for the artist would never go beyond sexual desire. Upset since the death of the empress, Vienna's strong man would dedicate the rest of his life to his duties towards the Imperial Crown. The following years were far from easy for Franz. He had to solve the problem of his succession by designating an heir. With the loss of Sissi, the Magyar people no longer saw the purpose of remaining loyal to the Habsburgs. Hungary began to agitate for its complete independence. Were added to this list of complications the start of World War I. In conflict with Serbia, the monarch announced the beginning of hostilities with this Eastern European country. After sixty-eight years of reign, Franz Joseph would die of pulmonary congestion. On November 21, 1916, at the age of eighty-six, he would pass away after receiving the last rites. The coffin of Franz would be placed near his wife's and his son's. The imperial succession would be taken over by his grandnephew, Emperor Charles I.

Still grieving her mother's death, Archduchess Marie Valerie set out to go to Possenhofen Castle. She was aware that the residence of her late maternal grandparents had symbolic importance. So many times had she heard about Sissi's blessed youth in Bavaria. To accept that she was gone, the daughter of the Habsburgs decided to stay in the neighbouring country.

On September 20, Franz's youngest child arrived in Munich by train under a torrential rain. She took advantage of her presence in the capital to make a detour to Ludwigstrasse Palace. When she found herself in front of the building's doors, she received no answer. The location had been deserted and no one seemed to be staying there. Despite the absence of the occupants, she walked around the premises to keep images of Sissi's universe in her mind. Her eyes did not know where to stop for her curiosity was insatiable. Each window or each door was related to a specific moment of the empress' childhood. Soaked to the bone, it pained the daughter of the emperor to see the ducal residence.

After about twenty minutes, Marie Valerie headed to the castle of the King of Bavaria under the heavy rain. A relative of the powerful man, she intended on asking him for a carriage and a coachman. Wasn't the ultimate goal of her trip to visit the estate of Possenhofen?

As expected, the sovereign provided her with a vehicle. Without wasting any time, despite the weather conditions, she got on the country road. She finally arrived safe and sound after a long itinerary which was slowed down by the deluge.

"Possenhofen!" exclaimed the archduchess when she saw the turrets of the castle through the curtain of rain.

The coach did not even have time to stop that the daughter of the late empress left running to the gardens. If there was a place that her mother had described to her so often it was this multicoloured flower bed. Amid the wilted plants, she fell to her knees on the wet soil. She cried her heart out; a moving scene for anyone who would happen to arrive unexpectedly. This very moment, Marie Valerie truly grasped that she would never see the woman who had brought her into this world again.

The wife of Archduke Franz Salvator of Habsburg-Tuscany would dedicate the rest of the life to charitable causes. Mother of ten children, she would keep a diary. On the pages of her notebooks, she would write poems just like Sissi had in her lifetime. The daughter of the monarch would come to experience the end of monarchy in her country, but would decide to live in a suburb of Vienna. Marie Valerie, who had grown closer to her father since the passing of the empress, would die on September 6, 1924. She would be buried in Sindelburg Cemetery after the Republican government refused to allow her to rest in peace with her relatives in the imperial crypt.

As for Gisela, she would go on living with her husband in the kingdom of Bavaria. Less affected by the death of Sissi, she would gradually grow apart from the Habsburgs. The princess and her children would be actively involved in working with people suffering from deafness and eyesight issues. She would even be one of the first women to attend the national elections of 1919. The eldest child of the late empress would die on July 27, 1932, on a sunny day. Her coffin would be placed inside St. Michael's Church, in Munich, as a testament to her unshakable faith in Christianity.

In early October of 1898, Irma Sztaray headed to Budapest, Hungary. Given the loss of her mistress, she no longer had a reason to work for the Imperial Crown. The lady-in-waiting had given up several years of her life loyally attending to Franz Joseph's wife. Turned widower before getting the position of favourite, today she had nothing to show for it. Childless, she had no specific goal to hold on to. Apart from her futile existence, the countess was stricken by remorse after Sissi's death. Since the passing of the empress, she hadn't stopped hating herself.

"Without my negligence, Her Majesty would still be of this world," she told herself constantly with tears in her eyes.

A month to the day after the death of the Empress of Austria, Irma was found dead. Her neck was tied to a rope and hung to a wooden beam in her room: the former attendant of Sissi had hung herself. Remorse had been weighing heavily on her conscience. Before she died, the Hungarian noblewoman had written a letter explaining her gesture to Franz.

> *On this tenth day of October, I confess my sin towards Her Majesty the Empress. If my benevolence hadn't failed on that tragic day, our beloved sovereign would still be among us. My mistake has deprived a nation and an empire of a remarkable woman. I cannot go on living my own life knowing that I am responsible for the demise of my mistress. My negligence has broken the heart of His Majesty the Emperor of Austria and has taken a mother away from Their Imperial Highnesses the Archduchess of Austria-Tuscany and the Princess of Bavaria.*
>
> *May God forgive me for my sin,*
>
> *Irma Sztaray*

The message, which was found by an employee of the hotel, would never reach its recipient. Contrarily to what the countess thought, her suicide only magnified the pain of Sissi's daughters. The Habsburgs, who were mourning the loss of their mother, would have wanted to meet the woman who had shared the last moments of Sissi's life. They would have liked to know the last words of Elisabeth of Wittelsbach. With her premeditated death, the loyal friend carried the precious secret of the famous sovereign to the grave.

ଓ THE END ଯ

Actual chronology

December 24, 1837

Elisabeth of Wittelsbach, aka Sissi, Duchess in Bavaria, was born at the Palace of Ludwigstrasse, in Munich.

August 16, 1853

Franz Joseph I of Austria and Sissi get engaged.

April 24, 1854

Elisabeth of Wittelsbach marries the Emperor of Austria and officially becomes empress.

March 5, 1855

She gives girth to Sophie of Habsburg, the first child of the imperial couple.

July 12, 1856

The sovereigns' second daughter, Gisela of Habsburg, is born.

May 28, 1857

The young Sophie of Habsburg, the eldest daughter of the emperor and the empress, dies.

August 21, 1858

The empress gives birth to Rudolf of Habsburg, heir to the Austrian throne.

June 8, 1867

Franz Joseph I and Sissi are crowned King and Queen of Hungary.

April 22, 1868

The imperial couple's last child, Marie Valerie of Habsburg, is born.

May 27, 1872

Archduchess Sophie of Austria, mother of the monarch, dies.

April 20, 1873

Gisela of Habsburg marries Prince Leopold of Bavaria.

March 8, 1878

The Archduke Franz Karl of Austria, father of monarch, dies.

May 10, 1881

The heir to the Empire of Austria, Rudolf of Habsburg, marries Princess Stephanie of Belgium.

November 15, 1888

Sissi's father, Duke Maximilian in Bavaria, dies.

January 30, 1889

The imperial couple's only son, Rudolf of Habsburg, commits suicide.

February 18, 1890

Count Gyula Andràssy, Empress Sissi's lover, dies.

May 16, 1890

Princess Helene of Thurn and Taxis, Sissi's favourite sister, dies.

July 31, 1890

Marie Valerie of Habsburg marries Archduke Franz Salvator of Austria-Tuscany.

January 26, 1892
Duchess Ludovika of Bavaria, the empress' mother, dies.
September 10, 1898
The Empress of Austria, Elisabeth of Wittelsbach, aka Sissi, is murdered in Geneva, Switzerland.

Acknowledgements

I took great pleasure in writing the historical fiction novel *Sissi: The Last Empress*. Good childhood memories associated with the popular television series about the Empress of Austria came back to me as I was writing this manuscript. The breathtaking images of the imperial residences kindled in me the soft melody of this era. Nonetheless, I had to seclude myself for hours at a time to devote myself to this book. This is why I wish to take this opportunity to highlight the exceptional support of a few people in both my professional and personal circles.

First of all, many thanks to Frédéric Daviault who has believed me in as a writer from the very beginning. He never stopped motivating me and encouraging me to keep writing *Sissi: The Last Empress*. His encouragement and moral support have always been of indisputable value. He is – probably – one of my most dedicated readers. My dream of becoming a writer was born thanks to his constant presence by my side.

Secondly, I wish to extend my gratitude to the members of my intimate circle (friends and family), who have shown me their undying pride since the beginning of my literary venture. Their presence is essential to fulfilling my life as a writer.

Finally, I wish to thank my readers who have been following me on this journey since the beginning. Without them, my career as a writer would merely be a dream. I encourage you to visit my website at www.dannysaunders.com or email me at writer@dannysaunders.com. You can also follow me on Facebook or Twitter. Your comments will be greatly appreciated. Do not hesitate to come meet me during public events such as book fairs and signature sessions. Never forget that without you, writers throughout the world wouldn't have the privilege of being read.

CPSIA information can be obtained
at www.ICGtesting.com
Printed in the USA
BVOW08s0833270817
493210BV00001B/13/P